T0067323

COUGAR RIDGE

Cooliage Family Series

Debbi Haskins

Order this book online at www.trafford.com
or email orders@trafford.com

Most Trafford titles are also available at major online book retailers.

© Copyright 2018 Debbi Haskins.
All rights reserved. No part of this publication may be reproduced, stored in a
retrieval system, or transmitted, in any form or by any means, electronic, mechanical,
photocopying, recording, or otherwise, without the written prior permission of the author.

Print information available on the last page.

ISBN: 978-1-4907-8651-3 (sc)
ISBN: 978-1-4907-8652-0 (hc)
ISBN: 978-1-4907-8669-8 (e)

Library of Congress Control Number: 2017918961

Because of the dynamic nature of the Internet, any web addresses or links contained in
this book may have changed since publication and may no longer be valid. The views
expressed in this work are solely those of the author and do not necessarily reflect the
views of the publisher, and the publisher hereby disclaims any responsibility for them.

Any people depicted in stock imagery provided by Thinkstock are models,
and such images are being used for illustrative purposes only.
Certain stock imagery © Thinkstock.

Trafford rev. 12/13/2017

www.trafford.com
North America & international
toll-free: 1 888 232 4444 (USA & Canada)
fax: 812 355 4082

For;
Claire & Hazel
And their continued adventures

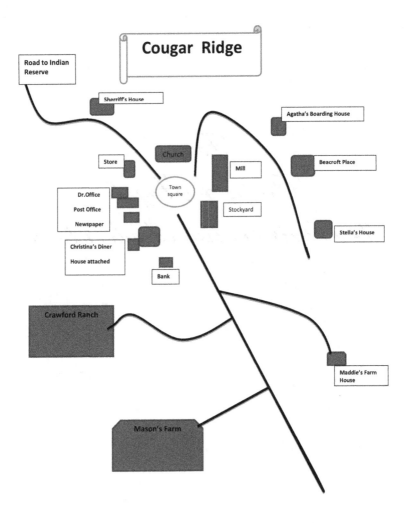

The sun shone brightly, cascading lace shadows across the patterned quilt folded neatly on the made bed. Even the birds singing their songs outside her window and the beautiful morning promised by the light warm breeze could not bring a smile to her face. For today she was leaving, returning home for good.

As she snapped the latch on the last of her bags she glanced about the small but tidy room that she has called home during her time at the university, making sure nothing has been forgotten. She then approached the mirror on the washstand, placed her peacock blue headpiece on her hair and secured it with a silver hat pin. The flower encased hat had wide blue ribbons which she tied beneath her chin, slightly off to the right.

After another long glance, she informed the footman that she was ready. Yes she was ready. For today, Claire Marie Cooliage of Boston Massachusetts will be returning home as a certified teacher. Today she had graduated with her class. Alone she accepted her diploma, as no member of her family attended her ceremony. She was not surprised. Her father thought it was a grand waste of his time and his resources since she will be wed and need to be a wife to an upstanding member of the society, not a meager school teacher.

Debbi Haskins

Her mother was not one to go against father's wishes, no matter how ridiculous they were. None the less, Claire was proud of her certification. She will miss the professors and the few friends that she had made while learning here.

The footman approached and picked up the last of her bags and followed Claire from the room. He couldn't help but stare. This young lady sure was a sight to behold. He doubted that she was even aware of how truly beautiful she looked. He could see the immense breeding instilled into her as she walked ahead of him. The way her back was straight, her head held high, the natural sway to her hips making a soft swishing sound by her blue traveling gowns. Those blue gowns were trimmed ever so slightly with small embroidered flowers along the cuffs and hem of her dress, and down the front of the matching tunic. Together with her matching blue head piece, Miss Cooliage was a true beauty.

Once out in the sunlight, the footman corrected his previous thoughts. Not a simple beauty. No. Miss Cooliage was a goddess! Her gorgeous red hair set ever so perfect, with just a hint of soft wispy ringlets escaping from beneath her headpiece and framing her face beautifully. A perfectly shaped alabaster white face, and naturally rose red lips. But it was the eyes. Yes, the eyes he would remember always, and dream forever of. For her eyes were emerald green and so clear and shiny they would make the finest jewels fade in comparison. Her eyes were bright and curious. She was a gem.

The footman handed the last of the baggage to the sharply dressed gentleman loading the personal carriage. The carriage was just as formable as the lady being helped inside. Black as the darkest night and highly polished. You could see a perfect reflection. Dust would not dare land on something so fine, the footman thought.

The opened windows had red velvet curtains trimmed with gold brocade that could be lowered to keep the sun and the weather out while protecting all that's valuable inside. The footman handed Miss Cooliage her small carpet bag that must be very personable as she insisted it ride inside with her. It was there he noticed how remarkable the inside of this carriage was as well. The floors were polished to the highest shine, the wood slats gleamed, and the seat cushions were of the same red velvet, so very thick the passengers surely would never feel the rough roads. There were even lanterns attached to the inside of the walls for a comfortable travel experience. Indeed this lady was made for such finery. As he closed the door and bid Miss Colliage good-bye, the footman took note of the two pure white stallions in blinding contrast to the carriage, standing ever so regal, waiting to carry the precious passenger inside. The coachman himself sat atop the rear storage compartment of the carriage adorn in his best grey finery with a top hat, red feather and all. Regal.

Secured inside her father's coach, Claire reflected on her time at the university. The hard courses she loved. All the long hours she spent, reading the musty and dusty books long forgotten in the large library. Even some of the information that she had learned in those books had already changed. So much in life she has already learned.

While the carriage gently rocked and bounced onward past the university library grounds, Claire fondly recalled one particular moment in that same library were she and a fellow teaching student, soon to also become a certified teacher, but most of all one of her most trusted friend, William became so animated on the discussion of freed slaves that he had fallen off his chair and at the same time toppling a fairly large stack of books. In doing so, they had gained the stare and condescending reprimand of the librarian, and sent to the headmaster's office. This memory brought a slight giggle and at the same time a single tear slipped out of her eye and slip down her cheek. She brought up her dove grey glove to capture and wipe away the tear.

They were still on university grounds as this was a large property. Only the best for a Cooliage, after all, Claire could hear her father's voice in her head. They were passing the grand hall now; this is where the graduation ceremony was held yesterday, and afterwards the evening party. Oh and what a special dance that was, her first real dance.

Well chaperoned, of course, but it was fascinating and frightening at the same time. The band was remarkable; the dresses the ladies wore were bright and beautiful. The men were dressed in their best suits. Professors became regular people that night. Not to be feared. The foods served were of the best quality as this was a celebration, a farewell.

Yes, farewell. The friends she made over the years here will remain in her heart. They all exchanged mailing addresses and promised to keep in contact. Claire doubted it would happen, but remained hopeful. She herself had made a personal promise to write to each and every one of those cherished new friends the moment she arrived home. To see how their journey to their homes went, and what their futures hold. Perhaps some of them have already gained a teaching position somewhere. That would be her dream. Once home she will need to send notice to the board of teachers to inquire on any availabilities suiting her degree. Something she knows will be met with much disapproval from her father.

It wasn't long after leaving the grounds that the rhythmic motion of the carriage lulled Claire into a dreamless sleep. The pair of stallions clearing miles of country side, while the sun sliding further into the west. Jonas, father's driver and most trusted servant, announced that they were rounding the turn towards the Estate and shall be arriving at the main door momentarily, what seemed like moments was in fact several hours. This was Claire's cue to straighten her tunic and hat, check her face and hair in the tiny compact mirror she always carried in her wrist clutch.

Claire raised the heavy red velvet curtain for this was always a sight she enjoyed, coming home. Seeing the grand Cooliage Estate from the main road of Boston, the gleaming white columns, the highly polished black shutters on the windows forever gave her a giddy feeling. She could see her balcony off to the side of the house and couldn't wait to be sitting on her chair watching the dogs run and play. Oh she had missed those silly rambunctious animals that her mother adored. Wolfhounds, large hairy beasts but so affectionate you could entrust them to the care of babies. Mother found the breed on one of her trips abroad, and brought back a pair to breed. She now has four of the mighty majestic beasts. Every one of them was a cherished family member.

The carriage ambled down the cobblestone drive and pulled up alongside the front entry. There the house footman exited the main entrance followed by a couple errand boys eager to be put to work. The baggage was unloaded, and the butler approached ready to help Miss Cooliage from the confines of the carriage. As Claire was helped from the carriage she heard the yelling of Toula, her maid. This made Claire laugh as Toula still treated her as a child, always ready to scold her then hug her and hand her something sweet. There was Toula now, standing at the doorway in her starched white uniform that she insisted she needed to wear. It enhanced her ebony skin and pearly white teeth to perfection.

Toula had been with her family as long as Claire could remember, and always had a special place held just for her. Unsure of Toula's real age, Claire just assumed she never aged for she has always looked the same. She was the mother that Claire wished her mother actually was. Toula would always tell Claire exactly what she thought, no matter how hard or easy it was to say and hear.

No sooner had Claire stepped onto the flagstone walkway she heard the unforgettable sounds of the hounds. She braced herself for the encounter that she knew was coming. Loud barking and heavy sounds of thunder approaching. Sure enough, her favorite wolfhound bounded towards her, bypassing the errand boys that were set ready to capture the animals before knocking their mistress to the ground surely. Jasper cleared the boys and launched himself towards Claire. Much to the horrified screams coming from the front door, it was her mother's screams Claire heard as she fell to the ground with over a hundred pounds of hairy dog flesh squirming and giving slobbery kisses, the beast landed his target.

What a homecoming! Now that she was thoroughly slobbered upon, dress was dirtied from the dog, and who knows what happened to her hat! Claire finally stood on her two feet and with the assistance of Jonas, walked up the stairs into that waiting arms of first Toula, then her mother. Stiff as a board, her mother grazed a kiss on each side of Claire's cheeks before turning and suggesting lemonade in the atrium. Jonas handed Claire's hat to Toula, and led the hound towards the back gate where the errand boys had managed to coral the other three hounds so they could not approach the greeting party on the front steps.

Claire felt an overwhelming sense of nostalgia, like always when she entered her home. It was a true southern mansion right in Boston. Nothing but the best, of course her father always said. Large columns on the wide veranda, eight foot tall double doors were swung wide open to receive her home. Her breath caught in her throat when she walked in the front door. The cream coloured marble floors were polished a mirror gleam, the grand staircase directly in front of the entry room sure was grand! Every time Claire enters, it is always like the first time.

Gleaming wood staircase, curving up and separating into two sides at the top of a balcony like walkway. One side leading to her parent's private set of suites, the other, leading to the many rooms located on the other side of the grand home one of which held Claire's suite. Black metal urns placed on either side of the staircase showed off her mother's passion for orchids. Bright and floral and expensive, they gave off such a wonderful scent. Off to the right was father's study, his office, where he was most likely nose deep into his ledgers and had forgotten all about her homecoming.

It was down the hallway to the left that Claire was being escorted, to the atrium, her mother's private personal space. This is where you could almost always find Catherine Cooliage. As Claire enters her mother's personal oasis she sees the silver tea set sitting on the oak and glass tea server to the side of the chaise lounge. Over towards the double glass doors that lead out to the gardens was a small white metal ornate table set for two.

Upon this table was a large pitcher of lemonade and two glasses complete with ice from the ice house. Cook's tea biscuits and preserves were on a tiny silver platter in the centre of this table, tiny spoons for the preserves atop each serving plate. Set on the seats of the matching ornate metal chairs were plush flowered cushions in the prettiest of pastel colours.

The entire scene was very warm and inviting. Catherine Cooliage came out from behind a large green plant in time to see her daughter enter the atrium. A warm smile filled her perfect features. Sleek faded red hair pulled in to a fashionable knot at the top of her head, exquisite gown in violet shades edged with darker purple trim, and a silver hair clip with a purple flower showed the true beauty of this monarch of the Cooliage family. The only jewellery was a simple strand of pearls and a cameo pinned to the high neck of the dress. Mrs. Catherine Cooliage certainly looked the part of wealthy upper-class Boston. She was very touched to have her only daughter home after so long. She raised her lace handkerchief to dab the corner of her eyes. She had missed Claire so.

The two exchanged embraces, and sat at the tiny table while a serving maid poured the lemonade and was then dismissed. It had seemed ages since Claire had been in this room and across from her mother. Talk felt strange as so much time had passed since her last homecoming. As Claire reached for the strawberry preserve to spread on her tea biscuit, her mother inquired about her time at the teaching classes. Claire set the tiny spoon down on her dish, and a happy smile showed that this was one of her favourite topics.

Her mother was secretly pleased that Claire enjoyed her time at the university. Hopefully, as much as she did many years prior, Catherine had very fond memories of wanting to embark on a lifelong dream of teaching. It did not end that way for her, as she soon married her husband, Claire's father Charles. And bore three sons, and then Claire, her only daughter.

Not that she was complaining she loved her life and her family. She kept very busy with the ladies of the town, the church and her husband's many dinner parties. Her children gave her the most pleasure though. Their first born son, Adam, is now a Captain in the Army and is away right now. Second born son, Micheal, has become a very renowned lawyer in Boston, and just recently made partner. Micheal just bought his first home and will be moving out of the Estate in the upcoming weeks. Now, to the third and youngest son Stephan, Stephan wants so much to please his parents. His dream is to eventually take over the family business. So much like Charles, he will succeed for sure! It was a few years before Claire came along. Catherine thought for sure she would never have a daughter. This could explain their reluctance to let Claire go to school and leave the house.

Talk soon changed to lively memories Claire was sharing on some of her professor's strange habits. She regaled stories of her exams, and studies, about the friends she made and the hopes that they would still remain in contact; Which reminded her that she would need a desk moved into her sitting room shortly so she can start her correspondence to those friends, so she asked her mother if they can shop for a desk later that day.

Lemonade and tea biscuits were enjoyed, conversation was relaxed and overall it was a nice welcome home. The ladies made plans to meet at the front entry hall for two o'clock to go to the furniture store downtown to select a perfect desk for Claire's rooms.

Claire set out in search of her father, Charles. He had yet to put in an appearance to welcome her home. This was normal, thought

Claire. As once her father closes his study doors, all time seems to stop. As she approaches the large double wooden doors she takes a deep breath and checks her hair in the oval gold mirror hung on the wall by the front entry. Making sure not a hair is out of place, she wants to look her best for her father. I guess once a little girl searching for daddy's approval..... Always that little girl. Nothing changes. Softly knocking on the door, she opened it. There he sat, her father, Charles Cooliage. Back towards the door, he sat on a heavy leather winged chair facing the fireplace, book in hand and pipe in his mouth, a glass of whiskey on the small table to the side. Upon hearing her entering the study, Charles looked up.

Seeming slightly shocked, he glanced at the grandfather clock in the corner by the massive bookcase and exclaimed how he must have lost track of time for he missed her homecoming. Charles stood and approached his precious daughter, his arms outstretched waiting for his little girl to run giggling into them. He had to remember that she stood before him a changed version of his little girl.

Gone were the round chubby cheeks and unruly red curls, for now stood an elegant woman. So much the picture of his wife from younger years ago, Claire has blossomed into a rare beauty. She glided across his orient carpet and into his willing arms. Silent tears were in her eyes, as she missed him dearly. Charles set her back from him just enough to place several kisses on her cheeks, and then back into a strong bear hug that lifted her feet off the floor as he spun her in a circle before releasing hold of her.

Charles and Claire head over to the overstuffed leather couch beside the bookcase facing the fireplace, where he offered his daughter a glass of water, which she accepted happily. Charles asked his daughter about her graduation ceremony and then made the appropriate apologies for not being there; using his business dealing as his excuse for missing the special day. Typical for Father, thought Claire. If it didn't fit into the grand scheme of things, then it really didn't matter to her father. Claire inquired about her father's business, in which he just brushed it off as if it was too confusing for a simple woman to understand. He switched tactics, asking about her future plans.

Claire was excited to mention her shopping trip with her mother at two o'clock to purchase a desk for her sitting room. Charles thought it was a huge waste of time and money, but kept that comment to himself, for now. Charles mentioned that he was planning on hosting a rather large welcome home party in her honour this coming Saturday.

Claire was to make sure that she visits the dress shops while she and Catherine were in town. To buy the best dresses available as Charles planned to show off his beautiful daughter.

As Claire was leaving her father's study, she realized that even though her father mentioned throwing a huge party to welcome her home, he failed to mention her degree in teaching. The whole reason she has been away for so long. Placing that in the back of her mind to be brought out and thought about later, she went upstairs to freshen up and change dresses, she ran back down the stairs and waited for her mother at the front foyer.

Precisely two o'clock and the grand dame herself, Catherine enters the hallway looking every inch the socialite that she is. Gone was her violet dress and simple pearl necklace. Now dressed in a peach town dress, with a gorgeous headpiece with feathers of the same tinted peach colour, diamonds adorned her hands, neck and wrists. She absolutely sparkled. Claire felt very mouse like in the same type of outfit that she had travelled in hours earlier. She has been away at school for so long she had forgotten how she is supposed to always be the belle of the ball in looks and behaviour at all times. She could feel the heat creeping into her face as her mother approached. Claire was about to apologize and ask to be forgiven then go change but her mother had other things in mind.

Simply stating that since her father is planning a large gala in her honour that they should spend a large amount of his hard earned money and set her up with a brand new wardrobe better to suit her changed ways. Claire had grown into such a lovely young woman she now needs the clothes to show that she was no longer a child. Catherine hugged her daughter close, and placed a soft kiss on her head. They then exited the home and into the bright sunlight to an awaiting coach. Being such a lovely day they chose to ride in an open coach with their parasols opened.

They chatted about silly things along the way. How the tree at the end of a particular street looked like an old man, how beautiful those gardens are. The poor nanny with the unruly boys she was trying to control. Simple silly talk actually, but it felt good and natural. Much too soon they had arrived at the first stop, the furniture shop.

As soon as they had inspected the desks available to purchase, they agreed and settled on a smart looking white Victorian writing desk with elaborate gold trim and a matching bench that easily slides underneath. Catherine instructed the proprietor to bill it to her husband and to have the desk and bench delivered immediately, and was to be placed into her daughter's sitting room overlooking her view of the gardens, for inspiration of course. Back into the carriage for a short ride to the next stop, the finest dress makers in Boston.

-2-

The pair of women were instantly met with excited screams when they entered the dressmaker's shop. There running directly towards Catherine and Claire were a group of screaming girls! Behind them slowly approaching were their mothers, moving less frantic, and more adult and aware of their station in front of the women who had just entered, The Cooliage women. The screaming stopped as the group of four young ladies swarmed Claire, fighting for the chance to hug her, crying and laughing at the same time. Claire was also very emotional about the reunion of her childhood friends that she has missed dearly during her stay at university. The young women chatted about everything at once; nothing made any sense or was even understood.

The girl's mothers retired to the lounge where they sat watching their offspring act so young, and secretly wished society allowed them to behave as so in public. Instead they sipped iced glasses of tea and nibbled tiny sandwiches provided by the store owner.

The store owner was sure of a large commission as she had heard of the return of the only daughter to the Colliage family, the only daughter that will soon have her coming out formal party to announce that she is soon ready to be wed. She could hear the cash drawer ringing away, she will need to hire on a few local girls from the rural areas to help with the sewing.

She sat back, waiting on the mothers and patiently allowing the group to have their welcoming before slightly clearing her throat to gather attention to the things at hand. She had two fittings ready for the lovely twins, and the dark haired beauty was interested in new gowns from Paris. Today will be a big money day for sure. Her husband will be very proud, and could work less in the butcher market this month. Very excited about the upcoming sales, she set about refilling iced tea and placing fresh tiny sandwiches out at the sitting lounge.

When Claire had entered the finest dress establishment in Boston her furthest thought was running into her childhood friends. But here they were! Running towards her the squealing group came. As if no time had passed, it launched Claire into the screaming frenzy of the past. Here were her cherished friends; her longest and best friend Margarite Stinson, beautiful dark skinned, raven black hair pinned high on her head and her sultry dark eyes looking very moist with unshed tears. Margarite has known Claire since younger schooling. Dearest of best friends. Margarite's family was of Spanish decent and they own several high class establishments throughout Boston. The Stinson's only have the one child, and Margarite is spoiled. Arriving from Europe with their fortune already, they easily fit into the upper-class society. Margarite's dark beauty turned a lot of heads. She knew it, and used it to her benefit. As Claire was bound to find out how her friend has changed over these past few years.

Next to get into the hugs was Jaquelin. Jaquelin Robarts has an older married brother and 2 younger sisters; she herself is a fine looking young woman. Claire met Jaquelin later in school and became fast friends. Jaquelin's quiet demeanor meshed well with Claire's outgoing personality. They balanced one another. Jaquelin had her long brown hair loosely tied at the base of her neck. She wore a modest coloured dress, as usual. Not one to draw attention to herself. Even though her parents owned several fine clothing shops, Jaquelin never wore anything special, much to her parent's

13

ire. Claire was under the impression that Jaquelin often wished herself to be sucked into the background where nobody will notice her. Well that just won't do after all, thought Claire.

Then there are the twins, of course, the twins. Where there is one... there is the other. Never to be elsewhere; always together; always dressed the same, always the same. Rosalyn and Elizabeth Riley, or as Claire affectionately calls them Rose and Beth; beautiful tiny in body structure, bubbly in nature, blonde twins with curls galore and crystal blue eyes.

Today they were matched in the frilliest pink frocks with lacy white gloves and matching parasols. Pink ribbons adorn their tight curls. The twins are only children to the Riley family. The Riley name goes way back. They are of old money Claire's mother once said, they are ship traders, and the twins father builds ships. Claire's father has bought a few of those ships for his trading company. Good sound ships her father boasts.

Soon the laughter had ceased, and they were discussing the latest in dresses. Something that brought the mothers to their feet, and alongside each of their daughters, to be included in the dress discussion. The shop owner set out her staff to take notes and measurements and sent an errand boy to the rural area to round up the extra help she desperately needs.

After several hours, timeless measurements and four new store bought dresses complete with stockings and undergarments, gloves and shoes, Claire and Catherine were tired and ready to return home. The ride back in the carriage was quieter than the trip into town. Both ladies were exhausted and in dire need of rest. Even though she was exhausted, Claire made an attempt to chat up her mother.

The conversation was about her teaching degree and how she was going to search for a position. This conversation visibly upset her mother and she instantly regretted bringing it up. It was out in the open and could not take it back. Catherine sat silently for a moment, then turned to her daughter and took her hands in her own. She had a sad look in her eyes when she spoke you could feel the tension, the love and the fear. She had to say it. Catherine mentioned how Claire had just today arrived home, can they not just enjoy her home coming a little while before the talk of her leaving for good takes over. Feeling chastised, Claire agreed and kissed her mother's gloved fingers and sat back on the seat to watch the city roll by. Soon the Estate came into view. The coach came to a stop and out of nowhere the footman was there to take the parcels to Claire's suite. Jonas mentioned to Claire that her desk had arrived; he had it placed where the Missus had instructed but if Claire had other placings in mind he would certainly change the location for her immediately. They entered the house and Catherine said she was retiring to her rooms for a nap and was to be awakened before mealtime to prepare herself; Could Jonas let Mr. Cooliage know they are home now.

Jonas went to the study, and let himself in without the expected knock. He knew the Master would not hear him knock anyways. Once inside the study, Jonas approached the master and informed him that the ladies have only returned from their shopping and that his Missus has retired to her rooms. Charles looked up from his desk, unsure of what he heard. He asked for Jonas to repeat what he had just said. Then he gathered a rather large box of items and instructed Jonas to have these items taken directly to his daughter. That they were items she would surely need with her new desk, then dismissed Jonas and went back to his writings.

Jonas carried the large box himself up the flight of stairs, down the hallway to the far end where Claire's set of rooms were located. He passed the first door which was the sleeping quarters and proceeded to the third set of doors. These rooms were designated Claire's sitting rooms. Jonas smiled to himself as he tapped ever so lightly on the door knowing full well that Claire would be in these rooms and not resting like her mother certainly would be.

15

Sure enough, Claire opened the door all excited about the desk and thanked Jonas for knowing where she would have preferred her desk be placed, and not in front of the garden window like mother ordered.

No, Jonas had placed her desk in the opposite room by the patio doors so the fresh air would flow in and the sounds of the estate could fill the air. Jonas has known her secrets for so long; sometimes she thought he knew her better than her parents did. Maybe it was true, for he knew how to place her beloved desk, and had a bookshelf installed along the wall that used to hold her doll house and many porcelain dolls. Her precious books were also unpacked and carefully displayed on those new shelves. How he had accomplished so much in such little time she did not know. But she was pleased regardless.

Claire was curious about the box and its contents. Doubly curious once Jonas said it was sent to her from her father. Jonas placed the heavy box on the floor close to the desk so that Claire could remove the contents. He mentioned to Claire that he will return to remove the box while she is at dinner. Claire hugged Jonas tightly and gave him a simple kiss on his cheek. For a big burly man he certainly felt small. Simple gestures like that were normal from Claire towards Jonas, and it always humbled him that she thought so much of him to grace him that way. He would protect her to his dying day. That's a promise.

-3-

Toula entered Claire's suite to help put her new clothing away into her closets. She carefully unwrapped each silk stocking and lovingly rolled each and placed into the lace lined cedar drawer built into the wall closet. After Toula rolled the stockings she moved onto the under clothing, oohing and aahing over each fine item, making Claire blush. The two women were joking and talking about each item, and placing them gently into another lace lined cedar drawer of the same wall closet. Toula reached for the gold metal latch to open the large cedar closet to hang the gorgeous dresses, gowns and cloaks. Mr. Cooliage will certainly see his only daughter in a brand new way for sure. If these were just the store bought dresses, Toula couldn't wait to see the designer gowns befitting her princess.

With the clothing put away, Claire and Toula sat out on Claire's balcony sipping iced tea and talking about her time away. How much Toula had missed having her little Claire at home. Having no children or family, Toula was over the moon happy to have found safety in this family.

She had served the Late Mr. Cooliage SR, and when Charles grew into a grown man and asked her to accompany him to his own household for the remainder of her days, Toula had felt like she finally had her family. Mr. Cooliage had provided her meaning, and stature, and a fine, fine family to raise.

Mrs. Cooliage is a wonderful missus to work under and her children are all special to her. But then, everyone knows that Toula has a very special spot in her heart for Miss Claire. Toula cleaned up the tea supplies and bid Claire farewell. She closed the door and walked happily towards the kitchen to speak to Cook about the meal plan to celebrate Claire's homecoming.

Claire admired the set of rooms from her balcony door and couldn't help but compare these glorious spacious rooms to her tiny cramped dorm room at the university to what felt like a lifetime ago! From these doors she sees the beautiful desk that she and her mother had just picked out. That was the desk she planned on penning a letter to the head of teachers and ask for placement. She sees the large comfortable chaise reclining sofa, pink and purple flowered pattern to match her mauve walls of the sitting room. Beyond the sitting room was her dressing room, in yellows and whites. Along one wall was a large closet made of cedar but painted white against the yellow walls, and tiny blue butterflies painted down the door, so tiny they look like little dots. A couple of overstuffed sitting chairs and a dressing table with mirror complete her dressing room. Just past the dressing room was her sleeping quarter. Her very large, king sized canopy bed had the most luxurious down comforter dyed in the palest of pinks, matching pillows adorned the bed, black wrought iron bed posts rose up towards the high ceilings and joined in a twisted magical explosion of artwork, framing the bed, upon this iron work was the same gauzy material tied back at each corner with pale pink satin ties that when released it shall cocoon the person inside into a soft curtain of whimsical wonderland; a beautiful, heavenly place to dream.

From the balcony, she walked inside but left the double glass doors opened wide, her white gauzy curtains flowing with the breeze. She could smell the lilacs that grew below her windows. Her mother made sure that her daughter's suites had the best of everything, even a breeze with aroma. Headed toward the forgotten box that

Jonas had delivered from her father earlier, Claire looked inside. Her father had mentioned that it was everything that she would need for her desk.

First item that Claire pulled from the box was a beautiful silver frame; inside the frame was a photograph of her as a young child sitting in the open carriage with her mother and father. Claire was unsure of her age, she was guessing around four or five. She could not remember posing for this photograph either. Tears sprang from her eyes knowing that her father must have cherished this photograph, and she had never laid eyes on it before. Hugging it close to her heart she walked to her desk and placed it on the corner, a place of honour.

There was a brand new ink well, a silver pen with her initials engraved into it, and a new paper blotter. Several pencils, a couple new ledgers, a wonderful stack of personalized letterheads, and finally a beautiful gold and silver desk clock. Claire was touched by the deep heartfelt emotions, knowing her father had thought ahead to have these items commissioned and ready for her return home. Claire was on her way to having a fully functional desk, thanks to her father's thoughtfulness.

As she lovingly placed each item on the desk and sat back to admire her task completed, Claire decided that tomorrow morning was her time to start her new life. Tomorrow Claire was going to sit at her lovely desk and pen her letters to her classmates and then her letter to the dean of teaching to ask for a positon placement suited for her degree. She wasn't going to let another day stop her. Life was wonderful, and Claire was ready to run full steam ahead!

Downstairs in the study, Charles was pacing the floor. Unknown to Claire, her father was putting his own wheels in motion in regards to her wellbeing. He was concerned for his only daughter. Charles did not want her running off to some God forsaken place to teach. Teach, His daughter? No, no way. He would not hear of it! A Cooliage will not be a teacher. His daughter will be married to a wealthy man, an upstanding gentleman and produce strong children. That is what his daughter will do; for he has played along with her silly dreams for long enough. Charles thought for sure that Claire would have come running home once she had a taste of school life, sharing a small living quarters. He had to pull a few strings to make sure that Claire had a private room. Be it small, it was still private. That still wasn't enough to have her return home. Charles had underestimated his daughter's strength and commitment to her studies. This will be harder than he originally thought. It was time to return to the drawing board and plan a new line of attack.

The dinner bell was sounded and Claire glanced at the new desk clock and was once again amazed at how time was advancing so rapidly! She quickly changed from her day dress to her dinner dress, splashed fresh water on her face, dabbed some lemon verbena onto her neck and wrists and ran her brush through her hair before descending the grand staircase and heading towards the dining hall. The smells were intoxicating as she followed her nose into the great hall. Gleaming oak table large enough to sit an entire army Claire thought, matching high back straight chairs set in the centre of this polished room. The fireplace on the outer wall was lit and crackling sending warmth and light in the large room. The table had been set for royalty instead of a simple family dinner, a gold and royal red table runner down the centre of the table. Three candelabras with white candles ablaze and casting flickering dancing shadows onto the china and crystal place settings, the silver shone as if brand new. Claire counted settings for five people. She tried to count in her head who the five would be. As she was figuring it out a very familiar voice announced that it was about time she graced everyone with her presence.

Joyfully Claire ran to the open arms of her darling brother Micheal. He placed a brotherly kiss upon the top of her forehead. As Claire's mother approached the pair she indicated everyone to take their seats. Once her parents were seated, Claire chose the seat next to Micheal so that they could continue their talk during the meal.

Just before Cook served the meal Stephan strolled in nonchalantly, not a care in the world. He greeted his mother with a brief peck on the cheek and a handshake to his father before sitting down across the table from Claire and Micheal. Stephan was pleased to see Claire, and said so. Father announced that the meal shall be served in honour of his daughter's return home. A celebratory meal, therefore there will be no talk of work only talk of Claire and her studies and her plans now that she is home. This dinner was for Claire, after all.

Cook had outdone herself, Claire sighed. Game hens on each plate, encircled by tiny cabbages and peas and carrots all glazed by some sweet sticky substance that she knew for certain, cook would never tell her the secrets. A small garden salad and fresh breads finished off the main meal. Sparkling cider was the drink for her as she was not yet old enough for wine her mother said. After the meal, mother said that the dessert was one of Claire's most favorite of all. A small chocolate cake with some powdered white sugar and tiny berries on top was placed in front of Claire. Toula came over to Claire and told her that next week will be a much grander cake for it will be her sixteenth birthday. She would then be a proper young woman.

After dinner and dessert, the family retired to the front parlor for quiet moments and to listen to mother play the piano. Memories flooded Claire as she sat on the floor at her father's side and listened to her mother singing so beautifully her brother Micheal joining in.

His deep steady tone only added to the angelic sound of her mother. Stephan sat on the piano bench beside mother like he has done since he was big enough to climb up on it. These were the happy times Claire will always remember. She hoped that she can hold these memories to heart when she finds a teaching position and will have to leave her home.

Sad thoughts entered her mind and she forgot where she was for a moment. It wasn't until her father touched her shoulder that she snapped back to the present. Claire had to ask her father to repeat what he had said, saying that she must have drifted slightly to sleep as it has really been a long day. Father said that he would really love to hear her sing and play the piano before they all head to their respective rooms.

Claire rose and proceeded to fix her skirts as she sat at the piano. Fingers poised over the ivory keys she thought for a moment as to what song she should play. A smile crept to her lips as her hands settled on the piano and started to glide over the keyboard like small butterflies. So elegantly and graceful, she began to play and sing a tune that she knew would please her parents. The song beautiful dreamer was spilling from her heart. For this was her parent's favourite song. She glanced over and caught sight of her father gently holding her mother as they danced slowly in the centre of the parlor, oblivious to anyone or anything else. That was true love. Everyone in the room knew it, and wanted the same thing.

Once the song ended everyone said their goodnights and went to their rooms. Claire was happy to see the end of the evening. Exhausted and excited she was at a crossroad in her life. Saying good-bye to the child that was Claire, and hello to the woman that Claire was now; she was a certified teacher, and a woman. Claire changed into her brand new sleeping gown and slippers and sat at her dressing table to brush her luxurious red hair. As she watched her reflection in the mirror with every brush stroke she was finding it harder and harder to keep her eyes open. She soon gave up, placed the brush on the table and rose to her feet, walking to the already turned down bed and doused her lanterns as she removed her slippers and slid between her silk sheets. Slipping into a dream filled deep sleep Claire finally relaxed, for she was home.

-4-

Morning shone into her opened window; the soft summer breeze, the singing of the birds and the lovely fresh scent of the flowers; it was the perfect way to wake up. Claire freshened up at the washstand, and changed into a beautiful day dress of pale blue. Heading downstairs to the breakfast room, set just off of the dining hall, it over looked the garden and gave a nice calm start to the mornings. On the buffet sat a selection of fruits and breads and cheeses. Cook came in with the hot platters stacked high with eggs and sausages and potatoes. Breakfast has been served. Claire was happy to see that her parents were a bit late in arriving, that gave her some time to have conversations with her two brothers. Both of which were already seated at the quaint table sipping their coffee. Claire chose to have tea over coffee and was buttering a slice of bread when Micheal informed her that he had purchased his very first home since she had been away. This caught Claire off guard. She was certain the brothers would never leave home. Very intrigued by this news, Claire inquired as to where the house was located and when Micheal plans on moving into it. Was there a special someone he had in mind when he bought this house? These were all the questions Claire was asking Micheal, without allowing him to reply before she asked the next question.

Micheal sat back on his chair, sipping his coffee intently listening to his little sister rapidly fire questions at him like a drill sergeant at a firing range. He smiled as he looked closer at his sister. She has blossomed, overnight it seemed. He will have to watch her closely and protect her from the greedy hungry men that will soon notice her as well. Now that Claire had stopped to take a much needed breath, Micheal decided to grasp the moment and begin to answer her questions. Yes, he did indeed buy his home here in Boston. No, he had no one in mind when doing so. Yes, he was ready to move out, actually in two days. Yes, he has had a lot of help from friends and their wives in choosing the furniture and colours for his home. Yes, Claire will be able to view his home later that day if she so wanted. Micheal was tired just from answering these questions. His sister hasn't changed that much after all, he thought. Still so full of wonder and always asking questions, in search of constant answers.

Breakfast was removed and Micheal set off to his office. Micheal had become a partner in a leading law firm in Upper Boston. Something he has been working towards for many years. He is a man of wealth both from family money and now his own. Claire was very proud of Micheal. Adam, Claire's oldest brother had made Captain in the army and was currently away. Mother didn't know when he would return home, but they receive regular correspondence from him, so they know he is safe still. As for the youngest of the boys, Claire's brother older by only two years, Stephan still lived at home. He had no desire to move out any time soon. As father's right hand man, Stephan was being groomed to take over the family business when father was ready to retire.

The Cooliage name was well known all over the world; father's father had started out in the trade markets, and father embellished on this by purchasing ships and trading worldwide. Cooliage was a name to be recognised. They were a different standard to the wealthy. Almost to the point of royalty, as word goes by.

Claire decided that she would head to her rooms and start writing those letters so that when she goes into town this afternoon she can post them. She had received a card this morning asking her to meet with Margarite for lunch. She happily sent word that she would be happy to do so. Taking a small plate with some fresh preserves and a biscuit to her room, she was already planning in her head what she planned to say in each letter to her school friends. Pen in hand, doors open to allow the fresh breeze to enter, Claire began to write the first of several letters. Time flew by, again.

Micheal loaded his last trunk into the rented carriage. He glanced over his shoulder at his home, this home in which he will be leaving forever in one short day. He motioned to the driver to take him to the address on the card he handed him. The carriage started with a jolt, and they were off. He was taking the last of his books to his new home, to be placed in his very own study. So much like his father's study; with the dark mahogany desk, heavy leather furniture and large sturdy book cases, a man's study. This was the one room in which he made all the decorating decisions. The beginning of his new life as a prominent lawyer.

Stephan watched as Micheal's coach pulled away. He closed the drapes to his father's study and turned to the man sitting behind the large desk. Stephan was speaking with his father on the subject of Claire. Charles had taken Stephen into his confidence and in doing this he was hoping to get the needed backing to put forth his plan to get Claire married and stop this teaching idea foolishness. Charles had decided that the Saturday following this Saturday would be a perfect time to hold a gala to both celebrate his daughter's birthday and to announce that she is of age to be courted, ready for suitors. Father and son set to task, planning the guest list and a list of potential suitors, all to be invited to the gala. Charles figured he would approach his wife later in the day with his plan. Catherine was happy in her life, and she gave up her idea of teaching when they wed, so why should it be any different for Claire? Stephan sat in the wing back leather chair across from father's desk, pen and inkwell ready, together they began their list of names to be talked about later.

Jonas knocked on Claire's door, and opened it as she bid him to enter. Jonas noticed how mature Claire looked standing beside her desk in her new day gown, gloves and hat in hand. Jonas reached for the stack of letters that Claire had written and her parasol then followed Claire down the staircase. Once at the bottom of the stairs, Jonas handed Claire her letters, parasol and wrist clutch. He walked her outside to the awaiting closed coach, and instructed the driver as to where to drop Ms. Cooliage off by handing him an address card. The carriage rolled away, and Claire became rather excited about her upcoming luncheon with Margarite.

The ride to town was not a long one so she sat and looked through her letters making sure she forgot no one. The driver indicated the diner where Margarite would be waiting and he helped Claire out of the carriage. He mentioned that he would return to this spot in a couple hours for her return ride home.

Before Claire went into the diner, she crossed the street to the postmaster office and posted the letters. While she was there the postmaster handed her a small bundle of mail that was to go to her home. It would save time having Claire take the mail, rather than sending an errand boy to deliver it. Mr.Cooliage usually sends a boy into the postmaster once a week, she thought this would save time and coin. Claire agreed, so she happily accepted the small bundle of tied mail and walked across the street to her awaiting friend at the fine diner.

Margarite sat at the tiny table by the front window. She watched her childhood friend exit the coach, and immediately had a sharp intake of breath. The woman walking across the street to the postmaster's office could not be her friend Claire. She carefully watched as the woman who exited the coach walked into the postmaster's, then walked back out into the sunlight. This woman walking back towards her was a much more grown and sophisticated looking version of her childhood friend.

-5-

This was slightly unsettling to Margarite. The woman who Margarite was so intently keeping an eye on was dressed in a beautiful pale yellow day dress, with tiny yellow buttercups embroidered along the hem and wrist cuffs. Her matching tunic had the same embroidery pattern with a yellow braided stitching along bright gold buttons, covering a starched white high neck blouse. Her luscious red hair piled high atop her head with long perfect coils trailing down to the back of her elegant neck. Perched perfectly on her head was a corn silk coloured straw head piece with yellow and white flowers around the brim and secured with a discrete silver hat pin. With a beautiful parasol of the finest white sheer fabric and lace and her matching gloves, Claire looked the sophisticated debutante that she surely was. Poise and grace, her dress enhanced her natural beauty, she didn't have to paint her face or dress in gaudy clothing to be noticed. Margarite felt a moment of jealousy hit her hard. So much so that she checked herself in her compact she removed from her wrist bag. Touching her fingers to her hair she was happy with what reflected back at her. She reminded herself that Claire doesn't have her dark exotic features that men beg for. Claire may be pretty, but Margarite thought SHE was Devine, every man's wish.

Claire entered the establishment, and located her dearest friend, approached her with a sincere wide smile. How long it has been since she was truly happy to see someone. They exchanged embraces, and Claire sat at the small table opposite Margarite. The two women unaware of how exquisite pair they were, sitting in the front of this small restaurant. The males walking by stared openly, the patrons inside wishing that they were at that table enjoying those wonderful smiles, and wanting to be in on the conversations which made these two lovely women so lively.

The older proprietor, having known these girls their entire lives, brought over their favorite tea with ice and small sandwiches on a simple china plate. She then placed two smaller plates in front of each young woman and returned to her other customers. Margarite and Claire talked and laughed together for a long time, having finished off all the sandwiches and tea. They talked of everything. They talked of nothing. It was just two great friends catching up on life. Claire had learned that Margarite will be in her second season this year, her parents eager to see their only child married and giving birth to their grandchildren. Margarite was not so sure that she wanted to get married right away. She was enjoying the male attention too much she admitted. That was why she could not settle on a suitor last year. Claire could not imagine having so many suitors that she would have to make a schedule like the Margarite was explaining that she needed to do. How exhausting that process must be.

As they concluded their visit, both women agreed to another visit, this time a less formal one at Claire's home in the upcoming few days. They both rose, and hugged good-bye and both left the building together. There on the boardwalk, Margarite thought that she will definitely need to stay ahead of Claire from this point on. Their other friends knew their place now, so Claire will have to be watched. She could be competition if she wanted.

Claire was being helped into the family carriage as Margarite called for a rental carriage to take her home, not waiting for her coach to arrive. She needed to hurry home and plan for the upcoming season. She needed to be the belle of every ball, no matter what.

The ride home from down town was shorter than Claire remembered. Maybe it was because she was lost in thought again. She seemed to be doing that a lot lately. Things were so simple at school. She didn't have to worry about matching her gloves to her hat, or remember to carry her wrist bag to hold her compact. No, at school she wore a simple frock, no hat required and as it was a learning environment, she never thought of looking for a husband. It was carefree. She was there to learn, to get her teaching degree, as were others there. Fashion took a back seat. She was simply Claire Cooliage. Now, here she was smack dab in the middle of fashion central. Now she needed to dress and act like the perfect daughter of one of the wealthiest families in Upper Boston. Here she was Miss Cooliage, and she had to remember that fact.

Claire noticed a couple of carriages parked outside the main entrance to her family home. As she was helped down from her carriage, Jonas immerged from the front door and informed her that her father had guests and they were staying for diner. Claire was expected to dress appropriately for a formal dinner. Wonder who Father had here? Claire made her way up the grand staircase towards her set of rooms. Stephan heard her and opened his room door stopping Claire in her tracks.

Stephan looked so much like Father, Claire thought. His hair combed perfectly and his suit immaculate, not a wrinkle to be found. Even his shoes were shined to a high reflective state. So much like Father, Look your best, at all times. You never know who will arrive, and the contacts that could be made. The first impression is the ONLY impression. Claire actually could hear those words being said in her father's voice inside her own head. She's been hearing those words her entire life. As Stephan surely had been groomed to fit Father's image, he oozed perfection. She felt like the ugly duckling in comparison.

Stephan leaned on his door frame and smiled, that boyish wonderful smile that Claire liked to think was her special smile.

It was the same smile they shared whenever they thought that they had gotten away with something massive. It was home. Claire smiled back and inquired as to the smile on his face. Stephan told Claire of Father's guests; big time business men from Europe staying with them for the weekend. Stephan was headed downstairs to be included in business matters and Claire was to spend the remainder of the time in her rooms, preparing herself for the big dinner, and dress to impress. Nothing but the best, of course, shows off his doll of a daughter. She's beautiful to look at, but never initiate a conversation, as women were to be looked at not spoken to. This was going to be a long dinner thought Claire.

She entered her dressing room and noticed Toula busily arranging her wardrobe. Her new gowns had arrived and Toula was making room in the main closet. Her day gowns were moved to the side wall closet, the main closet was reserved for the best, of course. How she longed for the quiet solitary room of her dorm. Toula fussed over the fine materials, the colours and the matching shoes to each dress and gown. She was trying to engage Claire in conversation regarding what dress she would want to wear for dinner, so she might press it and prepare Claire's hair to show off the jewellery for the gown. Claire honestly could care less, but she faked the excitement she knew she should feel. She hated being trussed up like a doll to be sat on a shelf. She chose the simple evening dinner gown in muted rose hue. Matching silk slippers and her outfit was chosen. Now for her hair, Toula insisted that they style it in a simple up do with trace wisps framing her face. Simple gold chain was the only jewellery needed to top off this sophisticated look.

Dinner was announced, so Claire made her way towards the dining hall. Claire pasted the usual smile on her face, one that said she was happy to be here. The table was set in the best the family had, obviously these businessmen meant a lot to her father, and Claire would have to watch her manners. Her mother looked gorgeous, as usual. She was in her natural element, forever the hostess. She was seated to the right of her mother, towards the opposite end of the large table from the men.

Brother Stephan at Father's right, as the right hand man should be; Father's pride. Claire was happy her brother was finally given the credit he deserved. He had worked so hard to gain an ounce of recognition from their father, and now he was being groomed in every manner to eventually take over.

Claire made the appropriate proper introductions, said all the right replies when addressed and remembered to use the right forks. As far as her parents were concerned, dinner was a huge success. To Claire, she barely could remember the gentlemen's names. Not that it really mattered, for after this meal she would not be required to show herself again. That was ok with her, how she hated these functions. To put on a grand show, not being yourself. She will be so happy once she gets a positon teaching and she can fore go these formalities once and for all.

Once dinner was over, the men retired to Father's study for cognac and cigars, while her mother begged off with a headache and went to her rooms. Claire went upstairs to change into her night clothes. Still not tired she slipped down the back staircase, the one usually reserved for the servants to use so they are not seen, she entered the kitchen and grabbed a chunk of cheese and bread off the sideboard, and headed out the veranda to sit on the porch swing in the darkness with only the moonlight to light her way. The sounds of the night always calmed her. She could hear carriages rolling down the street, and at this moment she heard the hounds heading her way. As they too hear the sounds in the night. Claire knew the beloved hounds would come, that's why she brought the cheese and breads. She was glad her father hadn't seen this spectacle, his daughter sitting in the dark feeding the beasts. It made her laugh out loud, and Claire felt more like herself than she had since her homecoming. She finished her time with the dogs and headed to her awaiting bed, finally feeling sleep approaching.

At morning tea, Catherine announced that Father is planning a welcome home Gala that coincides with her birthday. A double affair, Grandeur expectant and will take place a week from Saturday. Catherine was excited to be able to plan and host such a special event; this was to be her baby's coming out. To finally let the men know that Claire Cooliage was ready to be courted. So exciting, Catherine sat and drifted into past memories of her own courting days with Charles.

As Claire's mother seemed to be remembering happier times, Claire slipped out of the room. How could they be doing this to her? She didn't want a coming out gala! Didn't they realize that a future husband would likely not approve of her wanting to teach? That was Claire's dream; to finally teach. Surely her parents knew that, or why had they allowed her to stay away at school earning her teaching degree? The day was off to a horrible start. Claire went to her rooms and busied herself with replying to her letters that had arrived in today's mail.

-6-

The days during the following week went by without much excitement. Claire was busy with her mother planning each outfit to the last detail. She was being schooled on each suitor father had invited. Catherine had even went as far as to make up little cards for each eligible man that had written on it his name, station in Boston, his family and a few key points for Claire to remember. Claire pretended these were just learning ques for an upcoming test. Yes, view this as a test, for she was not in it to secure a future husband. She had a life plan, and this was just a bump in the road, so to speak.

Once her parent's saw that she did not click with these suitors maybe they will give up and let her carry out her dream. For now, she will go along with the role as debutante daughter. She will dress to impress, dance and smile till she hurt. But in the end, she will accept a teaching position.

The day of the first gala ball had arrived. The staffs were very busy polishing the entire estate from top to bottom. Toula had been instructed to prepare a rose scented bath for Claire, and set her hair. Claire emerged from her hot tub of scented water to be encased into the softest, plush towels held out to her by Toula. This was a very special day and Toula hummed her happy song all the while explaining how the house was all done up, and how Claire will be the prettiest of the girls there. She was sure Claire's daddy will be getting a lot of offers for her hand tonight alone. Toula was so proud of her little charge; she was just like one of her own.

The gown chosen was a fine ball gown, golds and ruby red accents with layers of petticoats to bring out the fullness. When Claire put it on she felt like a princess. Silk layers, gold lace, and off the shoulder puffy sleeves. The dress had a sweetheart neckline that showed a little more skin than Claire was comfortable with, but Toula assured her she looked perfect, and proper. Claire's natural emerald green eyes were sparkling brighter than the real emeralds around her neck. She was radiant. As she slipped on her above the elbow gold gloves, her mother entered the room to check on the progress.

Catherine stood statue still as she walked into the dressing room. There was her daughter, so beautiful so grown up looking. It took her breath away. Unshed tears formed in the corners of her eyes and she dabbed them with her gloved finger. Catherine walked toward her daughter and held out her hand. Palm up she held a small velvet box, she indicated to Claire that this was her birthday gift from her and her father. Claire reached for the blue box, held it for a moment before lifting the clasp to open it. Inside was a lovely bracelet of gold with emeralds and diamonds circling the bracelet, the clasp had a small chain with a tiny lock to keep it from coming undone once attached to the wrist. It was lovely, and went with her necklace like they were once a matched set. This thought was confirmed by Claire's mother as she removed the bracelet and went to place it on Claire's wrist. Catherine explained how the necklace once belonged to Charles' mother and once they were married he gave the necklace to her. Charles then commissioned to have a matching bracelet made. It was always Catherine's deepest desire to have a daughter, so she could hand down the set. Her dreams finally coming true tonight, her only daughter adorn with her emeralds, on her sixteenth birthday.

Catherine walked ahead of her daughter on their way towards the grand staircase. They could hear the music coming out of the ballroom. The gala was in full swing, time for the belle of the ball to make her grand entrance, thought Claire. She was curious as to the many suitors who had agreed to show up tonight. Also knowing that many single ladies will also be here to snatch up a future husband. Normally these types of affairs were more of a competition, than a happy event. To Claire, it was a means to an end.

She was here to show indifference to these men, and to make sure each and every potential beau knew that she was going to become a teacher. If they had a problem with that, then that's exactly it; their problem, for Claire Cooliage bowed to no man. With this thought running through her head, Claire was ready to make her entrance, a lovely natural smile played on her lips thinking of the faces of the men when she let loose her thoughts on teaching.

He father was waiting outside the closed ballroom doors, he held out his bent arm for her to hook her hand onto. Catherine stood to the other side of Claire. When the current song ended, a butler had announced that Miss Claire Cooliage was ready to be accepted. The ballroom doors swung open and Claire's nightmare was to begin.

The crowd was parted down the sides of the ballroom, like the parting of the red sea, this thought made Claire giggle under her breath. Her father tightened on his grip to her arm, which was a silent reminder to behave. Claire sobered and walked into the gathered crowd. She noticed a lot of familiar faces, those of her beloved friends, and then many more faces that she didn't recognise as well. Her father gave a nod to the band and they began a waltz letting the onlookers get a real good view of the lamb being offered up to slaughter, another giggle emerged.

After the first dance concluded the band was to take a break, which allowed for well greetings and happy birthday wishes to be said to Claire, as she stood at the front of the ballroom. It seemed more of a greeting line actually, with people vying for her attention. Claire thought it was all very well-orchestrated, almost comical really, for these people pretended to actually know her.

After the band had announced that the birthday cake was to be wheeled in, Claire had noticed that a long table had been set up along one side of the long room. There sitting in the centre of the table was an elaborate four tiered white cake with yellow flowers and pearls as the only decoration. It was a glorious looking cake; Cook had certainly done her best job ever. Claire started to mist over. The birthday song had been sung, and people were wishing her well.

When it came time for her friends to approach her, Claire was ready for the fake smile to slip off and be replaced with an honest happy smile. First up was Margarite, of course. Her raven thick hair pulled to the side and piled high on her head, long strands curled tightly and red roses were placed strategically throughout her hair with tiny white pearls threaded with them. Her dress was as red as the roses, which showed off a little more cleavage than Claire thought was appropriate for such a gala, but with her dark features, rose red dress with its white lacy petticoats trimmed in black lace peeking out the ends and her above the elbow red gloves she was a sultry beauty. She had taken time to make sure her lips shone and even painted sparkles onto her eyelids. Margarite came to stake her claim as the best tonight.

She was making a point to Claire. Her point was to make sure Claire knew she was second best, nobody out shone Margarite. Claire took note. She did feel like second best, and surprisingly that did not bother her. In fact, she felt sorry for her long-time friend to have to feel the need to try to out shine someone on their special day. When had Margarite become so insecure, so selfish? She will place this thought in the back of her memory for now, to be brought up front later for review.

The twins came next. Rose and Beth looked stunning! Of course dressed the same, bookends of beauty.; their blonde hair was twisted into a complicated design with black lace and small feathers entwined, gorgeous black gowns with pale blue satin showing, rounded low necklines and simple pearl necklaces and the blue satin gloves that rose to just below their armpits. Rose and Beth hugged her with honest sincere love. They were here to celebrate in Claire's honour. Not to compete. No flashy show from these two, no not at all. Claire was happy to have these two as her friends here tonight.

Last of her friends, Jaquelin came slowly forward. Almost too shy, she barely made eye contact. Claire wasn't sure why she was always looking down; Jaquelin was a good looking lady. She could likely use a better dress selection, but she still dressed nicely. For tonight her brown hair sparkled, it was left down with silver hair combs holding the sides, with baby's breath flowers on those combs. Her ball gown was a cream colour with brown laced bottoms and brown laced trims on the sleeves. It had a square neck cut across her breast, and tiny brown embroidery around the edges. It was stunning. She wore no jewels. Claire thought that Jaquelin's dress matched her to a tee; simple and elegant.

After the receiving line and a few refreshments, the band cued that the dancing was about to begin. Claire had received many dance cards, which her mother proudly held for her. Dance partner after dance partner, the night was flying by. One by one each of Father's suitors asked for her hand to dance. Every one of them lovely and prominent dancing partners; strong in the lead, and gentle on the hands and feet. Many of these men wanting to dance second and third times. Claire was getting visibly tired, so thankfully Stephan stepped in, and suggested that Claire take a walk with him to the terrace to grab a bit of fresh air. This met with the approval of both Claire and their mother.

Stephan led Claire through the large glass double doors onto the well-lit terrace. There were other couples out on the terrace but Claire didn't notice, she was overcome with giddiness from the dancing. Stephan remarked how lovely she looked dancing tonight, and how proud their parents looked. He also inquired about the many suitors fighting for a dance. Did she have a favourite? Stephan asked about each man, and gave his opinion on each man, as Claire regaled her promise to herself to no be impressed by the men her father chose. Stephan laughed as Claire told him of the horrified looks a couple of the men gave her when she informed them that her desire was to teach and that she has sent out for position placements.

Only one other dance partner seemed impressed by her claim, and this was intriguing to Claire. She was asking Stephan about this gentleman but could not for the life of her remember his name! He only danced with her the one time and then seemed to have disappeared. Stephan though about the men that Claire had danced with and asked again what this certain gentleman looked like. Claire didn't have to think long, because this one guy certainly made an impression on her despite her resolve to NOT be infatuated by any man tonight.

She told Stephan that he wasn't as tall as most of the men, not as handsome either. He was slightly pudgy, clean shaven, smooth hands with sandy brown short cut hair and hazel green eyes. He had on a brilliant dark suit with a yellow cravat, a diamond in the centre of this cravat and a single yellow carnation in the lapel. A rather larger ring on his finger as well. Oh yes, and he was a lawyer. Stephan thought long and hard over father's suitor list to match the description to a name. It was the last bit of information that struck a knowing cord, the lawyer. Yes it had to be him, Brian Stackhouse. Brilliant new lawyer to the same Boston firm in which their older brother Micheal was now partnering to. Brian Stackhouse, pompous idiot, thought Stephan. One of the many suitors that Father was hoping to secure. He had wealth, and the breeding that would fit nicely for Claire. Stephan had a different opinion, but Father wouldn't hear of it, Stackhouse was on the guest list.

They had been out on the terrace for longer than Stephan had planned but he was concerned about the way Claire spoke of Stackhouse, he really didn't want his sister getting attached to this man, as there was just something he didn't like about him; but couldn't put his finger on. The band was tuning for the next set of dances which was the cue to bring Claire back inside. The air was so fresh outside that so when Claire went back indoors she had a rosy complexion, which complimented her already gorgeous looks. Once inside and by her parent's side, Claire was able to watch the dancers for a change, having asked to sit the first dance out.

-7-

She watched the people on the ballroom floor gliding around, gowns flowing and everything so elegantly coordinated. Claire saw that both Rose and Beth were out on the floor dancing with a couple of gentlemen admirers that she had seen dancing with each of them earlier. There was Jaquelin, sitting off to the side of the ballroom with her chaperone, her mother. Why wasn't she dancing? Claire knew that a couple of men had approached her, but she had declined every dance offer. She will have to inquire as to why. And then there was Margarite, laughing at a group of men circling her wanting her to add them on her dance card. Flirting and carrying on, such a wanton display. Where was her mother during all this? Claire couldn't help but be a little put off by Margarite's behaviour.

The gentleman that Stephan called Stackhouse was approaching Claire's father. They exchanged pleasantries, then handshakes he said his good-bye and moved on to Claire's mother. Bent over Catherine's gloved hand he place one simple kiss to the back of her hand; a gentlemanly polite gesture that wasn't lost on either Catherine or Claire. After speaking momentarily to Catherine, this gentleman walked towards Claire. So unlike herself, she was actually sensing excitement in the thought that this man was interested in HER. Even knowing that she planned on securing a teaching position, he was still interested. Strange feelings were over coming her. When Stackhouse, as her brother had called him, stopped in front of Claire and asked her for this dance, she went willingly into his hands.

It was not the only dance they shared, it was soon easy to tell that Claire had preferred to dance with this man, so the other suitors bowed out, and moved on to the other women in the room. The night was drawing to a close and the final dance was announced. Several people had already left the ball, and Claire was surprised to have noticed that she didn't even say good-bye to her friends. The only one remaining was Margarite, and she was standing against the snack table looking extremely put out. Claire wondered what could have happened to make her friend look so angry, maybe because her mother was sending for their carriage and Margarite wasn't ready to leave yet? Yes, that had to be it. Why else could she look so angry?

The dance ended and Brian Stackhouse held Claire's hand as he escorted her back to her parents. Brian, she had learned his first name when he insisted she call him by it, handed her to her father and asked if he may call on her later this week. Claire smiled and looked to her father for direction. Charles looked very pleased and he nodded in agreement. That settled, Brian said he would call on her later, and he said good-bye.

The evening was over, the last guest was shown out and the lanterns were doused. Charles instructed the staff to take the night off and they can set the rooms straight tomorrow. He and his wife were headed to bed. Stephan had already retired to his rooms earlier, so it was Claire alone to her thoughts.

She walked down the long hallway towards the kitchen, knowing Cook would have a glass of milk and a large plate of cookies waiting for her. Something she has secretly done her entire childhood. Yes, there was her chilled milk, and plate of cookies waiting for her. As she nibbled a cookie she thought about her dance. Each man was nice, but none compared to Brian. He seemed to honestly understand her desire to be a teacher. That meant the world to her. To be treated as an equal, instead of a

Cooliage prize to be won. As Claire climbed into her turned down bed, her smile remained well into her sleep.

The day after the ball, Charles had gone into town to see Mr. Stackhouse. During their visit, Charles learned that Brian was interested in courting Claire. After a lengthy discussion about what both men were wanting from this arrangement, it was agreed that Brian had The Cooliage blessing to court Miss Claire.

Any other suitor would be turned away. Since this was agreed upon, Charles returned home that evening a very happy man. At dinner that night he had announced to his family seated around the dining table, that he had accepted Mr. Brian Stackhouse as a proper suitor for Claire and gave his blessing to the courtship. Catherine was smiles as she looked at the happy look on her only daughter's face.

Micheal, who had come home for this special announcement tonight was pleased, and also gave his apologies for not attending the ball as he was dealing with a troublesome court case at that time and could not get away for the ball. Knowing Brian from the law firm, he was surprised his sister found him intriguing enough to have court her. Micheal thought Brian was a pompous sort, and not at all what he thought Claire would like. Maybe his sister had changed while away at university.

The only person at the table that outwardly did not show their pleasure at this news was Stephan. He was not happy at all about the thought of that man courting his little sister. Father must have lost his senses. He will have to find a tactful way to speak to Micheal about his misgivings on this. Until then he only prayed it was a very long courtship.

The first time Brian Stackhouse showed up at her door the following week, proper etiquette stated that the meeting must be in her home and well chaperoned. Claire greeted Brian in the parlor with her mother and Toula in the room. Catherine and Toula tried to be off to the side and discrete, giving the young couple the needed privacy to talk and get to know each other.

-8-

Claire and Brian sat in the parlor for hours, talking about everything in their lives. From Claire's time away at school and the studies, her friends she made while there to her plans for her teaching future. Brian told Claire about how he came to live in Boston, starting out in different lawyer's offices until reaching the firm where he was now. As a junior law clerk, an upcoming trial lawyer he was sure he would become a vital part to the firm in no time. Claire noticed that he didn't mention her brother Micheal being one of the partners at this firm. He must have just over looked this point. Perhaps it wasn't a big deal. It wasn't to Claire, so she let the thought go. It was time for their first meeting to end, and Toula showed Brian to the door. Not before Brian asked Mrs. Cooliage if he may bring his carriage by the following week and take Claire for a drive around the park. Catherine agreed to this as it sounded like a wonderful idea and Claire seemed to like Brian very much. Her husband must be thrilled his matchmaking went so well. A date and time were set, Brian said his good-byes and left the estate on horseback.

The week seemed to be dragging along as Claire awaited her outing with Brian. Cook had packed a lovely basket with cold quail, fruits, cheese and breads. A container of cider and a quilt were added as an afterthought. Claire was almost ready as she heard the carriage approach on the cobblestone out front. Dressed in a camel coloured day dress with a mauve tunic and a camel coloured bonnet she looked especially excited. She grabbed her gloves as Jonas opened the front door to allow Brian to enter.

At the top of the staircase, Claire watched the two men exchange pleasantries. Brian looked uncomfortable talking to Jonas and checked his reflection in the gold mirror on the entry wall. He was adjusting his cravat and top hat, holding an ornate walking stick, Brian made quite the dashing look. Claire started to descend the stairs, and watched for a response from Brian. True to form, Brian smiled and bowed to her as she came to stand in front of him. He switched the walking stick to his left hand and offered Claire his right arm as they walked out to his carriage.

Brian helped Claire into his covered carriage and instructed his driver to load the basket that Jonas had, then to take them around the park. Once inside the carriage Claire got a really good look at Brian. His features seem to have changed a bit, he was clean shaven, and hair was freshly cut. He took great pride in his appearance she reflected. He had the most unusual ring on his finger. It was a gold lion head with large ruby eyes. When she commented on his ring, Brian smiled and said that it was a family ring, something that has been passed down to him by his grandfather.

Brian held up his walking stick to show Claire the lion head with the same eyes as the top of his stick. He had said that he had this walking stick made in the fashion of his ring. It will become his signature of sorts. Something people can remember the great lawyer by; his prowess in the courts just like that of the lion. Strange, thought Claire, but then again men of his stature can be quirky. Something she will learn to love.

They rode around the park a couple times before selecting a spot by the pond for their lunch. Brian's driver set the blanket down and the basket on top. He then returned to the carriage to wait. Claire was helped to the blanket where she started to unpack the basket placing items alongside. Brian relaxed on his side watching Claire.

Commenting on how graceful she was, how lovely she was and how lucky he was that she had chosen him to court her from all the other suitors. This line of talk made Claire uncomfortable as she was not one to have attention drawn to her.

She changed the subject by offering Brian a plate of food. They ate and talked of simple things, then fed the ducks some of the bread before placing items back in the basket. Brian pulled out his pocket watch and checked the time, he had better return her to her home. Claire was sad that their time was at an end, but Brian held her hand to the carriage and even inside the carriage on the way home. Once at her house, Brian kissed the inside of her wrist. That one act set Claire's heart racing. So intimate, so personal. Brian surely must have strong feelings for her.

Claire floated to her rooms where she sat in front of her dressing mirror in a love daze. She was lost in the glow. For the next few days she couldn't recall what happened. She was in love, she was sure of it.

And so it went. On and on just like this. Brian would show up, they would go out and be seen in public, at fine restaurants, and the park everywhere. They attended parties together and even a dance at a friend's place. All the upper class Boston had it on good notes that the sought after Miss Claire Cooliage was indeed going to be spoken for soon.

Stephan had made arrangement to have dinner in town with Micheal one Wednesday evening. Micheal approached Stephan at the table and they shook hands and embraced like the brothers always did. Stephan was nervous and Micheal could sense something was bothering him, but decided to let him get around to mentioning it. They had a before dinner drink, while waiting for their meal. During the drink Stephan asked Micheal about his cases, his new home and his dating. Laughing Micheal answered all the questions and stopped short of talking about dating. He didn't want to disillusion his younger brother. Obviously Stephan assumed Micheal dated a lot, truth be told Micheal was too busy to have a personal life right now. Micheal then asked Stephan about his dealings with work, and how he liked having Claire home again.

That was the opening that Stephan needed to breech the subject of Brian Stackhouse. Stephan informed Micheal that Stackhouse has staked a claim on their sister. This shocked Micheal as the man worked in his firm and has never mentioned dating his sister. On the contrary, Micheal thought Brian was a single man. Stephan and Micheal discussed their feelings on this Brian guy, both coming to the same conclusion that something wasn't right. Micheal agreed to keep an eye on things from his end, and Stephan said he would do the same on his side.

Together they would figure things out and meet back up later to discuss their mutual findings. Feeling better about having someone to share his feelings, Stephan was able to enjoy the rest of the dinner with his older brother. Micheal, though, was concerned.

Margarite draped the heavy dark cloak over her dark dress and exited her house. The rented hacky was waiting, as she climbed in she handed a piece of paper to the driver with an address on it. The hacky took off towards the seedier side of town. Knowing better to question the passenger or he knew he would not earn the huge coin she was sure to give. This was not the first time he has picked up the covered person, and delivered her to this address. Each time his purse gets heavier. He was instructed to return at a certain time as he watched the cloaked figure disappear into the doorway of the plain cottage, and then inside. As the driver pocketed the coin into his purse, he wondered at her urgency to get to this side of town, she is of wealth for sure. It was not his place to wonder he reminded himself.

Driving the cloaked woman to and from is feeding his family much better now than the many years prior. Who is he to question good fortune? With that he headed home to his missus and children. To feast, and drink and rest before returning for his fare to have her back on the wealthy side of town before the good people are awake. Perhaps she is a servant there?

Stephan and Micheal left the restaurant and went their separate ways. Micheal called a hacky, which was passing by and had him stop and take him to his residence. The hacky was happy to have gained another fare on his way home. This fine gentleman was not taking him far out of his way so he didn't mind, and started whistling a jaunty tune, happy of his money to be made. Micheal paid the fare plus a nice little tip as it was a bit out of the hacky's way seeing how he was headed home. Micheal thanked him, and the driver mentioned how tired his horse will be and how he will switch out his horse for a fresh one for his return fare later tonight. Micheal thought as he walked away how hard a man like the hacky driver must have to work if he was going to interrupt a good night's sleep to pick up a fare in the dead of night. Such a good man supporting his family in an honest way was hard to find in Boston.

-9-

Stephan pulled his horse up to the stables where he handed the reins to the groom. He walked slowly towards the main house still in thought about his talk with Micheal. Would his father be upset if he knew the brothers did not trust his choice of suitor for his daughter? More than likely thought Stephan. He will keep this to himself for now. Tired from the long day he had, and knowing he had a longer day tomorrow with his father; Stephan hurried to his room to undress for bed.

Claire's life continued as normal, Brian picking her up, courting her. This was getting more serious, as the weeks went by, turning into months. One evening Brian showed up unannounced at the Cooliage Estate wanting to speak to Mr. Cooliage. Charles had been waiting for this day, he showed Brian into his study. Brian paced the floor while Charles smiled into his whiskey glass as he sat by the fire in his leather wing back chair.

Brian cleared his throat and fiddled with the ring on his finger. Charles looked up as Brian approached his chair. Holding a ring in his hand he handed it to Charles. Looking down at the huge gaudy gold ring encrusted with rubies around a large diamond. It was an ugly ring thought Charles. He would most definitely never offer a woman such an eye sore. But perhaps it's a family heirloom and means a lot to him, Charles won't be judgemental. Brian announced that he wanted Claire's hand in marriage, that he has secured a proper home and will staff it with the best help he can find.

Charles was happy with the knowledge that Brian worried enough to make sure his daughter was kept in the lifestyle she was accustomed to, but one thought stuck in his head. He needed to cut to the chase and asked Brian what he thought about Claire's wish to become a teacher. Brian gave pause for a moment. He sat on the ottoman by Charles chair, and spoke slowly at first. He mentioned that his hopes were that after the wedding she will be too busy planning his house dinners and eventually raising their children to be thinking about teaching.

Charles was pleased to hear that Brian did not agree to his daughter's dreams of teaching. Being satisfied about his choice in Brian, he handed the ring back to him, shook his hand and gave him his blessing to wed his daughter. He wanted to know when Brian was going to propose to Claire, and if they should plan a formal engagement party. They had agreed on the formal party to be held after he asks Claire. He was sure she would agree, but will give her the time to be used to being engaged before the entire city of Boston hears of it. Charles and Brian had devised a plan that would require the help of Catherine, they would decorate the garden gazebo with lanterns and a round table set for two. A romantic dinner and small talk would be the back drop for this evening in which Brian would get down on one knee and formally propose. Now that the details would be left in Catherine's capable hands, the men finished off their last drink and rose to say their good-byes.

-10-

Leaving the Cooliage Estates, Brian heads to the rented home he has down town. A home he shares with his widowed mother. Brian was planning on keeping the rented home and supplying his mother with a staff and an allowance once he was married to Claire. He will be able to afford to do this with her added monies that he's sure to gain once they are married. He needed to plan a perfect day in which to propose to Claire. He needed the best outfit, must make sure his hair has been groomed and bring fresh flowers from the market. Whistling to himself, he felt like the world was finally aligning for him.

Today Claire donned a simple plain earth toned dress with matching tunic over a creamy coloured high necked lacy blouse. Her red hair piled high on her head and a simple head piece of tan colour with a bright white feather surrounding the brim. Elegant brown feathers entwined throughout the white feather. Secured with a pair of hat pins Claire was ready to head downtown to visit with her friends. All were meeting at a small tea house to discuss the upcoming parties that have been announced through the society. Claire walked down the staircase and as if on cue, Jonas appeared holding a brown parasol and her gloves. A welcoming smile showed her pleasure as she placed a simple kiss on his cheek. Jonas was always humbled at such shows of affection, but this was HIS Claire after all.

Claire exited the home and to the awaiting carriage. The short ride through Boston to the tea house was made even shorter by the thoughts swirling in her head. She seemed to be doing a lot of daydreaming lately, and about one man in particular. Brian, he seemed to always be taking up her mind lately. This was not entirely a bad thing, but she wondered how she ever got through the day prior to thinking of him.

The carriage stopped outside a quaint little house that boasted a sign on the front gate simply saying "Tessa's". Claire walked up the short walkway and opened the front door. She was immediately met by Tessa, tall willowy and beautifully dressed. Tessa was a bit of a mystery, nobody knew from where she came from, or her last name. For all Claire knew, Boston had sprung up around her! Tessa was a sweet older lady with superior patience and her teas were amazing. Each patron had their own little private area and larger groups were seated in the dining hall. This was a wonderful establishment for private chats with your friends.

Claire was led to the little alcove towards the garden, there she saw her friends seated on comfortable wicker chairs with soft flowered cushions. There was a small wicker table placed in the centre and an elaborate tea set sat upon this table. A three tiered tray loaded with sweets and sandwiches also on the table. Beth was first to notice Claire's arrival and she went to hug her friend. Not to be out done, her sister Rose came forward for her embrace. Jaquelin stood as Claire approached her and hugged her friend tightly. Margarite did not rise, but nodded in her friend's direction.

Claire did not find anything odd in this, but Beth looked at Rose with a concerned look. Rose shook her head as if to say, don't say anything.

Talk circled around the many parties, which invites to accept, which to ignore. What they should all be wearing and the people bound to be at these parties. General gossip and childhood stories filled the afternoon. All the while, Margarite couldn't help but pick apart every aspect of Claire's attire. Try as hard as she could, she just couldn't find fault. Claire looked lovely. It was a natural kind of elegance, where Margarite needed the added face paints and hours of hairstyling. When had her friend blossomed into such the beauty?

Jaquelin had decided to ask Claire about the many suitors that her father had set her up with at the ball. Claire blushed and said that she was overwhelmed with the number of available men, but luckily she had found one that stood out. Beth and Rose giggled with excitement and asked his name. Brian, Claire said, Brian Stackhouse. This conversation brought Margarite's head up with a snap. Claire finally had her full attention. Brian was a lawyer in a Boston firm and was a kind man with a calm soul. He was interested in her ideas and her teaching degree. She had a wonderful time when with him, and she was hoping to have met the man her father would approve of. This would make leaving for a teaching position that much easier. Maybe she could even gain a position in the Boston school for young ladies.

Dreamy eyes drifted towards the garden at the thought. Much of the rest of the conversation that followed was lost to Claire as she was in her own little dreamland once again. It wasn't until Tessa came in to clear the cups and plates and let the girls know that their carriages awaited them, that Claire remembered where she was. Embarrassed she apologized for not being a part of the conversation, and with friendly eyes, her friends all said they understood.

Loaded into her carriage, Claire asked her driver to stop at the postmaster's office so that she can gather that week's post for father. There seemed to be quite a lot of mail this week Claire noticed. One thing that Claire did not notice though was any mail for her. Wondering if she would ever hear back from the dean of teaching on a position, Claire's sunny mood soon faded. It was a disturbing ride home, thought of not ever landing a teaching position were eating at Claire.

When she arrived at the estate, Claire left the mail with Jonas and went directly to her rooms. Once there she went to her day planner on her desk and flipped backwards in the dates to find when her last letter was sent to the dean. Several weeks had passed apparently, and with no response. Should she pen another letter? Would it seem she was being too forward and pushy? She will broach the subject later tonight at dinner to her parents. Claire knew her father's reaction but hoped her mother could give her some sense of guidance on the situation.

The topic was not to be mentioned during dinner as Jonas announced that her parents were dining alone in their quarters so Claire and Stephan were left alone in the dining hall. Try as hard as she might, Claire could not bring herself to ask for her brother's opinion. Thinking for sure he would instantly side with the same ideas as father. So silently she sat and ate her meal. After dinner she had excused herself and retired for the evening.

Claire woke still troubled about the missing posts from the dean. She was still troubled about her parents not being available for her to ask their advice on the subject. Who can she turn to if her own parents were not available? Her brother Stephan was sure to side with her father, her mother was not one to go against her father either, but atleast mother could give her honest advice. Her oldest brother Micheal has since moved out to his own home and seemed so busy lately that she dared not trouble him. Who did that leave, Toula, the servants? Maybe she could talk to Brian, he is very supportive, and accepts her dreams of becoming a teacher and being placed soon. Yes, that is exactly what she will do. She will talk to Brian and gain some much needed advice from him.

Felling much better with her decision, Claire went downstairs to have breakfast and start her day with a new outlook; bright and sunny, just like the morning. Claire entered the dining hall and noticed she was the only one present. The food trays were laden with breakfast choices and fruits and breads. Claire filled her plate with a selection of fruits and cheeses and some bread.

On the table where she usually sat was set with jam and juice and the maid brought her a fresh cup of tea to go with her breakfast. Jonas entered and informed Claire that the rest of the family have already had their breakfast and are carrying on with their days. Odd, Claire thought, as she climbed the stairs to her rooms. Once there she had decided to start to pen the letters she hoped she would post, after she spoke to Brian of her decision to do so. If Brian thought it was a solid plan then she would have the letters ready and then take the to the postmasters office. The day drifted by.

It was the big evening, the Cooliage house was a buzz of excitement and Claire had no idea why. The staff were racing around, polishing and cleaning every inch. Her father was held up in his study all day refusing to even see her until just this moment when he had sent Toula to fetch her to the study. Claire let herself in and on nervous feet walked towards the fireplace where her father sat in his favorite leather chair. Charles motioned for her to sit opposite him, and that's when she noticed that her mother and both her older brothers were also seated here. It was definitely serious if the family were all there. Claire swallowed a hard dry knot of nerves. Searching each person's face for the horrible news she was expecting.

-11-

Claire sat on father's ottoman directly in the line of fire. All eyes were trained on her pale face. Unable to form a word, she waited. Charles cleared his throat, looked to his wife and sons and then finally to his only Daughter, his baby. When he spoke it was the softest, kindest tones that Claire had ever heard her father use. Had he said what she thought he said?

Hand in marriage to Brian Stackhouse? Surely she had heard him wrong, but glancing around and seeing the very pleased looks on both her parents she was certain those were the words she heard. Just to make sure, Claire had asked her father to repeat what he had said. Chuckling to himself, Charles stated clearly that he had agreed to Stackhouse's offer for her hand. Claire's mother Catherine took this moment to inform Claire that tonight in the garden gazebo Brian was going to formally propose to her with the family blessing.

Claire looked from each face in the room, looks of joy from her parents and conflicting looks from her two brothers. Before she could ask Stephan and Micheal if they had concerns, Catherine had insisted Claire go upstairs right away and put on the gown that Toula was setting out in her dressing rooms and to prepare for her evening.

Like a sleepwalker, Claire walked out of the study and up the grand staircase to her suites. Opening her dressing room door she was met with happy hugs and nonstop chatter from Toula and one of the young maids. Both seemed extremely excited for Claire and her upcoming evening in the garden. Toula talked of how the gazebo had a fresh coat of paint only this week and the bushes trimmed to perfection. Even the night flowers seemed happy as Claire could smell their scents flowing in through the open windows.

Brian was going to propose. To her. Why hadn't he mentioned any of this on the many rides they shared? Yes, she knew eventually that she would marry, but she was just turned 16, and was looking forward to teaching. Would Brian still be happy about her wanting to teach? Will he still be supportive of her dreams? Or would history be doomed to repeat itself, and she would lose out on her hopes and dreams as her mother lost hers once she married father? More confusion, just when she assumed that she was sorting out her life choices. Should she mention her letters to Brian still? Claire was beginning to develop a mild headache. Still she allowed the chatty women to fuss over her, fake smile in place; her mind whirled with unanswered questions.

Her mother never came right out and said that she regretted not teaching, but Claire wondered just the same. Fear was gripping her strong right now. How would she reply to Brian's proposal? Should she ask about her desires to still teach? She asked Toula her thoughts on this. Toula stared at Claire and sat down on the bench by the big mirror. Did Claire even want to marry Mr. Stackhouse? Certainly Miss Claire saw how happy the idea of this marriage made her father. Claire always looked happy when she left with Mr. Stackhouse, and always happy when she returned from outings. What did Claire think? Claire couldn't answer that. Yes, she enjoyed her times with Brian. Yes, she could see herself as his wife. He was a kind unselfish man, not as handsome as some, but kind just the same. She could not do better for a husband she thought. He got on well with her family and her brother Micheal had Brian working in his firm, surely he was trustworthy or Micheal would object. A smile came to Claire's beautiful face. Yes, she would accept the proposal, everything will work out. Brian was all for her teaching before they were to be married, why wouldn't he be the same after.

Dressed in a simple faded yellow light summer gown with a flowing material, her hair brushed into a shiny red mass of curls cascading down her back, the side held pinned atop her head with gold hair combs, Claire walked out into the dark garden and followed the path to the gazebo which was brightly lit by fiery torches, sending a warm glow across her skin. Her face flushed with excitement. There stood Brian, in a simple grey suit, tan breeches tucked in gleaming black riding boots, a starched white dress shirt and grey cravat with a ruby pin, his top hat on his tailored hair. He sat his walking stich against the pillar of the gazebo as she neared. Extended hand to Claire, Brian then removed his top hat and smiled warmly at her nervous face.

With Brian's grip on her arm, Claire managed to climb the few stairs into the gazebo. She sat on a white chair across from his with a table covered in a long white tablecloth adorn with tall candle sticks and silver covered plates. There was a vase of freshly cut roses off to the side of the candles; the scene was very romantic thought Claire. Brian suggested they enjoy the special meal cook had prepared, and they talked about their week. It was a very relaxing dinner and Claire forgot the real reason they were dining out on the gazebo with all the romance around them.

Once the maid removed the trays, and they were left alone, Brian turned to Claire. He cleared his throat and stood up from his chair. He rounded the table in front of Claire, adjusting his jacket and cravat, while holding onto her hands he looked her in the eye and lowered to one knee. Claire felt her breath stop, she flushed. This was it! He was about to propose to her. Brian cleared his throat and squeezed Claire's hand.

Miss Claire Marie Colliage, would you marry me? Simple, direct no sweet words of love, no promises of a happy life, Brian was direct and to the point. Should Claire say yes and then ask about her teaching? Or just say yes and cover that particular touchy subject later? Claire smiled at Brian and nodded her head enthusiastically. Oh Yes, she replied in a near whisper. Brian smiled, kissed her knuckles and rose to his feet. He then reached inside his coat pocket and withdrew a gold ring.

My goodness thought Claire, it was an ugly ring. But Brian looked ever so pleased as he placed it on her finger. Claire looked down at the monstrosity staring back at her. She must looked happy she thought, for this ring obviously meant a great deal to him, and must have cost him a small fortune, for the jewels alone took up her tiny finger. There was a single large diamond in the centre of a double row of rubies, and weighed a great deal. The gold was heavy and the jewels boasted of royal quality. Where had he commissioned such a gaudy ring, thought Claire? He certainly didn't know what her tastes in rings were, as she would have never chosen such a ring. It surely must be a family heirloom. She must be sure to inquire of its origins so she will be able to explain to her friends when she needs to show them.

Brian sat back on his chair and began to explain to Claire that on Saturday next week her father is throwing a gala ball for the sole purpose of celebrating their engagement, she had one week to get used to the idea of becoming Mrs. Brian Stackhouse, for they were to be wed in one month's time. Brian went on saying how after the engagement party they would begin to look at suitable homes for them to consider moving into. He will of course be keeping the rented home he is currently in, so that his poor widowed mother will not have to move in with them. He was sure a newlywed couple did not want an old widow underfoot. He would also need to secure a proper staff, for both houses and then set his mother up with an allowance as he will not be there to provide her basic needs.

All this seemed a bit much for Claire to take in right away. Had Brian mentioned something about having her monies transferred into his accounts? Why would she need to do that? Oh well, maybe she had heard him wrong. She will wait and see. Brian suggested that they return to the main house now as time was getting on and he really needed to get home to his mother.

Kissing Claire, he said soon enough they would not need to be apart much longer. Holding Claire's hand he guided them towards the house. Once at the side entrance, Brian kissed Claire soundly again and placed her in the house. He then walked around the side of the property to his horse grazing in the coral. Seeing the man approach, the groom prepared his horse. Brian mounted and rode off towards downtown.

This was Claire's first real kiss. She quietly walked up the stairs to her rooms. Thinking about the kiss while she undressed and put on her night dress, Claire sat at her dressing table brushing out her hair and then tied it with a ribbon before climbing into her bed. Once in bed she held up her left hand and looked at her ring again, trying to picture what her dream ring would look like. She tried to imagine that ring and Brian kissing her. Would she feel those butterflies everyone talked about? Was she just nervous and therefore blocking those butterflies? Who knows? Sighing, Claire doused the lanterns and flopped into the softness of her comforters. She fell into a deep dreamless sleep.

-12-

Birds chirping and sunshine filling her room, Claire woke still confused about the way her life was facing. On her left hand was a very heavy, unattractive ring given to her by a man whom she's only known a few months and that she will be legally wed to in a shorter time, all with her family's blessings. Deep in thought, she sat at her dressing table gazing at her reflection in her mirror. Claire rose from her sitting bench and walked to the wardrobe to decide on today's dress choice. What did she plan on doing today? Should she ring Brian and have lunch with him, to discuss everything she had hoped to speak to him about? Deciding that was her course of action for today, Claire rang for Toula and together they began to set her hair, laced with fresh little flowers to match her mauve day dress. She will look her best today as she feared the topic of discussion will not go over well with her newly betrothed.

Finally dressed and walking down the staircase, Jonas met Claire at the foot of the stairs. Notified earlier by Toula, Jonas assured Claire that a message had been sent to Mr. Stackhouse pertaining to the arranged lunch date. Hugging Jonas and saying thank-you she then asked her parent's whereabouts. Claire headed to the solarium to speak to her parents about the finer details to the arranged marriage. Claire approached the room to see her parents sitting across from each other at a small table arranged in the corner of the room, a chess set perched atop. Her father was deep in thought obviously about the next move; her mother was watching Claire approach with a happy smile on her lips.

Kissing her father on both cheeks as she said good morning Claire turned to kiss her mother and get a welcomed hug as well. Jonas appeared out of nowhere to place a chair for Claire to sit on. Once comfortable and having both of her parents attention, Claire cleared her throat and began her well prepared speech. Claire began by asking her father about the date of the wedding. Charles said that the exact date had yet to be secured, but the final details he is sure to go over with Brian, and that Claire will be given ample time to prepare. Thinking the topic was closed, Charles rose to leave. Claire attempted to stop her father by saying that she had a few other concerns. Her father turned to her, patted her on the head like a child, and said that the details will be sorted out by the men, and she should have no concerns. He knew what was best, and that Brian only wanted her happiness as well. He then turned and left the room, and the forgotten chess game.

Even more perplexed than when she awoke this morning, Claire expressed her concerns to her mother. Catherine was very sympathetic, listening to Claire's worries. Claire talked to her mother about the timing, stating that she really didn't know Brian that well. Her mother answered in a plain tone, saying that no one really knows anyone, that time will work everything out in the end.

Claire voiced her concerns about teaching, only to have her mother shift the subject to the actual wedding plans that they must begin soon. Realizing that she was going nowhere in her desire to have some answers, Claire was happy to hear that her carriage was ready and her lunch date with Brian was waiting.

Claire bid her mother good morning and followed Jonas to the main door. Bright sunshine and the shiny carriage were of exact opposite of Claire's mood right then. She was in a darker place than ever. Claire could barely force the smile she bestowed on the footman as he helped her into the carriage and closed the door.

The horse started off, the carriage rocked and swayed, and Claire focused on the hideous ring as the sunshine gleamed off the massive stones. It truly was an ugly ring she thought. A shiver ran down her spine, forbidding and cold.

The carriage stopped at a fine establishment that Claire had yet to dine at. The footman helped her from the carriage and walked her to the front door. Brian was waiting just inside the door, and extended his arm for Claire to accept. She removed her light summer cloak and handed it to the servant at the closet. The head waiter led them to their private table nestled in a very secluded area in the corner. Surrounded by tall ferns and pillars, the table was a cozy wooden table set with pale ivory linen, and white china plates. A single rose sat in a crystal vase in the centre of the table.

Looking at Brian, Claire tried to feel some sort of excitement. This was her fiancé after all. Shouldn't she feel giddy? She glanced at his features, trying to muster the love she should feel. Brian leaned forward to place a kiss on her red stained lips. No bolts of lightning, no butterflies, nothing. Is this normal? Is she still too nervous for those feelings to manifest? Brian was speaking, and Claire had to ask him to repeat what he had said.

Blushing from embarrassment, Brian took her blush as a result of his kiss, puffing up in the chest a little more, feeling very manly he did repeat his previous statement. He was pleased to have the lunch date, and looked forward to them getting to know each other daily as he was outlining their itinerary for the upcoming week.

Brian was informing Claire that he has discussed certain details with her father, and they were expected to show the town that they were engaged. Daily outings throughout Boston, to be seen together as a loving natural engaged couple. It all seemed so orchestrated to Claire, but what did she know of these things? Maybe this is how the whole thing really worked. Lunch was served, simple and tasteless. Claire chewed, swallowed and sipped her iced tea. After the meal she could not even remember what it was Infact that she ate. Brian walked Claire to the front entrance and collected her cloak; placing it on her shoulders he once again kissed Claire. Exiting the establishment, Brian suggested the stroll the boardwalk towards the park, and notified the carriage driver to meet them on the other side of the park.

Quietly walking along side Brian, her arm tucked securely in his, they walked towards the park nodding hello to passersby's and occasionally stopping to talk to mutual acquaintances. Just before they reached the park, Claire heard her name being called. Turing she found Margarite waving and smiling as she approached the couple. Brian tensed slightly and Claire wondered why. She gave her confused look to him, and he patted her arm as if to say its ok.

Margarite hugged Claire and placing kisses on each cheek, asked how she has been. Small talk ensued and Brian was looking very bored. When Margarite inquired on Claire's teaching position Brian shifted on his foot and cut into the conversation, stating that right now Claire is too busy to focus on her teaching as she has just become engaged and will be concentrating on her wedding day for now.

The shocked look on Margarite's face as she looked from Claire to Brian, and then to Claire's left hand as Brian held it up to her inspection a smug gleam on his face, was even more confusing to Claire. Surely her best friend should be happy for her, not look like she had just witnessed a murder. Stumbling over her hasty goodbye, siting a prearranged commitment she forgot, Margarite turned and left in a hurry. Brian reclaimed Claire's arm in his and continued on their stroll as if nothing strange had just transpired. Claire on the other hand, was left to her even more confused thoughts to be sorted out later when she was alone.

The pair walked through the park, commenting on various topics from the weather to the attires of different people as they passed by. Approaching the coach, Brian suggested meeting in the park each day providing the weather was decent, for walks and conversation.

His need to be seen in public was strange Claire thought as she agreed. Brian kissed her soundly and helped her into the carriage. Again, no butterflies; did they even exist? The weight of the heavy ring pressed her hand into the soft folds of her dress as the carriage bounces away from the park, heading back to the estate.

Sitting on the park bench, he wrote in his book everything that he had witnessed today, a lengthy list of activities for the past several weeks. If this keeps up he will need a new ledger for sure. He closed his book, placed it into his coat inside pocket and whistled a tune as he walked away. Unbeknownst to the kissing couple he was so intently watching a few moments earlier.

Margarite was still in shock as she closed her bedroom door. Her best friend was engaged, and hadn't told her? Tears streamed down her prettily made up face. Looking into her mirror, she dabbed at the tears, and prepared to fix the makeup damaged by those tears. Once her makeup had been repaired she went to her writing desk and penned a letter. Placing the letter into a plain unaddressed envelope, she called for the footman to deliver this letter. Margarite pleaded a headache to her mother and asked not to be disturbed the rest of the evening, she was not hungry and did not want anything brought to her. She wanted total silence and not to be bothered until morning tea. He mother, not seeming concerned agreed, and Margarite climbed the stairs to her room and shut her door.

Claire's coach arrived at her home in time for her to see her oldest brother Micheal emerging from the front door. She called to him, and he stopped short of getting onto his horse. Genuine smile showing on his handsome face as he walked towards her embracing, he congratulated her on her upcoming wedding and offered any services she may require.

She laughed and asked if they may have dinner or lunch sometime in the near future to talk. Micheal agreed and they set a date for next week. Feeling good about the upcoming lunch date with her brother, Claire said her goodbye and proceeded into the manor.

As darkness fell, Margarite donned her modest peasant attire, and snuck out the servant's entrance and into the awaiting hired hacky. Slipping the driver the coins and address on the paper, not speaking and not showing her face. The driver knew the address, as he had driven the woman there numerous times before. The driver wondered again if the woman's mistress knew of her sneaking out at ungodly hours and returning before the household woke. He thought of his wife once again, tucked warmly in their bed, and thanked God that his woman would never be caught out at these hours and heading into that part of town. But he is not one to judge as this woman paid him handsomely for his discreteness and timely delivery to and from her destination. They arrived at the tiny dark cottage, the quiet woman slipped for the hacky and walked thru the worn broken gate into the dark doorway. When the door closed securely behind her the driver left, and will return at the prearranged pick up time. He jingled the coins in his pocket, smiling as he headed home for a few hours of needed comfort from his wife.

-13-

A lone figure was in the shadows, watching the little cottage, writing in his little book the time and the happenings he watched. Knowing it will be a while before the people inside would leave; he headed to the local pub for a pint. He has done this routine before, he knew it well, clockwork almost. It was a sad time in these days when he could predict the comings and goings of certain people. He will return at the appropriate time, and watch from a safe spot. Like always, never to be seen. As the pub closed for the evening, the lone man walked the dark alley towards the tiny cottage, ready to watch ready to write down his finding. He already knows by heart what will happen, but he must follow through and witness the happenings.

He placed himself in the desired location to wait. It won't be long, he said to himself; as the hacky approached, the dark figure of the woman emerged from the cottage. She stopped in the doorway to place a very long and wanton kiss upon the man in the cottage. When they parted he retreated indoors while she proceeded into the hacky. The man in the shadows wrote in his book, and made a post note to speak to the hacky driver in the morning again, as usual, and to pay the hacky driver for his silence as usual. He waited about an hour longer for the man inside the cottage to come out. The man then went to the shed beside this cottage and brought out his horse. He mounted his horse and rode off at a fast pace towards downtown centre; to his residence no doubt.

The figure in the shadows climbed onto his horse that was tied in the shrubs not far away being watched by a grubby dock worker only too happy to receive his payment for sleeping while being tied to the beast to ensure the animal remained where the gentleman placed it. His payment was a small coin sack and a bottle of whiskey. That was the agreed upon payment and he received it gratefully. The dark figure rode off in the same direction as the man from the cottage. He knew the end destination so he was not in a huge hurry, but did feel the need to make sure the first man arrived so the time will be noted in his little book.

Claire settled into bed, her ring catching the glow from the lantern. She focused on that ring, the heaviness, the stones, the coldness emitting from that ring. She couldn't find any pleasure from it, and thought maybe it's a sign? She didn't have butterflies during kisses, her ring didn't bring her happiness, and shouldn't this be one of the happiest times of her life? So many confusing questions that she had, but every time she tried to talk to someone, she was made to feel very silly of her thoughts. Maybe she was just unprepared. She will try harder to find those butterflies, try harder to enjoy the ugly ring and to try harder to be happy about her fiancé. That settled, Claire took a deep breath and doused the lantern to fall into a restless sleep.

-14-

The next few days felt like a dream with walks in the park and lunches in the park, dinner at numerous business associates of Brian's all what Claire assumed being married would no doubt end up feeling like. One day molded into the next and before she knew it the grand gala to announce their engagement was upon her.

Claire awoke the morning of the gala to find a lovely sunny day complete with singing birds and sweet smelling flowers. Toula was bringing in a tray laden with savory smells emitting from beneath the silver covering which caused Claire's stomach to growl. That in turn caused a giggle to escape from her and both woman laughed loudly. Claire got out of bed and grabbed her bed gown cloak, and walked over to the table that was set up on her balcony to enjoy her breakfast of boiled eggs, fruit, cheese, bread, and porridge. There was juice and tea as well. Toula said she would return shortly to remove the tray and assist Claire in her preparation of her special day today. As Claire ate her breakfast, she day dreamed of her married life ahead.

Toula had arranged a hot bath drawn for Claire, complete with scented rose petals and special soaps and finally scented body creams for after toweling off. Her gown was laid across her bed, matching slippers with the slightest heel peeking out from under the bed. Her undergarments were draped over the privacy screen waiting for her to slip into.

Once Claire had the undergarments on she came out to sit in front of her mirror while one of the chamber maids brushed her red hair into the most gorgeous styles she had ever imagined.

Slipping into her emerald green gown, the big hoops making her giggle like a child. She commented that she looked like a princess and felt like a queen! Toula reminded her that she was indeed a princess, and held her necklace as proof. This brought out more laughter. Catherine entered Claire's room just as Toula was finishing Claire's hair with silver combs on the back.

The quick intake of breath coming from Catherine signalled to the other two women that someone was there. They glanced at the doorway in time to see Claire's mother wiping away a stray tear of happiness. Catherine approached her daughter holding her hands and bestowed upon her, a tear filled smile. Toula took this moment to sneak out to give the ladies some privacy. She smiled as she quietly closed the door without a single sound.

Catherine couldn't believe that this beautiful creature standing within arm's length was her little girl. Only recently being reprimanded for playing in the garden and getting dirty; now, here stood a woman, ready to be married. Her daughter, her only daughter and her youngest child, Catherine instantly felt her age. Claire could see the change cross her mother's features and was concerned about that change. When she commented on it, her mother brushed it aside to change the subject, as usual.

They walked to the grand staircase to ascend into the gathering crowd below. For Charles had gathered the guests to bear witness of his only daughter becoming an engaged woman, from start to wedding. This was her grand entrance into her next phase of her life. Time to shine, Claire's mother whispered into her ear as they started down the stairs to the applause and smiles of the guests.

Claire was greeted by everyone from all of Boston it seemed. All of her friends were there and they expressed their happiness of the engagement. Her father hadn't made the formal announcement yet, so these well wishes were done very quietly by her small group of friends. Brian was waiting just inside the main ballroom door, once Claire entered he took his place at her side, and didn't leave.

Charles was in prime form tonite, laughing and dancing. It was time for his grand speech. Everyone stopped talking and focused on their host. He called for his family to come forward and for Claire and Brian to step to the front. Once Charles was happy everyone was where they needed to be, he proudly announced that Claire had accepted Brian Stackhouse's offer of marriage, with the support of her family.

Loud cheers rose from the guests, and Champaign was being poured and offered for toasting. The side doors to the formal dining hall were opened to show tables and tables of foods and snacks. The party was in full form. Not intending to wind down until the wee hours of early morning no doubt.

Micheal stood back in the crowd watching from a distance. When he spotted a gentleman he needed to speak to, he excused himself and led the man to his father's study. He closed the doors once the gentleman entered. Jonas was instructed to make sure they were not to be disturbed. Jonas knew of this man from talks in the city, but had never met the man. Knowing his place in the household, he kept the matter private, and the two men were not disturbed. Sometime later, Micheal returned to the gala, alone. The other gentleman had left the manor all together into the night.

Margarite looked sullen during the entire festivities and Claire could not understand why. When she approached her, Margarite would somehow dodge her by reaching for another drink, or fetching some food and even grabbing a passing by gentleman for a dance. Perplexed, Claire gave up trying to speak to her and put her mind to the rest of the party.

The night wore on, the party goers started to fade into the evening, the gala was coming to an end. A very successful end thought Charles as he held his wife's hand while they bid goodnight to their last remaining guests as they left the manor. Jonas was instructed to let the staff go to bed to clean later in the day tomorrow. They all deserved a good sleep, even the staff.

Brian was already at the front door, hat in hand waiting for Claire to kiss him good night. She was actually dreading this part of the evening. She had such a wonderful night that she forgot about the kiss. It was bound to have to happen, and she avoided it all night. Now she could no longer avoid it. Fingers crossed, hoping for butterflies, she leaned in for the moist hot breath of her future husband.

The only man who has ever kissed her and the only man that ever will. Can she ever enjoy his kisses? Hot moist breath he leaned in, took her in his arms and pressed her against the gold mirror in the front hallway for his deep passionate lacking kiss. Claire felt his hands encasing her waist as he pressed his body fully against hers. Trapped by the wall of the hallway and his soft round body, his ringed fingers dug into her flesh. Inhaling a startled shocked gasp Brian eased up on his pressure a little bit, but continued his tongue probing assault on her lips and mouth.

Shocked at the urgency Brian was showing in his wet slobbery kisses, Claire was relieved when Jonas cleared his throat and announced that Mr. Stackhouse's Carriage was ready. Straightening her gown and hair, Claire looked at the floor as Brian walked away. No words of comfort or forgiveness for the assault, just walked out the door.

Claire fled to her room to wash her heated face. Certainly there was more in store for her than rough groping and wet stale kisses. She was hoping for those butterflies to finally show themselves. It wasn't going to happen. She doubted there were ever any real butterflies, it must be another childhood story created for dreamy school girls. Well it likely was, you wouldn't want to scare your daughters with tales of wet drooling tongues shoved into your mouth now would you?

This brought a round some nervous pent up laughter that sounded false and scary even to Claire. She stripped out of her gowns and left them in a pile on her floor. Put on her bed clothes and climbed into her chilled bed and cried herself to sleep. Dark nightmarish dreams of claws scratching at her sides and wet tongues all over her body were haunting her sleep. Morning couldn't come soon enough.

Out on the road to Brian's downtown rented house the dark shadow of a man could be seen leaning against a tree facing Brian's home. The coach pulled up to the house and an angry Brian stomped into the house slamming the door, scaring the coach horse. The coach left to head to the livery, and the dark shadow of the man was gone.

-15-

As the days past in a flurry of fitful nightmares and busy daytime routines, Claire was beginning to show signs of stress. She longed for her carefree mornings strolling in the gardens, playing with her mother's majestic beasts of dogs.

For now Claire must focus on becoming the perfect wife to a lawyer. Her own mother grooming her manners and showing her how to run a household for Claire will have a grand home of her own in a few very short weeks. Claire put her dread of her daily park lunches down to nerves. Stuffed away any notions that perhaps she wasn't ready to wed Brian.

Getting ready for yet another dreaded park stroll and luncheon, Claire donned one of her prettiest amber colored day skirts and tunic. Bleached white lace blouse with a very high Victorian neck and long sleeves finished off her attire. A beautiful straw bonnet with wildflowers around the band, shiny black walking boots and parasol completed her look. As she walked down the front hallway towards the ever awaiting Jonas she smiled the first real smile she dared in many days.

Jonas knew her deepest thoughts and he knew she was uncomfortable with Brian as of late. He wasn't sure why, but he could feel it. As he handed Claire her wrist clutch, he mentioned that Cook had prepared a lovely basket for the outing today, full of cut meats, cheeses, breads and fruits and a stout bottle of cider.

The foot man helped Claire into the awaiting carriage and Jonas handed the basket to her once she was inside. Toula came running out of the house out of breath as she handed a small bag to Claire. For the geese she said as she winked and went back into the house.

This caused Claire to give a small giggle, as it was a secret joke between Toula and herself, that if things got out of hand all she needed to do was toss some seed into the air or around the ground and the geese will calm things down immediately. She truly was grateful for Toula. Glad that Toula had agreed to move to her new home once married as well. Claire was sure that Brian would object, as he didn't care for the black woman at all, despite Claire's fondness of her.

Right on cue, the man in the shadow said quietly under his breath. Miss Cooliage carriage and there waiting by the bench was Mr. Stackhouse. Primped as a peacock, such a plump pompous bastard. Pulling out his little book he scribbled down a few words before heading to the livery for his horse and buggy. Today he had to drive to a meeting outside Boston, and could not be late. Too much was riding on this particular meeting.

-16-

Margarite put on the men's britches feeling very excited about what she was embarking. She paid a lot of money for the stable hand's clothing and then having to also get a horse and buggy without anyone knowing it was her; was a miracle. She had her long hair pinned close to her head and a big floppy farmer's hat pulled down covering her face almost completely. She now sat hunched in the old buggy trying to control the large plow horses. Couldn't she have found gentler animals? No, not for this; and now she needed to hurry or she would be late.

Claire had told her of her lunch date today and she didn't want to miss seeing things first hand. The way Claire described things she seemed like she was being offered for sacrifice to some demon or something. Margarite found that incredibly hard to believe. With a crack of the reins, she was off with a bouncy start, barely controlling the horses, headed for the park downtown.

Claire and Brian were seated on a patchwork blanket by the edge of the park overlooking the pond. Food was laid out and mostly eaten; Claire had the little bag of seeds ready just in case. She smiled and gave a slight chuckle thinking of this, and Brian assumed her show of humour was for the story he was regaling to her which caused him to boast ever so much more.

He asked Claire to walk with him towards the pond to toss some bread to the ducks below. She agreed and as she was being helped to her feet, the ground seemed like it was shaking. People were screaming, and as she turned to see what was causing such a ruckus she saw the look of absolute horror on Brian's face as he turned and ran towards the trees.

Claire turned in slow motion to see where Brian had ran away to, the exact moment a wagon being drawn by two of the largest beasts she had ever seen was bearing down the grassy hill directly towards her! The poor man at the reins had lost control of his team and they stampeded over Claire's picnic blanket tossing the basket and food high into the air as the horses plowed into Claire knocking her to the ground; they trampled her in their wake dragging her a short distance as her skirts were caught up in the wagon itself.

Finally freed from the run-away wagon and team Claire lay in a tangled mess of fabric, hair, dirt and blood; unmoving, so still. The wagon had kept going towards the other end of the park, people milling around the lifeless body of a young woman.

Brian could only stare open mouthed, unable to move towards the devastation that he was looking at. It wasn't until a scream escaped a woman that he knew he needed to get help. He ran towards the police officer and asked him to grab a doctor. The crowd was surrounding the helpless pile on the ground.

Beaten and bloodied, covered in dirt and grime, you could barely tell it was a woman. A kind gentleman shouldered his way through the crowd, and carefully turned the frail body onto her back. He pulled the bloody hair away from her face and with his own coat he began to wipe the blood from her face. She was alive, but barely. Where was her man friend? Coward, the old man was not only angry, but disgusted at the actions of her beau.

A small group of men helped load the broken and bloodied body onto a passerby's wagon and it was directed to head to the infirmary down the street. This kind man stated he would stay at Claire's side until the doctor arrived he then climbed in the wagon and told the other men that he will remain until some family member showed up. He did not want to see this young woman suffer alone.

He had seen his fair share of death and suffering during the wars and did not want this woman to be alone during her most trying time. Where was the man that was sharing her picnic? For sure he had not been harmed as he jumped and hid behind the large oak tree.

As the wagon made its way toward the infirmary, the man spotted this woman's picnic partner walking slowly behind the wagon. He gestured for him to climb aboard and sit with her, but the man shook his head, a look of pure fright still on his face. Shock, yes, he had seen enough of that in his past.

Hoping this man will snap out of it and be able to speak words to his young woman, words healed the soul. Healing from the inside made the healing on the outside easier. The good book also helped out, and once this little lady was in caring hands with the medical staff the man was going to hunt for a man of the cloth to sit with her. With a plan in motion, the man patted Claire's cold dirtied hand and told her she will be taken care of, he'd see to it.

The wagon stopped at the hospital, and a couple large men unloaded the small stretcher with Claire's motionless body on it. She was taken directly into surgery to see what damage had been done and what hope they had to save her life, if it wasn't too late. The charge nurse stopped Brian on his way inside and asked if he was the patient's husband. Brian, still reeling from the ordeal said that he knew the young lady and gave her full name and home address along with her father's name, and then he slipped out the door and walked briskly down the road to the livery to get his carriage. He needed to get to the Cooliage estate.

They needed to hear from him, not the constable, or word of mouth. They needed to know that there was nothing he could have done to stop this from happening. If for one moment the Cooliage Family even thought that he was at fault, why he could be ruined in this town. That cannot happen; Claire was his means to a better life. He has to make sure things go ahead as he had planned. He had worked too hard to get this far, and he had sacrificed too much to turn his back now.

-17-

Brian quickened his footsteps, and was happy to see that his carriage was waiting for him, ready. He turned his horse towards the upper class side of Boston and at a fast pace he was headed to the Estate. The entire ride to the Cooliage Estate Brian kept replaying the incident over and over in his head. The driver of that wagon was hunched over the reins trying to gain control of the runaway team.

The way the ground was shaking as the massive animals bared down upon their quaint little lunch, the sounds of the screaming, he saw Claire being trampled, and tossed like a child's doll. Her perfectly coiffed hair now a messy bloodied mass of leaves and dirt; her face was a grotesque mask, not the beautiful face he last saw. Her skirts were torn and shredded; bones were definitely shattered as she was lying in a most unnatural twisted pile after the horses were done dragging her. Brian shuddered at the memory. Relief flooded him as he stopped at the main door of the Estate. Jonas was opening the door to greet them, expecting to welcome his Miss home. Confusion crossed Jonas face at first, then fear and finally anger. Where was the Miss?

Brian pushed his way past the protesting Jonas and started yelling for Charles as he made his way towards the study, sure that this was where he would no doubt find The Lord of the Manor. He was correct, the study door opened as Jonas grabbed the upper arm of Brian. Mrs. Cooliage was coming down the hallway curious of all the commotion, and when she saw Mr. Stackhouse looking so untidy and the crazy look in his eyes as he was yelling for her husband she let out a scream and fainted; the Staff collected her and were caring her into the study to place their Missus onto the sofa by the fireplace. Charles guided Brian into the study and poured him a stiff drink of whiskey to calm his nerves and then wanted to know what was going on, and where was his daughter.

Stephan chose that moment to enter the study and saw the scene; he too had a bad feeling as he sat beside his mother patting her cheeks to awaken her. Brian welcomed the drink as a distraction, drank it in one swallow. He coughed as the liquid burned its fiery way to his stomach. He began to tell the tale of the afternoon, and before he could finish Charles was yelling to have his horse brought around immediately, and the coach readied for his wife as soon as possible, Charles was headed to the hospital.

Stephan looked at his mother and then at his father conflicted with emotions, should he stay with his mother or ride with his father, Jonas solved his dilemma for him stating that he will have Master Cooliage's horse ready at the same time as his father's and that he personally will see that Mrs. Cooliage arrives to the hospital in good time. Stephan was sure that Toula would also accompany them.

To save face, Brian said that he would ride back with the women, to answer any questions they may have. With everyone in agreeance, the Cooliage men set out on horseback towards the hospital. The carriage was being brought around and Toula had been called for. Jonas was beside himself with worry; Toula will most likely be in a state as well. He must make sure that the Missus is taken care of before he worried about himself. Just as he thought, Toula started to tear up, but tried to hold back as she held to her duties of caring for Mrs. Cooliage. Once the carriage was brought to the front,

Jonas secured the women inside and he climbed in as well, Brian chose to drive his carriage behind the family.

Charles and Stephan arrived at the surgery and were waiting for a nurse to update them on Claire's condition. A messenger boy had been sent from the estate to inform Micheal of the accident. Micheal had yet to arrive; he must have been in court today. The two men refused to sit, and they turned at every sound coming from the hallway. It seemed like hours as they waited, finally Mrs. Cooliage, Jonas and Toula had entered the waiting room. Seeing the distraught look on his wife's pale face, Charles went to her side and comforted her as they sat on the chairs by the opened window. Stephan was running his hand through his hair wondering how this could have happened. He tried hard to recall what Brian had said but couldn't put it into proper order; they ate lunch, the horses were running, they were looking at ducks, she's hurt, and it made no sense. Brian entered at that moment, and Stephan lost his demeanor, he advanced on Brian and had the man by the throat demanding answers.

If it wasn't for the constables and the kind gentleman that sat with Claire at this moment then for sure Brian would be another casualty. The constables removed Brian from Stephan's grip and as he rubbed his throat he was aware of everyone looking at the blood covered man standing in the doorway. The kind man introduced himself as Wallace. No first name, only Wallace. He shook hands with the men, and gave a slight head nod to Catherine and Toula.

Wallace was telling the group of people how he was sitting under the big oak tree by the pond reading the newspaper on his lunch break. He was the local blacksmith at the livery. He said he heard the yelling and the screams and that drew his attention. He saw firsthand the destruction, witnessed the horrific scene and knew he had to race to help the young woman.

Wallace stated matter of fact, that when he arrived people were milling around and the horse and wagon was already gone, driver didn't stop. Or couldn't stop. Wallace said he wasn't sure if the driver had complete control or not, he sadly admitted he didn't focus on the wagon… only the damage the horses left in their wake. He was sure that there was a couple enjoying a picnic nearby, and that was confirmed when he approached the terrible crumpled body.

Wallace looked Charles in the eye as he shared that moment with him, a tear slip down his blood covered cheek and his hands shook as he was lost in the moment, taken back to the memory of that morning. Catherine was crying, Toula was crying, Jonas was visibly shaken and holding back his emotions. Only Brian was showing very little emotion, but shock.

Charles was thanking Wallace with a strong handshake, and asked if there was anything they could do for him for his service. Wallace just asked if the family would mind if he waited in the hallway for word on the girl. Stephan approached Wallace and extended his hand, welcoming him to stay in the waiting rooms with them. He accepted as he wiped away tears.

It was several hours of tearful anguished waiting until a nurse walked into the room with a doctor. All eyes turned, silence was the welcome for the pair as they entered the room. The doctor approached Charles and Catherine, and said point blank that Claire was a very lucky young lady to have survived the horse's hooves. She came through the surgery as best as expected, but they are not giving her good odds to live. She was seriously injured, many broken bones, her head was split open, and internal bleeding.

The doctor mentioned how they had to cut her hair to assess the true damage done, and to stitch her face and scull back together. They believed they have stopped the internal bleeding and have set her broken bones. Only time will tell if she will pull through this. They will keep her sedated as best as they can, and she is being moved to a secluded area in the west wing where it will be quieter and a nurse will be bedside at all times. The Cooliage Family need not worry, Claire will be kept in the best of care.

Charles asked if they could see her, and the doctor agreed that everyone may walk in to sit with her, but not to try to speak as she must remain still. Toula asked Jonas to have the maids pack her a small bag as she intended to remain by her side until she comes home, and nobody would stop her.

This brought a sad smile to Catherine's face and she nodded her thankful approval. The doctor knowingly agreed as this was a royalty like family and their needs were to be respected. Showing the roomful of people to the west wing the doctor only hoped the young woman pulled through. Obviously a lot of people cared for her.

Wallace remained behind, until Stephan turned and walked towards him asking if he wanted to see his sister. He had earned the right to see it to the healing end. Wallace knew he needed to return to work, he'd been gone all day, but he just couldn't turn his back on someone so small and that desperately needed him at that moment today.

Stephan said he will send word to Wallace's boss to secure his job and to make sure that no ramifications were brought upon him today. With a sigh of relief, Wallace walked slowly towards the room at the end of the lantern bright hallway of the west wing.

Micheal finally got around to the message that the page boy had delivered during his meeting this morning. Glancing up at the man reading notes from his booklet to Micheal, he asked him to carry on with his reading. Micheal turned the paper over in his hands and finally opened it to read it. A gasp escaped his lips as he jumped from his chair sending it crashing into the bookcase beside his desk.

Micheal told the gentleman that he had urgent matters at the hospital, explained that his sister had been involved in a wagon incident and was in surgery. They would reschedule their meeting another day. With that, Micheal yelled orders to his secretary to cancel everything on his calendar until further notice. That he can be reached at the hospital. The other gentleman noted the events in his little book, and tucked it into his coat inside pocket and left the office heading towards the hospital himself.

The vision of Claire lying so still on the stark white bedding, pale face and bright red gash along her face from the top of her scalp along her right ear down her jawline was in deep contrast. The wounds were real. She was a broken shell of her former self. Gone was the rosy cheek fun little girl Charles was hoping to see. Here lying on this bed was something so grotesque looking that it made Brian turn his head. Catherine sat on the chair beside the bed weeping loudly while holding the bed covers afraid to touch her daughter. Claire's hair had been cut short to give access to her injuries, just as the doctor explained. She was bruised, her eyes swollen shut, the swelling on her face made her unrecognizable. Stephan felt so helpless at that moment, and he turned to Brian to ask how he had gotten away without a scratch? But no words came, as he was looking at an empty space where Brian once stood.

Micheal made his way to the west wing with the directions from the nurse. He entered the room to find his mother weeping, his father looking lost and his younger brother showing signs of rage. There was Jonas standing off to the side, and the ever present Toula on the other side of the bed and some unknown strange man looking out the window.

Micheal walked slowly to look down at his sister, her broken body lying lifeless on the bed. A cold chill ran down his spine as he reached for Claire's hand. Wallace turned at that moment, and was happy to see this family coming together. But where did the other man go? He was about to speak those words when the new man that recently entered spoke them first. Everyone looked around, but nobody knew where Brian had disappeared to. The doctor came in and asked everyone to leave for the day, to allow Miss Cooliage to get some much needed rest. The room emptied, except for Toula, who placed a chair beside the bed facing Claire. She sat, watching, hoping and praying.

Wallace asked if the family would mind if he could ask the nurse desk daily on Claire's condition, this was more than ok with Charles. He then headed back towards the livery to speak to his boss, and hoped he still had his job. Even with the assurance from Mr. Cooliage, Wallace knew how his employer was; he demanded a full day of work for barely a full day wage. Nightfall was fast approaching, and he had horses to care for and a cold meal to eat.

Brian sat in a dark cold room, he didn't even light the fire to get the chill out of the closed up tiny cottage. The place had been closed and had the closed smell. Usually he sends a local lady to open the shutters and sweep the rooms to bring some light and cleanliness to this drab little place, but not today, for he felt he needed the dank smelly darkness to match how he was feeling. A soft knock at the door as it opened, there was a dark cloaked figure entering. Walking straight towards Brian, he rose and held out his arms. The cloaked figure went willingly into his opened arms for the embrace they both welcomed. Outside in the shadows the man wrote in his book, snuffed out his cigar, and climbed onto his horse knowing the pair inside will be there awhile.

-18-

Days turned into weeks, bandages and dressing changed. Claire's swelling was subsiding, the bruises remained. Still she did not wake up. Toula refused to leave her side, if they took Claire out of the room for test, Toula went with them. She ate her meals beside Claire's bed, and only left her side to freshen herself. The wound on Claire's face was an angry red slash, and the bruising was a blackish purple now. It was a horrible mask on a pretty face.

The hospital staff was very sympathetic towards the family when the stopped in daily, giving them their needed space and time. Even Mr. Wallace stopped by the nurse station every day on his lunch to check on the progress. The constables have checked in to see if she was awake and able to answer any questions yet. Everyone seemed to be checking in on Claire Cooliage, except her fiancé.

Brian had been a no show since the very first day at the hospital, when he disappeared. He had not even reported to work in those weeks following the accident. With the wedding announcements placed on hold, Catherine was sure that Brian was devastated and just needed time. Well Brian's time was running out, thought Stephan. Why wouldn't he be beside the woman he claimed to love so much? He hadn't even asked about her from the nurse's desk. It was all very confusing to the entire family.

Micheal sat back in his chair, reading from the small notebook that the gentleman handed him. Date's times, comings and goings; not once was it noted that the whereabouts were at the hospital. Anger was quickly replacing the concern. Slamming the notebook onto the desktop, Micheal reached for his pen and inkwell. He began to pen a letter. The gentleman sitting across from Micheal sat back in his chair and crossed his arms over his chest. He knew what was going to come of this letter, and that meant a road trip and more money for him.

Micheal handed him the letter, he read it and nodded. He needed to pack and plan his trip. He was happy he no longer had to hide in dark alleys and shadows. Leaving the lawyers office into the busy streets of Boston he headed to the train station to check schedules and buy his passage. From the station he could send a telegram to the end of his trip to secure a room and a horse for his needs. This will be a much welcomed trip. He whistled as he walked towards the train station.

-19-

Margarite had stopped by the hospital a couple times, just like the rest of Claire's friends. But none of them had ventured into her room. They were all told of her changed appearance and could not bring themselves to actually see that. For this reason all of the girl's parents were happy. Today would be different, as Margarite planned to see firsthand how her best friend fared the accident. Deep down inside her she felt like people were making it all up and that Claire would be sitting propped up in a bed with flowers everywhere enjoying all the attention.

Shocked hit her full force as she walked into Claire's room. No flowers, no perky friend enjoying all the attention. No; instead of her beautiful friend, there was some freakishly monstrous creature lying on the bed in a sleep like state waiting to devour her if she came too close. A startled shriek of fear came from her as she spun around crashing into Micheal on her race to exit the room. Micheal steadied her as she slammed into him. Excusing herself shyly, she maneuvered around him and left the hospital in tears.

Micheal did not turn to look where Margarite went, for he thought very little of his sister's best friend. His sister's best friend, who cannot even stand to be in the same room as his little sister. Anger once again reared his head inside of Micheal, and he needed to take a few steadying breaths before he dared enter his sisters space. Only calm and supportive people need be near her now.

Micheal walked slowly towards the bed, Toula smiled up at him. Toula seemed to have aged a lot during these past few weeks. Fragile looking herself, she needed to take care of herself as well as be there for Claire.

Micheal suggested that Toula go out to the garden for a breath of fresh air while he sat with Claire. Toula smiled and nodded. Maybe a sprig of fresh blossoms in the room will bring some much needed sunshine to her little Claire's face.

Toula walked out of the room and into the garden, she sat on a wrought iron bench and let loose the tears that she has held in for so long. The tears would not stop, and she allowed them to pour out, to cleanse her soul so she can return stronger. She sent a silent prayer to the heavens, and sat quietly to calm herself. She was watching the birds frolicking in the fountain and she smiled. The first smile in many weeks. It felt strange to smile, almost unnatural in a way. The birds continued playing in the water without a care in the world.

Watching them brought a peace to Toula, she needed this. Spring blossoms would perk up the room for sure. Maybe she will ask Master Micheal to have some flowers brought in too. Miss Claire loved the scent of flowers. Toula decided it was time to wake up her little girl, one way or another. Enough of this sitting around waiting for her to die. They needed to focus on her to live. And you need happiness and flowers to live. A plan in hand, Toula sat smiling a genuine happy smile.

Micheal sat on the edge of the bed, and ran his finger down the red gash so vivid against the pale skin. He then touched the shorter locks, curled naturally as they were no longer weighted down by the longer length. Still so beautiful he thought, but why so still? Her broken bones were healing, and they are not worried about any further internal damage, so why hasn't she opened her eyes?

As if on cue, the doctor walked in to check on her. The doctor shook hands with Micheal and informed him of her progress. The doctor told Micheal how they have kept her slightly sedated so that her body could heal, more though so that her mind could relax so her body could heal. He said that next week they would slowly be backing off on the sedation and begin to hope she wakes up. This was wonderful news and he smiled as he stood to shake the doctor's hand before the doctor left the room. Still smiling, Micheal bent down to whisper in Claire's ear that she better wake up soon and start on her wedding plans. Even speaking those words brought a vile taste to his mouth, but he figured she needed something to hope for.

Toula walked into the room to see Micheal whispering in Claire's ear. Such a tender moment she didn't want to intrude. Where was the beau during all this time? Micheal heard Toula walking in and straightened his suit; he was smiling as he told Toula what the doctor had said. Joyful glee showed on her face, she placed the fresh cut blossoms on the bedside stand and hugged Micheal.

He said he would head to the estate to personally inform the rest of the family. Before he left, Toula mentioned her desire to have fresh flowers here for Claire. Micheal agreed, and wondered why he hadn't thought of that himself. Walking out the hospital door he headed to the local florist to arrange for the flowers to start arriving this moment.

Micheal left the florist shop and headed to the livery where he was going to rent a horse instead of having his coach and driver summoned. Reaching the livery Wallace saw Micheal approaching and met him with a steady handshake, inquiring on Claire's progress; even though he planned to go over on his lunch like he always does every day. Micheal happily told Wallace of the doctor's intentions and both men laughed at the good news.

Hearing that Micheal needed a good horse for the day, Wallace went to the stables and saddled the best for him himself. No charge he told Micheal, good news deserves good deeds. With a grateful nod in Wallace direction, Micheal rode off towards the estate with a happy heart.

Seeing Micheal leave the livery on horseback at a fast rate of speed gave Brian cause to pause his footsteps. Had something happened to Claire? That could be the only reason for Micheal to leave the office in such a hurry. Brian continued on his walk to the hacky waiting by the general store. He needed to refill his provisions and get a shave then a clean proper suit will be ordered before he left.

Enough time has wasted hiding out in the dingy little cottage. After this weekend he will return to his own house with a story of having been called away to tend to an ailing family member. His mother will surely back his claim. Until then he will head back to his cottage and await his nightly visitor.

He smiled at the thought. And wondered how he could ever give up this visitor once he was single again, for Claire was surely near death's door now. He had heard how poorly she was, not regaining consciousness. He should feel sadness but he only felt relief. He never wanted to marry the girl, but never wanted her dead either. He was trapped in the marriage plans and was hoping once wed, he could gain control of her money and have the life he deserved amongst the wealthy. He could play happy husband in public, and have his little cottage that nobody knew about. He had the life he so wanted. But now with her death, how was he going to be the wealthy husband? Now he can only be the grieving fiancé.

He needed to start to look the part, he wasn't sure if the Cooliage family would accept his absence for the reasons he will give, but he had to try. He will send a telegraph to his colleague in New York and have him send a reply back to his house informing him of the death of the sickly family member that he went there to care for. Yes, that should make his lie seem real. It was easy to lie, he had been doing it for so long it came natural. Hopefully his place at the law firm was still there, junior clerks were always scratching at the door to get in.

He figured the head boss was too busy to really notice he had been absent, and he had his page boy picking up work from his desk and delivering it to the city clerk office once he was complete with it. So it would look like he was still working. Nobody would be the wiser. If they did happen to notice he was not physically at work, he could always use the family excuse, or the injured fiancé route. Plan in motion, Brian climbed in the rented hacky to be taken to his dirty little cottage on the wrong side of town.

-20-

Two men met in the saloon, sharing a pitcher of beer, they talked business. He pulled out the letter and handed it to the sharp dressed man across from him. The other man read the letter, tucked in in his vest pocket and handed the other man an envelope. The fancy dressed man tipped back his mug of beer finishing it off, dropping a couple coins on the table he rose and bid the other man a good day. He left the saloon and walked to the sheriff's office across town. The man alone in the saloon finished off the beer and added a couple more coins to the already hefty pile on the table. The saloon girl salivated at the tip she had received.

Walking into the sunlight he adjusted his hat, this was a tiny little dirt town and he was glad the stagecoach was waiting and he could now leave. Head back to civilization, back to the city. Back to Boston, his home. The stage left on time, it would still be over a week before he would be back home. He was paid handsomely for this trip and would even have a nice sum of money left over.

Working for rich people did pay off. He rarely questioned his orders, just did them. This job however held a personal touch to it that he appreciated doing. He was hoping the outcome would benefit him also in the end. Providing he was able to see it to the end. Most jobs, he did not see the full thing through. This one job he has been in on since the beginning so he was pretty sure he would see it to the end.

With that thought he stretched his legs out in front of him and pulled his hat lower over his face and slipped into a sleep with the rocking motion of the stage coach.

Micheal arrived at his parent's home, jumped off the horse and ran inside yelling for them to come to him. The startled stable boy had never seen Master Micheal act like this before and set off to the stables horse in hand to let the rest of the hands know what had happened. Surely Miss Claire was worse off. Charles was first to arrive in the hallway, followed closely by Jonas and some of the other house staff. Stephan was on the upstairs landing looking over the railing and Catherine came out from the kitchen area. Everyone stood deathly still afraid of the news that Micheal was about to give. Catherine reached for the chair back knowing her legs will fail her once he speaks. Seeing Catherine in distress, Micheal ran to her hugging her and laughing. Everyone surrounded them wondering if he had finally lost his remaining marbles.

Micheal set his mother back on her feet and holding her face he looked her in the eyes and said that the doctor was planning on waking up Claire. Joyous cries bounced off the walls. Happy tears were flowing. Charles ordered a fine meal be prepared for his family is going to celebrate. The staff was given their orders and they were over joyed to fulfill them right away. Word reached the stable and sounds of cheers rang out. Claire was a much loved member of the family and the staff included.

The house was a buzz with activity once again, a happy sound in a long silent home. The family sat down to decide on a plan for when Claire could finally come home. They would have everything in place so when the day came it would be seamless. Questions came out about Brian, where has he been and why has he not been to visit Claire? As Toula has mentioned that there has been no word of him. This was troubling to Charles as he had hoped that perhaps Brian Stackhouse was just visiting in the night time after work.

Hearing from Micheal that although most of Brian's work was being completed, he himself has not been into the office at all since the accident, and nobody has seen him. Stephan even went as far as to visit the Widow Stackhouse to inquire on her son's whereabouts. To each visit she said that he was dealing with the accident of his fiancé very hard and needed time to adjust. That reasoning seemed fair enough at the time, but as the weeks went by and still no Brian, the Cooliage brothers had other thoughts. Thoughts that they chose not to divulge in today's conversation. That will be left for another time if needed.

After a wonderful meal was had, the family all said their goodbyes. Micheal returned on horseback to the livery and his home, Charles informed the staff that they were to share the meal with themselves and worry about cleaning up in the morning, everyone celebrates tonite. Catherine was holding in so much over these past few weeks that exhaustion finally overtook her and she fell asleep quickly. Charles retired to bed as well, leaving Stephan to his own thoughts in the study.

Glass in hand; Stephan sat in the leather wing chair by the roaring fire. Thinking on the past events and what the future could possible hold for his sister was hard to focus on. They had no idea if she will even wake up, let alone be his sister once again. They had no idea how severely damaged she actually was. Would she be able to function normally? Will she be able to be a good wife? And why the hell hadn't her loving devoted fiancé been by her side? He has heard rumors of him sneaking into the general store, and has been seen looking less than put together but those were rumors. He had no solid proof of anything and that was upsetting. If he had proof that the bastard was hiding from reality and neglecting his duties as his sister's fiancé then he would happily deal with him personally. That thought brought a snide grin to his face. Finishing off his drink, he stirred the embers of the fire and went to his rooms.

-21-

The days ahead were hard on the family, each day they sat around the hospital room patiently awaiting Claire to wake. Each day returning home defeated by the fact that today wasn't that day. Toula forever the brave one, accepting that when Claire was ready she will wake up. The doctor was no longer administering the sedative to Claire, so it would be up to her to wake up.

It was into the second week of no sedatives that Catherine noticed Claire blinking. Shrieks of joy, tears of happiness and loud yells for the doctor erupted for both Catherine and Toula. Word was sent to Micheal at his office and he then sent his personal page boy out to the estate to gather his father and brother. Micheal ran the entire way to the hospital waving off the hacky standing by for just this reason, instead he sent the page boy in the hacky.

Standing alongside of the bed while the doctor and nurse tended to Claire the people waiting were all holding their breath. Claire was indeed waking up. She was now looking back and forth from the doctor to the nurse as he was asking her to do small commands with certain body parts, asking her questions that were meant to be easy for her to answer. Once the doctor was happy with her responses he turned to the waiting family members and smiled, saying that she is fully awake and seems to have her memory intact, a huge relief to the entire room.

Claire had lost a lot of weight while she was asleep, and she was very weak, but at least she was awake. Not wanting to exhaust her, each member of the family approached her slowly and hugged her carefully. Claire shed a few tears and her hand went first to her hair, then ever so slowly towards her marred face. Her mother stopped her hand mid-air, she didn't need this right now. A silent plea went out to Toula. Message received, as Toula caught Claire's attention saying that her hair needed to be shorn so that her wounds could be seen, hair grows back and once she is at home Toula herself will cut it into a pretty style for her. This seemed to calm Claire and her hand fell to her side. She was tired, that was easy to see. The family said their goodbyes and said they will see her tomorrow. Toula, of course remained by her side.

Claire asked Toula about the length of time that had passed since that picnic day. Even though she could not recall the actual events of that day, and she really didn't want to know all the facts, she wanted to know how much she had missed out on. And where was Brian? Had he been injured as well? Trying to word things as to not hurt Claire too much, Toula explained how that day went, and how long it has been since then. She talked around the issue of Brian, not really saying much. That fact in itself was enough for Claire to figure out that Brian her fiancé has not been waiting for her to get better; he had not even visited her bedside. Not sure if she felt hurt, surprised, angry or sad Claire decided not to dwell on it. She was sure that once he heard that she was awake now he would show up. Confident in those thoughts she drifted off to sleep.

Days molded together as far as Claire was concerned, she couldn't keep her days straight and that was making her angry. Toula told her it would take a bit of time for her mind to catch up to her body, as her mind has been asleep for so long. That didn't help Claire's current mood. She had a steady stream of visitors daily, her childhood friends all stopped in saying how great she looked and Claire could see the horror in their eyes when they said this. So much so that she asked them not to visit her in the hospital anymore. She would call on them once she is settled at the estate.

Knowing full well she didn't want to see the look of pity on their faces anymore, she decided no calls for visits will be made.

Claire wanted to see how she looked so desperately. She tried to convince the young chamber maids to bring her a mirror, but they didn't speak to her or look directly at her. When she would ask Toula for a hairbrush and mirror, Toula obliged her by brushing her short locks herself saying why drain your energy when Toula can pretend that you are little again and attempt to tame your curls again. As it brought back fond memories for them both, Claire allowed Toula to take over and smiled as the older black lady hummed a childhood lullaby as she brushed her hair.

The day came when the doctor let Claire's family know that she could go home by days end. The coach was prepared with many pillows and comforters to add some much needed padding to aid in Claire's comfort. Claire was sitting up on the side of her bed waiting to be discharged; Toula had left the room in search of a wheeled chair to help get Claire to the coach.

The sound of a sharp intake of shocked breath caught Claire's attention and she glanced up expecting to see her family ready to get her home. Instead Claire was looking at the horrified expression on her best friends shocked face, Margarite's delicate fingers rising to cover her mouth as the gasp escaped. She was not prepared for the horrible face that now took the place of her friend's beautiful features. Her friend had been replaced by a true monster! Margarite turned and ran from the room. Claire lowered her head, wondering what she really looked like now.

A new desire to finally see what she has become over took all of Claire's thoughts, she frantically looked around for anything shiny that she can look into. Tearing open every drawer in her room and the wardrobe as well, she could not find a single item to assist her. Defeated she sat down to wait for her ride home. Once there though, she will have many mirrors to view herself in. that was a promise. She would make sure of that.

Toula arrived with the wheeled chair; Claire positioned herself in it and was whisked out the side door to the awaiting coach. Gosh the sunshine was bright, it felt so warm too. Toula noticed the sunshine was bothering Claire, so she handed Claire a bonnet to place on her head, careful not to disturb her scars.

The bonnet was helpful, but very uncomfortable, and Claire promptly removed it once inside the coach. Jonas was inside the coach with Toula and Claire. Micheal was riding his horse alongside, and mentioned that the rest of the family was patiently waiting at home for her arrival.

Claire was glad that the rest of the family remained at home, she felt insecure as it were with the people already looking at her, watching her every reaction to things. She even noticed that nobody ever mentioned Brian. Why was that? She will have to send word to him that she would like to see him as soon as possible to start planning their wedding. Yes, she should start living as normal as possible, return to her life once again. Too much time had been wasted being in the hospital.

The coach came to a slow rolling stop in front of the estate, normally the staff were on hand to greet the member of the family if they had been absent for some time, where were they today? Once she stepped out onto the ground she awaited the hounds. Nothing; not a sound, where were the dogs? Has everything changed so much?

Her mother was first to greet her once inside the manor, a large quiet meal was planned for her homecoming, and she was excited to sit at her family table and share this meal with the ones that matter the most to her.

Happy smile on her face she turned to head up the grand staircase to her rooms and rest before dinner. As she turned, one of the maids screamed and dropped her tray of silver. Claire saw the sheer fear showing on the young maids face as she bent to retrieve the dropped tray. Charles was ushering the young woman through the study door and closed it quickly. Stunned by the response, Claire was even more eager to finally see her face. She knew that was a large gold mirror at the front entry, she headed right for it before anyone could stop her. They tried, but she was already there; staring with wide frightened eyes, staring at the hideous creature looking back at her from that mirror. Panic settled deep inside her soul, and Claire started shaking from deep within, she heard a kitten cry as the world went dark and silent.

Claire opened her eyes to Toula wiping her face with a cool cloth. She immediately turned her face away from her, and demanded she leave her room. Toula was hurt, but she understood the shock Claire must have felt so she left the room silently. Claire was beside herself, she began to smash every mirror in her suite, even the small compact mirror she knew was in her wrist clutch. Screaming as she set to destroy anything that would give a reflection, anything to show her how hideous she was now, drew the attention of Toula. Toula came bounding in capturing Claire from behind pinning her arms to her sides, Toula was crying hard and allowing Claire to scream in anguish, knowing that she needed this release.

Jonas was next in the room, surveying the damage with wide eyes. Her parents and Stephan followed Jonas. Utter shock was sowing on everyone's face at once and this caused a painful sob to escape Claire's clenched teeth. How was she ever going to marry Brian looking like a monster? He could never love her now. All her hopes and dreams died that day in the park. Claire feared she was doomed to a solitary life hidden away from everything and everyone.

It took several hours for Claire to calm down enough that she would drink the foul tasting drink offered to her by her father. Charles had laced a small amount of sherry with a mild sedative that the doctor had left with them for such occasions. Claire drifted off to sleep as Jonas tidied her room. Toula forever at her side, vowed to make things better for her charge. The room was cleared of all the debris, and set to right.

Morning arrived and Claire woke to find Toula sitting at the little table that had been set up with a few light breakfast choices. Claire was in no mood to see anyone or to eat and she said so to Toula in a not so nice tone. Toula did not let it phase her, she just stood up in front of Claire and told her that she needed to eat. She could either eat on her own, or Toula would feed her like the baby she was acting like. This shocked Claire into submission for Toula had never spoken to her in such fashion. Claire sat at the small table and noticed that there was nothing reflective on the table, no tray or any silver.

Actually there were no utensils at all. Puzzled Claire asked about this. To which Toula calmly stated that she did not wish the staff any further cleaning from a spoiled destructive child, and she continued eating her cheeses and bread. Claire stared open mouthed for a few moments then started to laugh. Toula was thrilled to hear the laughter but would not show her pleasure, let Claire think she remained mad.

Claire refused to eat with the family, choosing to eat in her rooms with Toula instead. She had also informed her mother that her rooms were to be off limits to all staff, and that no member of the staff is to look at her if she were to walk by, heads were to be bent and eyes to look at the ground. She did not want to feel pity from staff, as it was bad enough feeling it from her own family.

It went on like this for many weeks, Claire hiding in her rooms and on the odd occasion that she wanted to walk in the garden she covered her head and face with a dark shawl or cloak with a dark veil. Numerous unanswered letters had been sent to Brian and no reply, of course, he was repulsed by her looks and she should release him from there planned vows. Claire was starting to settle into a depressing routine.

-22-

Brian had been back at the office for about four weeks when he was summoned to the main office. He couldn't figure out why he would be asked to see the head guy, his excuse of a dying relative had been accepted by everyone to excuse him from being around. Even Charles Cooliage seemed to accept his reasoning for not being around the hospital while Claire was healing. He still hasn't been able to gather the nerve to go see her yet to this day and he felt he was running out of excuses.

Brian notified his secretary that he would be going to see the senior lawyer in a few moments, she looked shocked and inquired as to the reason why Mr. Micheal Cooliage would send for you when you could just pop over to see him whenever, seeing how you are almost family. This stopped Brian in his tracks. What did she say? Micheal was his boss? He had been working here well over a year and did not know that his fiancé's brother was his boss? This changed everything and he needed to leave this office right now to figure things out.

Obviously Micheal has found out his lies and will call him out for the unforgiving nature of denying his sister of a face to face visit. Brian could not face Micheal today, so he grabbed his belongings and important papers and took leave early.

He rushed home, yelling for his mother. When she showed herself, Brian let her know that he will be out of town on business for a little while and she will be taken care of.

This was ok with his mother as she could not stand having him underfoot any longer; always whining about life being unfair, not willing to work to get what he wanted… but rather expecting it to be handed to him. Just like his beautiful fiancé, handed to him on a silver platter; and he doesn't even want her. What a waste of a son, she whispered as he walked out the door.

Brian stopped at the general store and placed a rather large order to be delivered by rented hacky, he said he will have the driver stop to pick it up and knows the address it is to be delivered to, the less people who knew where he was the best. Next he went to the post master and penned a very short note, sealed it and placed it for delivery. He went to the livery and had his horse saddled and departed for the other side of town, to the little dark cottage. How he loathed that place, but it was paid for and nobody knew he owned it. It was his private getaway, and he needed it right now.

Micheal waited for an hour past the scheduled appointment time, and still there was no Brian. He decided to walk to the adjoining building to see what was keeping him. This building housed the junior clerks waiting for their chance to prove themselves and hope for a chance to move to the next building.

This was why Micheal did not notice that Brian worked for him, he seldom came into this building, and these clerks did the gopher work for the higher lawyers. Rarely did paths cross.

The looks he was getting as he walked into the building assured him that the junior clerks knew who he was, even though he could not name even one of them. When he walked to the secretary's desk to ask Brian's whereabouts she fumbled her words. She was sure he had already left for the other building over an hour ago. He did leave and she just assumed that was where he left to.

Micheal asked to be shown his desk area, and she led him to a corner desk that looked as though it had been recently ransacked. All his personal files were gone and only trash remained. Without saying a word, Micheal stormed out of the building and headed towards the livery to get his horse. He rode hard to Brian's townhouse he knew he rented, tied his horse to the rail and knocked loudly on the heavy door.

The knock was answered by an aging stooped man who stepped back to allow Micheal entry. The widow Stackhouse walked to the door to see who came to call, she never had visitors and was curious. When Micheal introduced himself, she instantly beamed and asked how Claire was feeling as Brian had mentioned she was ill.

Ill? Was she for real, thought Micheal? Micheal didn't feel like getting into anything with this woman, he only came here to strangle her son. When he asked where Brian was, she looked even more confused, saying that of course he should know as he himself had sent her Brian away for business.

Micheal said she was mistaken and asked his question one more time. This time she looked worried as she repeated what her son had told her. Realizing it was far from the truth she asked again about Miss Claire, if her son lied about a work assignment maybe he was never engaged. Micheal plainly stated that his sister and Brian were enjoying a lunch picnic a few months ago when a runaway wagon bore done on his sister and caused her to remain in the hospital these past months, and that since she has been home she is doing much better.

Micheal then inquired why neither she nor Brian had even visited her in the infirmary. The widow Stackhouse looked paled and claimed she knew nothing of this accident and that her son has a lot to account for. Micheal decided to leave at this time, and look for the lying bastard himself. Headed to his home, Micheal was planning on calling for his friend to be used again. Mounting his horse, Micheal again rode hard back the way he came.

Once in his office he put pen to paper and enlisted his friend's help once again. Sending the sealed letter to the postmaster by errand boy, Micheal decided he would need to speak to Father and Stephan as well. Today was just a good a day as any, he thought as he tidied his desk. Letting his secretary know he would be gone for the day, she was to cancel all appointments.

Heading back to the livery to let Wallace know he would hire a hacky instead of his horse and that he was to set his horse to the corral. Wallace nodded as he waved to the awaiting hired hacky to come for the gentleman. Climbing aboard, Micheal was giving directions to the Cooliage Estate for the driver, not noticing Margarite watching from the doorway of the general store across the way.

Margarite felt ashamed for watching Micheal so closely. Women were not supposed to be so brazen. Giggling to herself she wondered what her uppity mother would think of her latest behaviours, if she would be cast from the family and scorned for bringing shame. Shaking off such thoughts she straightened her hat, opened her lace parasol and walked into the busy boardwalk heading to the fancy tea house to meet with Jaqueline and the twins. Dreading the topic that she was sure to happen; Claire and her predicament, Margarite tried to think of a much more pleasant subject for the friends to discuss. Smiling broadly she opened the little shop door and walked inside to sit with her friends that were already seated at a cozy table by the open windows.

-23-

Sitting in the study with his father and brother, Micheal wondered how he would bring up the subject of Brian Stackhouse, so he asked how Claire was doing instead, hoping it would happen gradually. Micheal was saddened to hear how Claire was hiding in darkened rooms, not allowing staff to enter her room unless she was wearing the scarf or head shawl. She no longer wore her fancy bright coloured dresses instead choosing to wear drab smocks, with hats that had dark veils.

He hadn't seen Claire's face in a few weeks, but he had hoped for some sort of improvement to her demeanor. Obviously that hadn't happened. The three men talked of ways to help her through this, and how the whole situation was taking a huge toll on their mother as well. Micheal asked if Claire had any correspondence from Brian during her time home, and that was met with tense silence.

Once the three men had finished their drinks and cigars, Charles suggested that Micheal go upstairs to see his sister, maybe seeing Micheal will brighten Claire's morning. Nothing seemed to brighten his daughter's days anymore, and Charles wondered what had happened to her loving fiancé? Stephan, on the other hand was thrilled that Brian hadn't been underfoot. For some reason Stephan still didn't trust the weasel. He will speak to Micheal about some of his thoughts after dinner, away from Father.

Knocking on the door to Claire's room Micheal waited for a response. When he did not get one, he turned the knob and walked into a dark, closed in room. Heading for the balcony drapes he pulled them wide open and turned to survey the heartbreaking sight. Claire's once proudly elegant room was now a shadow of despair. The wall treatments were scarred and torn, tables were toppled and mirrors shattered. Her beautiful desk was turned on its side and papers scattered everywhere.

Micheal walked into the next room where he saw his sister sitting on the floor in the furthest corner with her back against the wall. Looking up at Micheal she stared at him with dark hollow eyes. Micheal couldn't help but see the jagged red gash she desperately tried to hide from his view. Kneeling down beside her, Micheal reached for her and held her close. The pure love that emitted from him caused her to weep. Months of unshed tears poured from deep within Claire. Micheal sat back cradling Claire on his lap letting her cry.

Once he was certain she was spent, he dried her face with a corner of the bedsheet that was draped behind them. He gently held her face in his large hands and turned it for his full view. Her eyes closed, waiting for his intake of frightened breath, it didn't happen. Instead Micheal stated matter of fact that it was healing well. He stood and placed Claire on her feet, then told her to get ready for dinner for tonight she would be dining with her family and not alone in her room.

Shaking her head violently back and forth, with a crazed look she began to retreat to the darkened corner again. Micheal stopped her by holding her arm, looking her deep in the eyes, he pleaded with her to join them. Toula was in the next room, crying at the deep grief she was witnessing. Lord how this child needed help. She approached the brother and sister and said that she would help Claire ready herself for dinner. But they would have to accept Claire's new choice of wardrobe. This made Claire a little less frightened about leaving her room. She could wear her costume, and cover her face.

Toula selected a brown smock for Claire to wear for dinner, but she put her foot down when Claire wanted to wear the heavy dark veil. These were her family members, surely they would not be judging her she said to Claire. Instead Toula pulled out a long beige scarf, she then sat Claire on the sitting bench and showed her how to place one long section of this ornate scarf on top her head and draping it down the scarred side of her face just covering the red gash, leaving the rest of her beautiful face open. Toula then wrapped the ends of the scarf around Claire's neck loosely, it was a very elegant look, and her bruising was not as noticeable this way. Claire was pleased with the look, and was actually excited to go to dinner with her family, to see their reaction. For they only ever saw her lately covered completely.

Catherine was over joyed at seeing her daughter at dinner that night, as were the other men in the room. The staff was instructed to remain outside the dining hall, only Toula and Jonas were allowed inside the grand room during the meal. This was Micheal's suggestion, to try to let Claire relax some more. It was working, she almost felt like her old self for a few moments.

When dinner was done, and everyone was sipping their iced tea, talk turned to Claire and what she wanted to happen in the next little while. Claire had no idea what she wanted, she wanted to be left alone but that was not going to happen, as Micheal had already told her. He had said that her mourning and hiding was done, she needed fresh air and to be around people and her friends again.

Panic showed on her face as she recalled Margarite's reaction to seeing her that day in the hospital. The day after Brian had laid horrified eyes on her in the hospital bed and hadn't returned since. Months have passed and she no longer waited for Brian to call on her. Not sure if he ever will, she wondered where that left her, is she still considered to be engaged? Or is he a free man now?

Claire spoke the words out loud, and the silence was deafening. Her mother looked around at the three men nervously, her father cleared his throat. Stephan began to wipe the corners of his mouth with his napkin as he was about to speak; Micheal cut him off. Micheal rose from his seat and approached Claire. He sat in the empty chair beside her and looked at her as he spoke.

Micheal explained how he had just recently realized that Brian Stackhouse worked as a junior for his firm. How he had sent word to him to attend his office one afternoon so that he could ask Brian what his intentions were towards you, seeing how he hasn't shown his face in a while. Brian failed to meet the appointment. When Micheal was sure that Brian wasn't coming to the meeting, he went to the offices next door and found his desk deserted. He told Claire, and everyone at the table about how he went to Stackhouse's residence only to find an even more confused mother.

This was both shocking and sad for Claire to hear. Somewhere deep down Claire guessed that Brian would eventually come around with apologies for his behaviour, begging forgiveness. Didn't look like that was ever going to happen. Brian has flown the coup, and nobody seemed to know where he went.

Claire rose from her chair and looked at the ugly ring on her left hand. Removing it, she placed it in Micheal's hand and asked if he could return it to him if they ever find out where he went. As far as she was concerned, he was freed from his wedded obligations to her. Crying Claire left the room and headed up the grand staircase slowly, broken even more, to her safety of her rooms. Knowing Toula wouldn't be far behind, she left her door opened as she closed the drapes over the balcony doors.

-24-

Micheal looked at the ring he held in his hand, a new anger burning inside him. His sister showed such restraint and poise as she left the room with her damaged head held high. Clutching that horrid ring in a tight fist, he slammed his fist on the table causing the water tumbler to fall, spilling a trail of water across the white linen table cloth.

Micheal took this time to attempt to breach a subject of touchy matter. He had been thinking of this for a while, but not prepared to express his thought so soon. Asking the family to gather in the study, for more privacy he said he had something he wanted to discuss with everyone. They walked quietly into the study and Micheal closed the doors silently behind them. Perched on the edge of the settee by the fire sat his mother, lace handkerchief in her hand ready for tears. Stephan looking ever so much like their father stood facing the fire one arm braced on the mantle. Lastly was Charles, stood lovingly behind his wife with his hand on her shoulder. Micheal cleared his throat and poured himself a brandy from father's cabinet. Taking a long sip, he faced the family.

He was worried how they would take what he was about to say, but it needed to be said, and they needed to put it into action. For Claire. Micheal started by asking his mother how her widowed Aunt Maddie was, this was answered cautiously by Catherine when she said last post received was a month ago and she was doing well. Why did Micheal ask that?

Well, now that he started, Micheal began explaining that he had been in touch with Aunt Maddie, and told her of the accident and how Claire was deep in depression. It was his idea to see if Claire could be sent to Cougar Ridge, to Aunt Maddie's place to heal, where nobody knew of her, and she won't worry about the looks from people around here, the pity and the false politeness. At Aunt Maddie's place she would have all the privacy she could want, on the large farm property.

Maddie mentioned that she doesn't get many visitors anymore, except the Reverend once in a while and she goes into the town daily and to church every Sunday. Maddie had welcomed the idea of little Claire coming to her for rest. As long as the rest of the family was ok with the idea, then she would be more than happy.

Micheal looked at the faces staring blankly back at him. Catherine was first to speak, she wanted to know when they would be sending Claire. Father was slightly angry about his daughter being sent away like a dirty secret, but soon realized this was not the intention. He wanted to hear more of these plans that Micheal was so secretive about.

Stephan nodded his head in agreement saying it would be best for her to heal away from the city. Fresh air and good people is what she needs. Who was going to let Claire know what the family is already agreeing on? Micheal began explaining that he had everything worked out, Toula will travel with Claire and tend to her needs, while on the train car he will secure them a sleeper unit for ultimate privacy, but the stage coach into Cougar Ridge was a different storey. He couldn't guarantee privacy on that. He did try to hire a private coach for the last leg of the journey, but due to the distance he realized the stage would be the most comfortable way to go. Catherine seeing that Micheal had thought of everything asked him who was going to break the news to Claire, and when would this take place?

Micheal said that if everyone was in agreement that this was best for Claire then it would be one of the immediate family that would break the news to her. Micheal would get on the arrangements right away, so that she could leave by weeks end. The train would take about a week to its destination, and another three days by stage. A very long tiring trip, but they all hoped for the best end results.

Agreeing that Catherine would be the one to inform Claire of the decision in the morning, they parted ways for the evening. All were to be back in a couple days time to settle final preparations. Stephan figured he better forewarn Toula of their meeting, so she will be prepared to handle Claire if she were to have an outburst.

Heading up the stairs to the last set of doors to Claire's suite he knew Toula would be there. Bypassing the knock, Stephan opened the door softly and motioned for Toula to step into the hallway. Once there he told her of the meeting in the study. Toula took a couple minutes to let it all soak in, then she smiled big and wide. Happy for the chance to help out Claire, she nodded in agreement and slipped back inside the room. With newly found hope, she finally slept a peaceful night's sleep.

Morning sunlight poured in waking Claire. Unsure why the drapes had been pulled she sat up startled to see Toula holding out a day dress of mild creams and that scarf for her hair. Knowing she shouldn't question Toula as it will do no good, Claire let Toula wrap her hair and face in the pretty scarf. Toula was humming a lullaby as he arranged the scarf to cover the red scar, and fingered the bouncy curls poking out from the seams of the scarf. Downstairs for breakfast with your mother she has whispered to Claire, as she led her into the hallway and down the stairs towards the atrium.

Expecting screaming and a childish tantrum, Catherine made sure that breakfast was a light affair, not a lot of breakables. Claire and Catherine ate the light breakfast, speaking of neutral topics; the gardens, the dogs and how Claire was feeling. Once these mundane topics were spent and breakfast was finished, Catherine decided to broche the idea of what the entire family agreed to do. Claire took the news relatively calm, and no fuss was made.

Instead, she sat quietly and spoke softly when she asked when she would be leaving. Inside Claire was screaming and wondering why her family was sending her away. Were they disgusted to look at her? Unshed tears welled up in her eyes, but Claire refused to let anyone ever see her cry anymore. It was bad enough that her best friends could not stand to visit her, to call on her to see how she is doing. It was bad enough knowing that your fiancé was hiding away from everyone because he can't face you.

But now to know that your family is also wanting you gone, it was too much to handle, so she will accept their decision and move to her mother's aunt's home, far away and somewhere she knew nothing of; to a woman she only vaguely remembered as a child. She had no family anymore. Shunned by her fiancé, friends and now family; Claire knew she was a hideous beast to be set free in the wild. She stood, placed a fake smile on her face and said she shall start packing and would be ready to leave as soon as plans have been set.

Walking as if in a dream, Claire went up the stairs, down the hallway and into her room where she immediately broke down and cried on her bed. Toula standing outside the bedroom door saw all of this and her heart was breaking. Hoping they were doing the right thing, she vowed never to leave her side. Claire will never feel alone as long as Toula was breathing.

Plans were set, and the day arrived for Claire and Toula to start their long journey to Cougar Ridge. Even the sound of this unknown town was untamed, and not knowing where it was made it even more wild. Over a week for the journey, her family might as well be sending her to another world altogether.

Trunks were loaded in the second coach; Claire was dressed in a dark heavy cloak with wide hood. Under the cloak was a dark brown woollen dress and a dark brown bonnet with a dark veil. To an onlooker it would seem that she had just attended a funeral. In a way it was true, Claire was mourning, her life as she knew it.

-25-

Entering the first coach with Toula by her side, Claire refused to face her family gathered by the front of the manor. She would not acknowledge the people who didn't care enough for her; but only to send her away so they didn't have to look at her disfigured face and watch her awkward limping walk. Toula said she would send notice of their arrival once they ended their journey. Waving to her family she cared for all these many years, Toula couldn't help but shed a few tears. This was her home she was leaving, and she had never ventured so far before. Yes, she was a little scared, but she needed to be strong, so she can protect Claire.

The coach ambled down the Boston streets towards the train station. Being a Cooliage did have its perks, they did not need to wait inside the station, instead the coach pulled up directly to the second last car of the train where they were met by the conductor himself. Helping the women from the coach, he extended his offer to anything they would need, all they need to do is ask him and he will make sure it happened. The baggage was loaded into the car, and the women escorted to their sleeper berth. Once settled in the train car, Toula closed the glass door to the sleeper car hallway, and drew the red curtain used for privacy.

Claire pulled down the train shades and removed her cloak, leaving the bonnet and veil on. The train whistle blew, sounding the beginning of their lengthy journey. Tears ran down Claire's face as she felt her life slipping by with each rocking lurch of the train. Soon the train was moving at a steady fast pace, chugging her into an unknown future. Emotions have been so strung out for so long Claire drifted off into a restless slumber. Toula sat across the seat from her young charge, hoping and praying that they had done the right thing.

During the week long train trip, the conductor had wondered about the identity of the woman traveling with the black woman. She must be of some importance to have been loaded without the line ups usually at train depots, and to be travelling with a black woman inside her sleeping berth. Nobody could recall the woman even peeking out of the sleeper car unit, she did not venture out of the small room when they made their regular stops for water and foods.

This woman dined in her car rather than enjoy the fine dining car exclusive to the higher class of passenger's pleasure. Instead, her companion brought the trays of food to their room, and promptly removed the trays when they were finished. Checking his roster, the conductor noted that her name was listed only as "Miss Cooliage and companion" and that they were headed to Slayter. From Slayter they would take the stage coach to their final destination.

Such a long expensive trip she was embarking on, he could only wonder why. Not wanting to speculate any further he blew the whistle to notify the passengers on the platform that their leg stretch time was ending and the train was filled with water and wood and ready to leave the station.

Claire glanced at the small gold watch pinned to her tunic, five more hours and they would be off this train. Claustrophobia was beginning to set in, and she could not wait to breathe the fresh air again, to stretch her arms and legs, to feel the sunshine on her body. The only saving grace to their sleeper car was that she did not have to keep covered up, as Toula was used to her marred face and Toula didn't mind leaving to get their foods. But the next leg of their long journey would be the hardest she thought. A few days on a stage coach, with other people in close proximity, stopping in little towns along the way, dining at those same small towns. Claire doubted that they would be able to avoid eating inside the establishments, which meant that she will need her face scarf, and shawls to hide her disfigurement.

Not something she was looking forward to; she hated seeing the looks from people as they tried to figure out what was wrong with her. She sat back and instead tried to concentrate on her Aunt Maddie and what type of property she owned. Will it be large enough to help hide her if there were visitors? How big was her house? Will she need Toula to go purchase more materials so they could make more scarves as she really liked the cream coloured one Toula had found for her back home.

Drifting off into a light sleep she dreamed of having a beautiful perfect face, and being married. Even in her dream she could not see her husband, probably because even her brain could not dream of that. Toula was tapping her awake saying that they have arrived in Slayter, their stage coach will be ready to leave within the hour the conductor had told her. Gathering their meager totes inside their car, Claire arranged her heavy cloak with the bonnet and veil on her head she was ready to leave the confines of their sleeper.

The conductor helped the two women from their car, and told them he took the liberty of having their trunks transferred to the stage for them. Toula thanked him as they walked onto the train platform. He watched them walk away, again wondering about the silent form walking with such pride and obvious beauty by the way of her walk. Shaking his head to clear it, he turned and walked into the station to get his list of passengers, forgetting all about the mysterious woman with the black companion.

Walking down the plank walkway from the train station towards the stage coach, Toula made light conversation about this small town. They passed a small dress shop and normally Claire would have loved to walk inside to purchase something. Not today, she didn't even bother to glance towards the window display. There parked at the general store was the stage coach. A very rough looking contraption, nothing like the coaches they were used to in Boston, Toula was a bit nervous.

She heard stories about how black people were treated differently out here, not as civilized as in Boston. Hopefully those were just stories, as she did not want to place any more hardships on Miss Claire. They walked up the stairs into the general store to purchase a few food items to snack on, and inquire when the stage would be leaving. Hopefully they had a schedule for her to take note of.

According to Master Micheal, they would be on this stage for three days until it reached a small town of Cougar Ridge. Toula wondered if this town could possibly be smaller that Slayter? She had not been in such a small town before, and was showing her nervousness now. Claire glanced her way to which she gave a bright cheery smile to her young charge. No sense upsetting Claire with her nerves.

With their purchases tucked into her carpet bag, they went out onto the veranda to wait for the coachman. Once he arrived they were loaded into the coach and with a yell to his team of six huge horses they were off. My goodness it was going to be a very long and bumpy ride thought Claire, as she waved the dust from her dress.

Claire was looking at the written schedule for this coach, and noted that the next scheduled stop was later that evening, a dinner stop and to have a hot meal and spend the night at the local hotel. Rooms had already been reserved for them as part of their travel plans. The two women needed to share a room, as they did not allow coloured people to stay there, unless they were the servants of the paying customers.

Toula chuckled to herself as she remembered how uneasy the shopkeeper seemed as he told Claire about the hotel regulations. Yes, they were really stepping back into a much more wild part of the country. Basic comforts were not going to be readily available. She only hoped that they had water closets! Unsure if Miss Claire would even know what an outhouse was, this made her laugh softly out loud and brought Claire's attention to her. Trying to figure out what to say to explain her laughter, she motioned to the only other passenger in the stage coach with them. A portly looking middle aged man his hat had fallen off and what looked to be a toupee slightly askew on his balding head as he snored loudly between bumps. Claire nodded and laughed a little too. It felt good to hear her laugh, thought Toula, maybe this trip is what she needed.

Arriving at the bedtime stop over, the ladies walked up the tight staircase to the room they were to share. There was one sad looking bed, and a cot that the owner had provided for Toula to use. Shaking her head at the thought of Toula having to sleep on that thing, Claire said that she will share the bed, just as she used to do as a scared child during storms.

Toula smiled, and as if on cue, a loud bang of thunder shook the windows. Both woman laughed and walked down for dinner. After their meal, retiring to the room for a much needed sleep knowing that this would be the last good sleep they will get. According to the schedule, the next day and a half will be straight riding, with short stops to change out the horses and gather new passengers. It will be a rough ride after today's bumpy trip. Neither were looking forward to it.

Barren terrain, wild and wondrous was all they saw. Gone were any inklings of civilization, atleast what they considered as such. They did stop in tiny towns as the coachman called them. To both Claire and Toula, these stops were barely a shack and dirt roads. Seeing these towns Claire started to have major misgivings about Cougar Ridge. Her mother had said Cougar Ridge was a tiny place, and that Claire should be prepared. Well if that was a tiny place, what had they just left ? Surely the past couple stops for mail pickups and a passenger her and there were not really classified as towns were they? So onward they went, every rut in the road jarring her bones, her backside would surely be blue with bruising by the time they were done this trip.

The second and final day of this torturous stage coach journey was upon them. The coachman yelled out that next stop was Cougar Ridge in about 15 minutes. He said there will be about a half hour stop over for those continuing onto the next stop. Anxious to see where she will be living, Claire watched the scenery flash by her as the mighty horses flew into the tiny town centre.

-26-

They passed a cute little stream and over a small wooden bridge. Claire heard the clomping of each hoof as the passed over the bridge. The horses slowed, knowing they were getting a chance to rest under the big tree thus signalling to Claire that this was the town of Cougar Ridge. Not sure she would call it a town, there were no sidewalks, only dirt roads that the few scarce buildings sat on. The stage pulled up to the stockyard and began unloading their trunks. He mentioned that their baggage was ok to sit on the deck here until they could remove it, and pointed across the way to the Diner saying they could wait there for their ride. With that he unhooked his team to let them loose in the corral. He then sauntered towards the town square to the store.

Claire looked across the road to the small diner. She could see the entire town from where she stood. From the deck of the stockyard she saw a mill beside her, across from this stockyard was the diner, and a small house built on the back of it. To the far side of this diner there was a smaller building with bars on the door and windows, she thought she could read the word BANK on the bricked wall. The other side of the diner were three more small buildings. Further up from the diner, where the coachman was seen walking into was the general store. And at the far end of the centre of this town, the town square as the driver called it was a church building. As for the town square it was nothing more than a small grassy patch surrounded by a small white picket fence and in the centre was a beautiful white gazebo. Large enough for a small band to preform or to hold a small gathering or dance. Funny how it looked so cute sitting in this isolated town.

Where had her family sent her? There weren't any sidewalks or proper stores, she could only hope that there was more to this town somewhere. Toula and Claire were making their way to the diner when they heard Claire's name being shouted. Turning to see who was yelling, they saw a strange looking wagon approaching, and a large man with an even larger hat on barrelling towards them. When he stopped his wagon in front of them and jumped down, he removed his hat and it was then that Claire noted the star on his vest. This must be the sheriff, why was he coming to them?

He extended his hand to the women and introduced himself as Sheriff Randal Lynwood. Randy, as folks around here call him, he laughed. Sheriff Lynwood explained how he heard that Miss Cooliage was due to arrive and offered to collect her, Miss Toula and their belongings and give them a short tour before delivering them to Miss Maddie. Claire thought that was very nice of the town's lawman to do such a thing. So he helped both ladies into the back bench on his wagon and loaded their trucks into the rear. He climbed up on the front bench and proceeded to point out the buildings as they passed by.

As Claire had figured, the small building was the town bank, open on Wednesdays the sheriff said. There was Christina's Diner, great food; a newspaper office, post office and doctor's office. Just past that as they were circling the square, he said that the road just after the store before the church led to his place and the jail, and further out that road was the Indian reserve.

This brought Claire's head up quickly and she asked how close they were to the savages? Sheriff Lynwood laughed out loud at the use of the word savages. He explained that the Indians were a peaceful tribe and frequently came into town, they have yet to cause any problems, and she had nothing to fear from them. As they rounded the town square right in front of the bright white church, the sheriff pointed to another road on the side of the church and before the mill leading away from town. He said that road would take you to the boarding house and a couple other homes only. It was not really a road, but more of a large laneway.

Passing the mill and the stockyard where they were dropped off from the stage coach, they headed back out of town from the way they entered. The sheriff told them that there were only two roads in and two roads out of Cougar Ridge, so she shouldn't get lost. A short ways away she noticed that the road branched off, and they were taking the first left. Just a brief distance up this rough track of road sat a cute looking farm house, with a wide veranda and a couple large wooden rocking chairs sitting there waiting for someone to rock away the day.

There were wonderful huge ferns hanging and swaying in the breeze. Black shutters stood open along all of the opened widows. It really was a welcoming looking place. As the wagon approached a woman stepped out the main door wiping her hands on her apron, a hound dog was sleeping on the porch and the sound of horses woke it, and began to bark, promptly being hushed by the woman. Sheriff Lynwood jumped down from the wagon, gave the woman a hug and asked if she wanted him to put the trunks inside. The woman gave him directions to two rooms upstairs to place the trunks.

As the sheriff was helping the two women off the wagon, he introduced them to Miss Maddie. Smiling the older woman approached and hugged Claire tightly before hugging Toula just a tight. Slightly thrown off guard by the hug Toula was at a loss for words. Shushing the old hound dog as they walked up the front porch stairs and into the house, Maddie was all talkative about how Claire had grown, and how sorry she was to hear of the accident. She went on and on about Claire being able to heal properly here and nobody would bother her, unless she chose to be bothered.

Maddie then said that she had rooms made up at the top of the stairs, separate rooms, but there was a connecting door; if they chose to leave it open. She then asked if the ladies would like some refreshments or go to their rooms. They chose to enjoy the outdoors with iced tea. Sheriff Lynwood said farewell to the ladies, and how he will see them all at church come Sunday, then he left. Rocking on the big wooden chair, Claire couldn't believe how green it was here, and so quiet.

The old hound placed his heavy head on her lap and she scratched the top of his head absentmindedly as she thought about the city life and the differences. It was so quiet; you could almost hear the grass grow. Aunt Maddie was telling the ladies a few funny stories of her life in the old farmhouse, never married, she longed for a family. How happy she was that she could have this chance to spoil Claire.

Dinner was a simple meal of fried chicken, vegetables and rolls with some fresh cold milk to top it off. Claire hadn't realized how hungry she was until she noted the amount of chicken bones on her plate. She blushed slightly embarrassed, and Aunt Maddie said she was over joyed to feed people. Night fell fast out here, and it was so dark. Aunt Maddie said she had a water closet installed a couple years ago so she wouldn't have to find her way out back in the dark.

Toula was happy that this woman had opened her home to her as well as her niece, not everyone viewed a black woman as an equal and this woman made Toula feel very welcomed. Maybe this will work out just fine to help Claire find herself all over again. Claire needed to forget about Brian and focus on healing.

Climbing the stairs and headed to their rooms, Aunt Maddie said breakfast is informal, just like everything else. Therefore Claire can leave her facial coverings in her room if she wished. A new fear gripped Claire at the mention of her face. She certainly would not be seen without her coverings that just would not do at all. Sleep over took her quickly, and she slept in well past breakfast, neither of the older women had the heart to wake her. The two sat out on the veranda talking like old friends; such an easy life out here in Cougar Ridge.

The day started later for Claire, as she woke after noon meal was served. Coming down the stairs she apologized for sleeping so late. She could not understand why she had done so. The other two women exchanged knowing looks, and Toula voiced her thoughts. Perhaps it's the very fresh air and the exhaustion from the trip. Claire nodded her agreement, figuring this was the likely cause. Aunt Maddie was talking about the church picnic this Sunday and how this will be a wonderful time for Claire and Toula to be introduced to the town. A little frightened of this notion Claire was looking for a polite excuse to give for not attending church and the picnic afterwards.

Toula saw the hesitation and spoke quickly saying that sounded wonderful. The two older women set up a plan for the foods that they would bring to this picnic. Toula suggested the wonderful fried chicken they enjoyed the previous evening, and then said that she made the best potato salad around. Pies were next topic of discussion, as to favorites and least favorites. Claire was of no help to the talks of preparing meals, she had never even learned to make biscuits. When Aunt Maddie heard this she almost fell off her chair in shock. Well, that just won't do, Claire will need to learn to cook while she recouped here, Aunt Maddie said.

-27-

The next few days passed with Claire learning to collect the milk from the old cow, and eggs from the chicken coop. She even learned how heavy a basket of freshly wash was when she was asked to hang it on the clothes line out back. Luckily for Claire, Aunt Maddie had an indoor pump in the kitchen, or she would be hauling buckets of water from the well. As it was, she did need to haul buckets of hot water for her baths, something she was not used to at all. It felt rather satisfying doing these things, and Claire had a natural happy smile on her face for the first time in a long time.

Sunday was fast approaching, and the morning of Claire trying to fake being sick so she didn't have to go and be placed on display. Toula saw right through this and told Claire she had exactly ten minutes to be ready and downstairs for breakfast, or she would be going to church in her bed clothes. Knowing Toula never gave idle threats, Claire prepared to get dressed to head down for breakfast and then to the church for the freak show display.

Walking outside Claire looked for a coach or wagon to get them to church. When she didn't see one, she asked her aunt where it could be. Aunt Maddie laughed and said it was a great day for a walk into town, it wasn't far and it would do them all some good. Claire tried to remember how far it actually was to the church house in town, but couldn't. Well, she figured if her elder aunt could walk it, so could she. Off they went down the long driveway towards the road into town.

Church was a small affair, not the large show she was used to. There was no organ here, no music at all, and the men wore work clothes, not proper suits. Claire felt very over dressed in her city church attire, and realized that must be why people were staring open mouthed at her. She wore her face veil, and a smart beige dress and tunic with her high necked starched white lace blouse.

After the church services were close to end, the reverend announced a welcome to the two newest members of the community; Miss Claire Cooliage from Boston and her companion Toula. They were of course staying at her Aunt Maddie's place. A warm welcoming hello was spoken by the church members. Church was dismissed and everyone was headed to the town square for the church picnic. Tables had been set up using planks from the mill, checkered tablecloths were draped over the planks and plates were used to hold it in place.

A larger table at the front was being used to place all the different foods on, and people were milling around loading their plates and sitting on blankets on the ground or at one of the makeshift tables. Claire couldn't believe all of the food choices, she picked through and had a small plateful when she was done. She headed to the blanket that Aunt Maddie had spread out under one of the big weepy willow trees. A slight breeze was softly blowing the scent of strange flowers into the air.

Claire could not think of anything but the intoxicating scent for she had never smelt anything so heavenly. Lilacs, Aunt Maddie said, as she pointed to the large bush to the edge of the square. They were beautiful, purple ones and some white ones. Claire asked if they could pick some on the way home to place in a vase. Of course, and aunt Maddie said that there were plenty more all over the area, even on her land.

Reverend Cooper was approaching the ladies as they were cleaning up from their lunch. He asked if he could sit a few moments. Of course this was ok with Maddie, not so with Claire, but she just kept her head down cast. The reverend sat on the edge of the blanket and began to express his happiness at welcoming the two into his church, and hoped they felt welcomed. Toula said she certainly did, and when Claire did not speak, she spoke for her.

This was interesting to Reverend Cooper for Miss Maddie had mentioned how chatty her beloved niece was. He didn't see it right now, in fact she looked terrified. Trying to calm Claire, the Reverend tried to get her to raise her head by reaching towards her chin. Screaming in shock and stumbling backwards Claire tried to flee, only to be calmed and stopped by the strong arms of Toula.

Toula held Claire in her arms for a moment until she was convinced that Claire would not flee. Aunt Maddie told the reverend how Claire had undergone a very traumatic accident recently and was still recovering from it; and was unsure of people moving quickly and did not want to be touched.

Nodding in understanding, the reverend apologized and hoped his actions would not change her mind about the church. Excusing himself to see to other parishioners he tipped his hat and left. Claire was visibly shaking and Aunt Maddie suggested to Toula that they head back to the farmhouse, that Claire had enough excitement for the day. The ladies gathered their blanket and picnic stuff and headed out of town towards the farm house.

The days were moving on with no interaction from the town people, Claire was fine with that; actually didn't mind that fact. Claire was beginning to enjoying the very simple lifestyle here in Cougar Ridge, and she spoke to Toula one day about needing to get some different clothes as her city attire was a bit too formal for the people here and she didn't wish to stand out any more than she already did. Aunt Maddie suggested a trip into the general store the next day to see the dresses on display there, and if they didn't have what Claire was looking for, then maybe some fabric and they would have the dresses made for her.

The general store had so much stuff in such a small place. They had everything from food supplies to farm equipment, in a corner near the back were racks with clothing hanging on them. No separate ladies and gentlemen sections, everything was on the same racks. Very different from what Claire was used to. Claire was used to separate stores for ladies fashions, and was shocked to hear that there was no ladies store here; but to find out that everything was sold in the same store was a lot to comprehend.

As she was glancing around the crowded store, she noticed the selection of hats, heading over there she spotted a nice looking yellow straw hat with purple violet flowers on the brim. There was no price tag on the hat, so he replaced it on the shelf to ask about it after. Joining Aunt Maddie by the clothing rack she saw that the selection was very lacking. She did see a plain brown dress that was her size. She chose that much to Aunt Maddie's horror, the colour was all wrong for such a pretty young girl, no it wouldn't do.

Aunt Maddie suggested getting the material and having a few dresses made within the week. Claire agreed but only if she could also buy this dress. She then asked about the price of the hat, and noted some veil material also. Once the purchases were tallied, the shopkeeper said he would have everything boxed up and brought out to the farm later that day. Aunt Maddie said that would be acceptable and they left the store to walk to the post office to check for mail.

Claire had sent a letter for Toula to post when they first arrived, it was addressed to her family and it just basically said they had arrived safe and sound and were adjusting to the farm life. Nothing less, nothing more. Claire still was bitter about her family ganging up on her and sending her away. She was just as sure that Brian would now have received his dreadful ring back and now be relieved to know he didn't have to marry the beast she had become.

There was no mail today for Maddie, or anyone else at the farm for that matter. That was fine by Claire, she didn't think anyone would write to her. They are all too happy to have their perfect lives back with her being shipped so far away.

The door to the newspaper opened and the proprietor stepped out to say hello to Maddie. The three ladies stopped and Aunt Maddie made the introductions of her niece and Toula to Marcus Skylar, owner of the local newspaper. A kind looking gentleman, and very well spoken. He asked how the ladies were enjoying the small town life after the ways in Boston, then he asked if he could do a small write up on their arrival as an introduction to the community. Claire said that surely there were more interesting things to write on then two women travelling to Cougar Ridge. He assured them that the people here would love to know more about them. Against everything inside her, Claire had agreed to Mr. Skylar coming out to the farm the following day to ask his questions for his article. They waved goodbye as they walked down the road leading out of town towards the farm house laneway.

Dinner was a simple affair that evening, cold fried chicken, potato salad, pickles and freshly baked bread. They decided to eat their meal outside under the large tree in the back yard. Maddie had pulled the old table from the barn to the tree that morning and Toula had offered to scrub it clean. Claire was learning how to do laundry that day, so she was attempting to hang the clothes on the line, to no avail. She just couldn't figure out how to hold the heavy wet garment and try to pin it at the same time. This wasn't lost on the other two as they chuckled under their breath while positioning the table for later that day.

Dining on their outdoor meal with the slight summer breeze blowing the scent of freshly washed clothing, Claire couldn't help but look back on the past few weeks since their arrival. They have met quite a few interesting people during church, most of which Claire could not recall their names. For such a small town the people here were very close and very friendly. With the meal finished and the table cleared, the ladies drank iced tea on the front porch watching the sun set and the night sounds begin.

A wagon was approaching, and Maddie stood to welcome their visitor. Claire automatically raised a hand to make sure her face was covered. Resisting the urge to flee into the house she buried her face into the newspaper she had placed on the flower stand earlier. The wagon had stopped just shy of the steps and Claire heard a strong deep male voice speaking to Aunt Maddie.

-28-

The male voice said that Tom Southwold had some deliveries for Miss Maddie and being as he was her neighbor and all, he brought them to her to save Tom the drive. Claire had heard the man state. Then he asked if she wanted the couple heavy boxes around back in the kitchen. Toula stood to make her introduction and offer some help to which the man declined. When Claire heard her name she glances up slightly from the paper and noticed the man held his hat in his hand and nodded towards her when Aunt Maddie introduced her and Toula.

What did Aunt Maddie say his name was? Was it Mason or Jason? Oh well, it doesn't matter. She won't be conversing with him any time soon.

The shock she received when she looked him fully in the face; was like a punch to the stomach. Mason or Jason had to be well over six feet tall and she would bet he was close to two hundred and twenty-five pounds. All muscle as she could tell by his chest showing from a deerskin type of vest, and a pair of trousers with a belt. Claire had never seen a man dressed like this, she heard of the savage Indians wearing the skins of animals and barely anything else, and this man was wearing what she would assume was indeed Indian attire. His hair hung loosely on his shoulders, shiny and dark, his skin had been darkened by many years shirtless in the sun, and the muscles proved he lived a healthy hard life.

His face was darker skinned as well, kind blue eyes, that she could look into forever, and a scruffy growth of the beginning of a beard caressed his high cheekbones. It was his smile that stopped her in her tracks though, beautiful lips glided over even white teeth as he smiled his welcome to her. Dimples and twinkling eyes, wow Claire needed to remember to breathe.

Toula nudged Claire and she gave a soft hello to him as he carried the first box to the rear of the farm house into the kitchen. Claire had to ask Toula the man's name again before he returned for the second box of supplies from the mercantile. Mason; yes that fit the man for sure Claire thought dreamily; such a strong name for an even stronger looking man; a strange looking man, but very interesting all the same.

Mason retrieved the last of the boxes and was taking it to the kitchen when Aunt Maddie suggested he stop for an iced tea or she could put on some coffee. Mason begged off the drink offer, and asked if he could perhaps take her up on it another time. He needed to get home; his horse was due to foal any day now and he really wanted to be there. Smiling at the ladies, he placed his tan leather hat on his head and climbed aboard his wagon and headed down the driveway.

Claire had many questions she wanted to ask her Aunt Maddie about this man, but society didn't allow her to speak in such a matter. She was so relieved when Aunt Maddie started to talk about Mr. Mason Barker. Mason lived on the ranch to the south of hers, across the other side of the road to town. He lived alone, was a wonder with animals and especially any troublesome horse. People around here respected Mason for his horsemanship and the way he treats everyone. He was also the Indian Liaison she stated, to which Claire asked what that meant.

Cougar Ridge was built beside the Indian reserve as a way to introduce the natives to white people. Nobody really knows how the town began, but Mason had his ranch here before the town was built, rumor had it that he was part Indian, but it was never confirmed as no one has ever had the nerve to ask him of his past.

Folks just took it that he was part of the reserve, and the town was built with him helping in every matter. Mason was a town founder of sorts, never married, no children and no special lady; ever. There was even talk that he had real wolves on his land that he would run with at night, barefoot. Like the natives. Mason didn't dress like a white man, but did not look one hundred per cent native either.

This was a mysterious man Claire thought. Her interest was piqued for sure. She had not felt this interested in anyone in a very long time. She had given up on the idea of every being interested in a man, but on a knowledge finding quest, she figured she was interested purely for knowledge sake.

Mason was very curious about the woman on the porch. The black woman, Toula, was very outgoing but he sensed a protective note she had towards the younger quiet woman trying to blend into the newspaper. She was covered from head to toe in very unflattering attire with the biggest hat with the ugliest veil he had ever seen. Why did she feel the need to hide her identity in Cougar Ridge? He definitely wanted to find out more on her.

Reverend Cooper had mentioned to him the other day that Maddie Anderson's niece was staying with her for an undetermined amount of time supposedly to heal from a devastating accident that we weren't supposed to mention, as it might scare the young girl back into her shell; a shell that Widow Anderson had been trying very hard to crack wide open. When Tom from the mercantile mentioned he was taking a delivery to Maddie's farm Mason jumped at the chance to meet this young lady.

Taking the boxes to Maddie's farm, Mason was trying to figure out what to say if the young lady was not present, for that was the reason he was coming to the farm today, to meet Miss Cooliage. It was well worth the trip Mason said out loud to his horse as he unhitched his wagon at the barn. Turning his team loose in the coral, Mason whistled a couple shrill tweets and out of the tall grass came a very large dog like beast, barrelling full tilt towards Mason and finally launching itself off all four feet and landing smack dab in the centre of Mason's chest to be caught and hugged tightly.

Placing the grey and white wolf on its feet, Mason scrubbed the animal behind its ears as he spoke to him about the young lady he just met. She was small in structure, and he thought he caught sight of a few tiny wisps of red hair tucked inside that repulsive hat she wore. Maybe she was a person that did not take to sunlight well. He had heard of women from the city who always were covered. Not sure of this, he thought maybe an invite to an evening meal will show him more of her features. With that thought he and the wolf walked towards his house.

Unpacking the boxes that Mason had placed on the table in the kitchen, Toula and Maddie placed the food items on the table and removed the material to place it on the chair. So many different shades of material Claire was certain she didn't need all of that.

Last item to be removed was wrapped in a brown paper and tied with a twine string. Claire knew she had not purchased the item, and was pretty certain that Toula hadn't either, so she wondered what was wrapped in the paper. Aunt Maddie smiled at Toula as she handed the wrapped parcel to Claire. Claire was slightly confused as she sat at the table to carefully untie the string binding the small parcel. Once untied, she unfolded the brown paper and withdrew a lovely simple dress and a pretty scarf.

The dress was of a pale blue, simple with small while dots all over the material. No ruffles or hoops, just a plain dress. Her mother would call it a peasant dress, but Claire thought it was lovely. So simple, and useful for where she was now living. It was the same type of dress that the other women in the small town wore.

The same kind of dress that Aunt Maddie had said she was going to have the dresses made from the material she just purchased. Tears slid from the corner of her eyes. Her Aunt Maddie was a very caring woman to see that her city dresses were cumbersome here in this rural setting. And she was thoughtful enough to even add the head scarf knowing Claire's revulsion to be seen without her covering. Hugging her aunt tightly she kissed her on the cheek.

Maddie was sure this was the beginning to bringing her niece back to the family as her normal happy self. She had yet to see for herself the damage that was done to Claire, but she figured that when Claire was ready to share that with her, that would be soon enough. Seeing her niece smiling was perfect end to her day.

Claire was trying to come to terms that the town women were coming to Aunt Maddie's today to help with the measuring and then the sewing of her many dresses. Toula had assured her that the women would not be detoured by her face, that Infact they would be more detoured by the fact that Miss Claire hid her beauty so.

Claire did not agree and had worked herself into a mild panic stage, so much that Aunt Maddie needed to be called in to see if she could talk some calm and sense in to her. While Maddie entered Claire's small bedroom, Toula decided to head downstairs to set out some cool drinks for the ladies arrival. Once in the kitchen, Toula looked out into the bright sunny back yard, and prayed to her Lord that Miss Claire will find His healing powers here in this wild country so far from everything that they knew as normal.

The six town ladies arrived on foot, each carrying a basket of supplies and chatting up a storm as they climbed the front porch stairs. Being from Boston, the proper show of manners would be to wait for the home owner or house maid to welcome you inside to the waiting parlor; but here being neighbors meant you smile and yell your hello as you walk in the front door. Toula smiled and laughed as she headed to the front door to welcome the ladies and to show them to the large dining area that they had decided would be best to lay the fabrics out.

While the ladies were looking over and touching each chunk of fabric, Aunt Maddie was upstairs trying to calm Claire. Claire had been in Cougar Ridge for a few weeks now, and had yet to discuss her accident with anyone, even Aunt Maddie. Thinking now would be a good a time as any, Claire asked Maddie to have a seat by the open window in her room. Maddie knew what was about to happen, and was nervous and ready for it. Bracing herself against the past and the still raw memories, Claire began her tale of love lost and future lost.

She began her story by telling Aunt Maddie all about her schooling time and the homecoming. How her family was not very supportive of her teaching degrees.

Aunt Maddie put in the needed oohs and aahs knowing Claire needed to hear this to relieve her tension. As she slowly began the horrific tale. She went on about the story as it happened. The way Claire spoke, so sure and precise about every tiny detail, from the description of her fiancé to the ugliest ring ever thought Maddie, this story was a hard one to tell, but Claire looked out the window and kept going. Almost like a river flowing over the rocks, faster and faster she was unable to slow herself or even stop. The dam was opened and she began the terrible memory of the accident itself. Claire was visibly shaking as she recalled the ground shaking and the pain of the wagon then the blissful peace and quiet that followed.

Aunt Maddie was crying into a handkerchief she pulled from her apron, unbeknownst to Claire as she kept on with her story. Wild eyed and back in the moment, Claire screamed as she fell to the floor. Toula heard the scream along with the other ladies. Asking them to stay in the kitchen she ran upstairs to find Claire in a heap by the window and Aunt Maddie cradling her head in her lap. Gone was the protective head piece, and Claire's red hair was being wiped aside by Maddie. Waiting for the scream or look of disgust to show on Maddie's face, but Toula never saw that. What she did see was love and caring. Pure understanding. Toula shed tears as she approached to help comfort Claire.

To help Claire avoid any embarrassment over her face being revealed, Aunt Maddie excused herself to tend to the ladies waiting downstairs. An unspoken understanding passed between the two older ladies in regards to Claire. Toula will help straighten Claire and together they will come down when she is ready.

Walking down the stairs, Maddie couldn't help but feel a deep pride and over whelming urge to protect her niece. Hearing firsthand the horror the young girl endured and seeing the aftermath was hard enough, and she didn't have to live that life. How brave her charge was for coming all this way to rebuild her confidence once again. Wiping the remaining tear from her eye, Maddie smiled to the ladies and mentioned that they did have a breakthrough, finally. Happy smiles and hand holding were happening and promises that this storm will be over and the sun will shine again.

Toula was helping Claire wash her tear stained face and place her bonnet and veil back in place. Claire was not aware that Maddie had seen her scarred face, and Toula wasn't ready to reveal that fact. Not just yet, let Claire think that her secret is safe, for now. Hat in place, dress straightened and Toula by her side, Claire felt she was about as ready for this as she would ever be. Let's get it over with the sooner the better.

They walked downstairs towards the sounds of lively chatter and clicking of fingers on the table. Claire stopped at the doorway and took in the sight of all these strangers planning on making dresses for her, a perfect stranger in their town, and they are happy to do it. Strange people here in the wild, thought Claire; back home in Boston, we looked at the dressmakers as servants, and went about giving orders and expecting it to be done. Here, these women gather together and happily help out, not expecting anything in return. Humbled by this, Claire approached slowly, head looking towards the floor as she did not know how to act in these strange surroundings. Toula sensed her shyness and prodded her forward laughing about the shy girl in the room to the others who were watching them walk in the room.

The ladies noticed Claire's shyness and tried to set her at ease. They mentioned her lovely city dresses and expressed to her how much lighter the simple dresses that they were going to make her would feel. This brought a smile to Claire and she engaged in the conversation, slowly but still engaged.

Hours went by and it seemed like moments, next thing Claire knew was a wagon pulling up out front. Aunt Maddie walked to the front door to find Reverend Cooper's buggy being hitched to the porch rail. Reverend Cooper removed his hat when he saw Maddie at the steps welcoming him in for a cool glass of lemonade. He gratefully accepted and followed her inside.

Seeing all the local women gathered in the kitchen brought a wide smile to his face as he greeted each with a warm smile and welcoming handshake. Noticing all the material on the table, Reverend Cooper suggested perhaps they all take a break and enjoy the lemonade outside under the big willow tree in the backyard.

Glasses in hand, everyone stepped out the back door and headed to the lawn under the grand tree. Claire held back saying she felt she needed to sit inside for a bit, to catch her breath from all the excitement. Toula started to return to the house, but Claire said she should go enjoy the cool breeze outside that she would be fine upstairs lying on her bed for a bit. With that, Claire turned and closed the door as she headed to her room.

Outside under the big weeping willow tree that sat beside a quiet babbling brook the ladies gathered and sipped their cool drinks and waited to hear what had brought the good reverend by today.

Nobody said anything for some time, it was Aunt Maddie who cleared her throat and asked what brought Rev Cooper this way. Rev Cooper took a small white cloth from the inside pocket of his black jacket and wiped his sweaty brow before speaking.

He started off by saying how wonderful it was to hear word in town today of this small gathering of ladies to help out our newest member. He wanted to personally see if there was anything that they may need him to do, and then he turned to Maddie and said he did have another reason for coming out here. A rather personal reason. It had to do with Miss Cooliage, actually.

This statement brought all eyes up at once and looked directly from the reverend to Maddie. Toula glanced towards the house, out of habit, searching for Claire. Maddie asked whatever reason did he need to include her niece in anything, it was beyond her. Rev Cooper started to mention how Miss Stella Rhodes, the local school teacher, had received word that her sister was soon to be married in a couple months and wanted to attend the wedding. She would be gone for a month, maybe two.

Stella had heard that Miss Cooliage had her teaching degree and wondered if the reverend would come out to see if she could or would mind taking over the school during her absence so the children would not miss out on any lessons while she was gone. Of course Miss Cooliage would be paid for her teaching time, and Stella wanted to know if she could possibly attend a few classes before she accepted, just so she could see how things went out in a rural school like Cougar Ridge had.

Maddie thought her prayers had been answered! Toula looked happy as well, but then they both sobered and looked towards the house behind them. Miss Maddie said that she will mention this to her niece tonite at dinner, and will have an answer for Stella soon. Rev Copper smiled broadly and clasped Maddie's hands in his as he bid everyone farewell, saying he will see everyone at Sunday services and not to forget the picnic afterwards. All present nodded and said they wouldn't miss either.

Gathering their glasses and walking back towards the kitchen talk changed back to the dresses. Each lady was going to take a swatch home and work on the dresses; they were hoping to have them done no later than a couple days. Plenty of time before church on Sunday where Claire can show off her lovely new dresses! Maddie secretly held back material from each pile so she could make matching scarves for Claire's hats. Something she wished she didn't have to make, but if it made things easier for Claire then it would be worth it.

Once the ladies had left, Maddie set out to make dinner with Toula to help her. It was so nice to have people in her home once again, life out here had been so lonely and she never really noticed it until Claire arrived. Maddie was very happy having them here, and regretted the time when they would eventually want to go home to Boston. Maddie was expecting Marcus Skylar for dinner as they had welcomed his offer of a story for the paper.

-29-

Marcus arrived on horseback; he tied his horse to the porch railing and climbed the steps to knock on the screen door removing his wide brimmed hat at the same time. Toula went to answer the door a wide welcoming smile on her face. Maddie asked Marcus to sit in the front parlor as dinner was not quite finished yet. The two women chatted with Marcus while they waited for Claire to come downstairs.

Claire heard Mr. Skylar laughing downstairs and realized she couldn't stay hiding up in her room any longer. Checking her scarf, and straightening her dress she walked down to the parlor. Upon her arrival, Marcus rose and said his hello. He then pulled out his notebook and pencil ready to ask questions for his article. The questions were varied, and unusual but exciting to answer. There were no deeply intrusive questions regarding her reason for being in Cougar Ridge.

Marcus, as he kept reminding her to call him, had asked about life in Boston; what her parents company was like. He asked about her travel to Cougar Ridge, about the lengthy train ride in a sleeper car … how exciting! He asked how she enjoyed the stage ride from the train station and then he first thoughts on arrival at their little place. Marcus was really interested in her thoughts, and how she was enjoying her stay with Ms. Maddie.

He then began to ask Toula about her positon with Claire's family, and how she enjoyed her trip so far. He didn't treat Toula as if she were just "hired help". Marcus actually cared about what Toula had to say, this made Claire smile.

Talk continued over dinner and soon everyone was laughing and joking like long-time friends. Maddie had to turn on the lanterns as it was becoming dark in the farm house, this was Marcus clue to say good night. He waved over his shoulder as he rode down the lane, and promised to let the ladies see his story before he went to print, so that if they wanted anything changed he could do it. That was so different than the newsmen in Boston, They did not really care if the people they wrote about approved of anything. Claire wondered if this little town knew how lucky they were to have each other. With a heavy sigh, Claire announced she was going to bed. She had to think of an excuse not to go to church in the morning.

A few days later, Marcus had left a short story on the front porch of the farm house. Claire picked up the handwritten page and sat on the step to read it. He had said that if any of them would like changes made, they only had to write on the paper and drop it by the office and he would make the needed changes. If they were ok with what he had written, then they wouldn't need to reply, he will go to print in two days.

The story read wonderfully. She was from Boston, her family ran a well-known business and Toula was a warmly regarded family member. The two ladies are staying with Aunt Maddie for an undetermined stay, and are enjoying the time spent in Cougar Ridge. There was nothing about her need to hide her face, so unlike the Boston Herald when they mentioned Claire's horrific brush with death. Relieved of this, Claire smiled and went inside. The town ladies were due today with her dresses and Claire was going to set out some snacks on the kitchen table.

Even though the dresses the town ladies had made for her were lovely and fit her perfectly, Claire did not want to go to church today. She had only been to the church the one time, and she had felt very out of place. She also declined the picnic invite afterwards. Saying she would be fine at the farm house, she really wanted to practice her bread and biscuit making. This was an excuse not to be seen in the town and Maddie saw right through it but didn't have the heart to force her to do something that she knew was so scary to Claire. So she told Claire that Stella Rhodes is planning on stopping over for Sunday dinner along with the reverend tonite.

Claire went rock still, and held her breath for a moment. Fear was settling inside her again and she tried to quell this fear with her breathing, like Toula was teaching her to do. Claire turned to her aunt and smiled, she said she hoped they wouldn't mind if her bread isn't perfect, and wished her aunt a happy Sunday as she went to the pantry for the flour.

-30-

While Aunt Maddie and Toula were at church services Claire decided to perfect her bread skills. Dark smoke was filling the room as she had burnt yet another loaf. Opening the front door and the rear kitchen door and window she tried waving around a towel to help rid the room of the stench and smoke. The smoke filled house was making her eyes water, and she was coughing as she tried airing the house out.

Seeing smoke from the road Mason ran full speed towards Maddie's farm house fearing the worst. His faithful companion ran ahead knowing something was wrong. Claire was stepping onto the front porch wiping smoke from her eyes. When she opened them she was face to face with the biggest beast she had ever seen. Standing on all four legs this brute of an animal stood higher than her hips, its piercing yellow eyes staring directly through her.

Not willing to move in case she provoked this wild beast, Claire stood still not breathing; hoping to God above that a chicken ran past. Anything to catch this animal's attention! That's when she saw Mason, or was it Jason, approaching fast from the grass to the side of the porch. There was no way he would see the beast, she needed to distract the animal and warn him at the same time. But how?

Panic took over and she flung the towel that was in her hands towards the large animal and begun screaming to the man running

145

towards her that there was a wild animal here and he was to save himself.

The wolf shook off the offending towel that landed on his huge head and slowly was approaching Claire with a curious look to him. Claire was backed to the wall of the house too far from the door to escape she started screaming. This only excited the large beast and he began to bark and howl as he jumped around. Mason stood on the porch laughing at the sight of his wolf attempting to play with Claire. Never had he witnessed his wolf interacting with anyone before, he was a loner, and avoided contact with humans as best he could.

The sound of the huge beast preparing to eat her, and then hearing a man laughing brought Claire to force her eyes open and to stop her screaming. Sure enough, there was the beast front end bowed to the ground and the large back end standing upright ready to what Claire was sure would be a pounce stance, and that man just laughing. Mason calmed the situation by calling off the wolf with a shrill whistle. He gave Claire a couple minutes to compose herself before he apologized for the laughing.

He explained how he saw the smoke and assumed Maddie was under a fire, so he ran which alerted his friend to act as well. Mason called to his wolf to approach, and he sat at Mason's side. Claire was amazed this large frightful beast was tame. She said so aloud, and Mason corrected Claire by saying the wolf was not tame, but they had an understanding. This brought back the reason why Mason was here, so Claire had to say she had been burning loaves of bread all morning trying to bake.

Another round of deep laughter rumbled out of Mason, which in turn caused Claire to giggle a bit. The wolf seemed to tire of this and headed off towards Mason's Ranch. Both watched the majestic animal leap clearly over the hedges and disappear into the tall grass. Claire offered Mason a glass of cool water to which he accepted.

Watching Claire walk into the house, Mason couldn't help but notice that she was younger than he first thought and slimmer now that she was not wearing all those layers of city clothing. She was quite striking in her own way, and he was glad for the opportunity to share a quiet glass of water with her, to get to know her better. No woman had ever piked his interest the way Miss Cooliage did, and this intrigued him. She was a puzzle he needed to solve.

She was beautiful, he assumed, and couldn't figure out why she hid herself so. He needed to find out her past, her present and see what made her the way she is. Yes, Mason was intrigued for sure. Claire returned to the porch chairs with two glasses of cool water and a small plate of slightly burnt biscuits. Laughing Mason took a biscuit and shoved the whole thing in his mouth. While he could taste the burnt uncooked morsel he ate the entire thing and even had another. This fact wasn't lost on Claire, she herself had attempted to try to eat one, but it was so foul she nearly gaged. He must be starving to have eating not just one but two of the retched things!

They sat on the front porch talking about life here in Cougar Ridge and the differences Claire is dealing with having come from a rather large city to this town. Noticing Claire seemed to be tiring; Mason suggested they continue this conversation at a later day so that Claire can rest up for her fiery day. The way Mason said this made Claire smile then start to laugh.

She agreed to another burnt offering in the near future. Claire was just as smitten with this wild man as he seemed to be with her. Not once did Claire try to adjust her scarves or shield her face away from Mason, a thought that Claire herself failed to notice.

That evening during dinner, Claire had a hard time keeping up with the conversation at the table between Stella and the Reverend. Her mind kept drifting to the handsome man who came charging in to rescue her from a fire. A man she both feared and wanted to see again. Mason Barker was unlike any man she had ever met. He was unlike any man she had ever thought about. Mason Barker was a man all to himself. A wild creature, just like the wolf companion he had. Both were wild and mysterious, but gentle in a scary way.

Just thinking of Mason made Claire's skin prick with tiny goosebumps and her heart raced a bit. This bringing a flush to her pale cheeks. Thankfully her veil hid this. So she hoped. Toula could sense the changes in Claire, and kept glancing her way to make sure her missy was ok.

Talk soon turned to schooling, which perked up Claire's attention. Was she hearing correctly? Did this woman sitting here just offer her a chance to teach? My word, thought Claire, I must be dreaming. It was a real offer if Claire wanted to accept the offer then Stella wanted her to accompany her to class someday to meet the children before she agreed to anything.

Stella knew her classroom was not the normal type of school room most teachers think about, and that was one reason why she wanted Claire. She saw something missing in this woman's being and hoped that her special class could also help heal her as it had helped heal Stella when she needed it.

Claire agreed that next week she would come to the classroom and view it from the back, not wanting to disrupt the teachings and then she would make a decision about accepting the temporary placement. The table was cleared and the guests left. Toula and Maddie were sitting outside listening to the nite sounds and enjoying the quiet. Claire came out and sat with the ladies. She had mentioned that she would like to write a letter to her family, at the mention of her family the two ladies turned to her.

For over these several months Claire refused to mention anything to do with Boston; and here she wanted to write to her family. Perhaps she was beginning to heal inside as well as on the outside? Pleased with how things were progressing, Maddie figured she would also pen a letter to her niece in Boston to update her on what she is witnessing. Hopefully to get a return letter.

It was strange that her niece had not written to Claire or herself since she arrived. Very strange indeed. And what of that fiancé she heard about; why hadn't he shown up? These were only a few of the questions Maddie was thinking. This poor soul, alone in a strange place so very far away from everyone and everything she knows, only her maid for company.

What was her family thinking sending her out here so far away? Perhaps Claire was right when she said that they shipped her away because she became an embarrassment to the family. Hoping she was wrong in her thinking, Maddie retired to bed for the evening, shortly afterwards so did Toula and Claire.

Out in the darkness, a figure turned as the lanterns were snuffed and the house went dark. Mounting a horse, rider and horse headed towards town. Silently and unnoticed for yet another evening. Returning to the boarding house to get some needed sleep. For tomorrow a long journey was in store, before returning back to Cougar Ridge.

The horse and rider headed back towards town silently in the night's darkness. Bright yellow eyes watched from the tall grass, a low growl emitted as the horse and rider rode away.

Morning came and after a quick breakfast Claire stated that she would like to walk into town to mail her letter. Toula wanted to walk with her and Maddie suggested that they all go in together, order some supplies and then have lunch at Christina's Diner. This was a wonderful idea and the three set off talking up a storm, about nothing at all. It was lovely. Claire felt free for a change. So much that she failed to notice that he scarf was falling to the side and her face was almost in full view to all.

Dropping off her letter at the post office, Claire was introduced to a beautiful native woman. Her name was Hazel Every. Very quiet but with kind eyes, Claire knew instantly that she liked her, and hoped that they would become friends. As she smiled to Hazel she had asked if she'd like to join them for lunch at Christina's. Hazel smiled like the sunshine just appeared. She agreed so fast that everyone laughed, including Hazel. Claire commented on this fact when they left the post office, and Maddie mentioned that Hazel was part native therefore didn't actually fit in anywhere. This seemed odd to Claire and she asked why.

Apparently the natives see her as mostly white, and the whites see her as native. People are ok with her being employed, and she even comes to church, but very few claim her as a friend. People just aren't sure how to approach her. Claire commented that Hazel seemed like a very nice woman, and she would like to be her friend. Maddie smiled as she linked her arm in Claire's as they walked towards the mercantile.

Hazel watched these women walk away and wondered if the quiet one knew her scar was visible, and wanted to know the story behind it. The lady seemed to have deeper scars than the one on her lovely face. This made Hazel sad, but at the same time excited about the upcoming lunch with them. Singing as she went about her postal duties she kept a close eye on her clock so she wouldn't be late for lunch.

Walking towards the store from the post office, they passed the newspaper office and Mr. Jack Stiles, the owner of the Mill that sat across the way, was just walking out. He tipped his hat as he said good morning to the ladies. Claire instinctively reached for her scarf and adjusted it as she looked to her feet. Sheriff Lynwood chose that moment to come out of Doc Wellington's office beside the newspaper. He had to speak with Jack about some disturbances he had been hearing about, and wanted to know if Jack had heard anything. Excusing themselves, the men walked across the town square towards the Mill and the Stockyard where Jerimiah Crawford was waiting for them.

Wondering what these disturbances were, Claire asked her Aunt Maddie if she had anything to say on this subject. Maddie had no idea what the sheriff was speaking of, but she was sure to ask around. If anyone would know anything, Maddie was saying, it would be Agatha Clark. Agatha ran a boarding house, and hears and knows all. Maddie was saying that today Agatha was going to be in town ordering supplies as well, and she will see if she would join them for lunch also.

The three women arrived at the store to find Mr. Marcus Skylar leaving with a bundle of notes. Maddie said good morning to Marcus, and he in turn tipped his hat and hurried off to the newspaper office. Tom Southwold was behind the counter as the women entered the store.

Seeing the three come in he smiled and came around to greet them. Knowing that Maddie would be getting her usual supplies, Tom had his pad of paper ready. Inquiring on her usual order, Tom also asked if there was anything extra she would need. Or if the other ladies required anything to be delivered. Thinking on her upcoming school venture, Claire headed to the book section of the store to see what they had for learning books. Not very impressed by the lack of teaching supplies, she made a mental note to see what the school could use so she could purchase it as a gift to the students.

Having the purchases ordered and Tom saying that he can have everything ready and delivered later today, the ladies decided to walk around town then head to the diner. Leaving the store, they turned left at the street and walked towards the church. As it wasn't Sunday it was being used as the school. Claire could hear the children laughing as they were playing outside. Must be recess she thought as she carefully glanced towards the children. Interested in seeing the children she may be teaching her footsteps began to slow.

Suddenly she came to a complete stop, alerting the two other ladies that she was no longer walking with them. Toula came to stand beside Claire and asked if something was wrong.

Claire pointed to the children; there were a couple boys with longer black hair and no shirts on. They were barefoot and wore deerskin britches. She was shocked to see native children freely frolicking with white children. She mentioned this fact to Aunt Maddie, and Maddie smiled saying things were handled differently here in Cougar Ridge.

Children were children and color didn't matter much to them. Some of the native children wanted to be schooled and the school welcomes them. The way Stella ran her school, she doesn't want to change the native children, just teach them some different cultures. Claire thought this over the remainder of their walk. She wasn't sure how she would be able to teach savage children. Can they understand our ways?

So many different things she was seeing out here so far away from home. It was exciting and frightening at the same time. All the stories she had heard about savage Indians didn't seem to be true from everything she was seeing first hand. So confusing. Before Claire knew it, the trio had walked around the pavilion in the town square and were standing outside of Christina's Diner nestled between the modest bank and the newspaper building.

Joining them outside the diner were Hazel and Agatha. Both women happily accepting the invite. The small party of women walked into the small cozy diner and chose a table at the front by the big window with the pretty but faded lace curtains. The diner was quaint, tastefully decorated and had the most delicious smells you could ever think of. The owner, Christina Lewis emerged from the back and came to ask the women what they would like to have to eat. She gave them the specials, no menus were needed because Christina's served the best of almost anything. Every day she had a special, and then you could have either fried chicken or stew. Today the special was steak and eggs.

All the women ordered the special along with cold lemonade. Christina brought out a large pitcher of lemonade and five glasses, she then returned with a basket of warm rolls and fresh churned butter and placed it on the table for the women to snack on while their steaks were cooking.

Talk turned to the disturbances that the sheriff had mentioned. Agatha's eyes sparkled and lit up as she spoke about what she had overheard two days earlier at the newspaper office. She went into detail about Sheriff Lynwood noticing little things around town gone missing, then when other town members starting noticing other things, and the stockyard was unchained some nights allowing the cattle out. Well then the good sheriff was going to bring the men of Cougar Ridge in to form a look out, to make sure our town remains safe. He was going to speak to Mason also to have him speak to the Indians on their behalf. Just to make sure that they are also kept safe.

The mention of Mason's name brought Claire's head up and she was even more alert to the conversation. Hazel was intently watching this strange woman and was even more interested after seeing how the mere mention of a name stirred raw emotion from her. Not noticeable to others, Hazel had a gift of noticing things that other people over look. She really wanted to get to know this beauty. Such an interesting person she seemed to be. Maybe she will talk to Mason, see what he thinks of this new comer. Mason would be out at the reserve tonite, she will talk to him then. That settled, Hazel went back to buttering her warm roll while smiling to the ladies, watching Claire closely.

The steaks were cooked to perfection; if Claire didn't know better she would have thought she had been served in a fine dining establishment in Upper Boston. It was that good.

The walk home will do them all some good. Agatha had to get back to the boarding house as her long time boarder; Mr. Beauford was leaving today on business and will be returning in a couple weeks. She needed to clean his room from top to bottom so it's ready for his return stay. Tom let Maddie know that her order was ready and will be brought out shortly. The walk home was filled with lively chatter and conversations about the local flowers. Many of which Claire was picking to place in a jar of water when they returned to the farm house.

Hazel arrived at the reserve in time to see Mason talking with the Elders, she sat back to wait for him to finish knowing he will look for her to say hello as he always does. She turned her attention to the children chasing the dog through the tall grass. The boys were getting so tall, and the girls were becoming beautiful young women. She noticed two young boys sitting on a stump reading a shared book. Obviously on loan from the school teacher, these boys were handling it like a precious gift. Hazel wanted to ask the boys how they were liking the white man's school.

Running Horse and 2 Feathers saw Hazel walking towards them, and sat up straighter as they set the book down. Story had it that Hazel had been left behind by her mother when she was forced to choose between her Indian life and her white husband's life. Her mother and sister had agreed to raise Hazel but she was to remain on the reserve and not follow into the white man world.

Never being a full native woman, never quite fitting in Hazel was a very quiet woman, a mystery to most of the natives there. The young braves were wondering why she would be approaching them.

Hazel smiled at the boys and asked how they were adjusting to the Cougar Ridge School. They both started talking at once, in their own language knowing that Hazel could speak it also. They found it easier to put their words in their own tongue than to try to form English words. They were learning a lot at the school, and bringing that entire knowledge home to the reserve, teaching the younger children; while hoping that their learnings will benefit everyone at the same time. They held a lot of respect for Ms. Stella as she told the boys that they may come to school wearing their regular clothing, just as her other students were able to wear what they wanted. Their teacher treated all the children as children, no differences at all.

Hazel also learned that Ms. Stella was leaving the school for a trip to her family home to attend a wedding. In Ms. Stella's absence the new comer lady in town with the face coverings will be teaching the school.

Hazel was excited to hear that Ms. Cooliage was interested in teaching the children. She will be sure to ask her if she needs to know anything about the two boys from the reserve she only needs to ask and Hazel will be sure to help out.

Leaving the boys to their reading, Hazel noticed Mason leaving the Elder's tee pee. A woman on a mission, Hazel walked straight to Mason waving at him to get his attention. Mason smiled his wide smile when he saw Hazel heading in his direction. Such a shy woman, not really fitting in anywhere, Mason thought they had a lot in common.

Getting past the morning pleasantries, Hazel knew that beating around the bush was not something either of them were good at. She simply asked Mason what he knew of the new woman staying at Widow Andersons place. Mason stood for a moment thinking of what to say. When he did speak it was in gentle tones, he commented how Ms. Cooliage must have a deep need for solitude and that she came along way for it. He felt that she needed to be here to heal from some accident and perhaps that's why she wears the face covering veils. Other than that, she seemed to be a very quiet lady and he was just getting to know her slowly.

Hazel expressed her interest in getting to know Ms. Cooliage better, and asked Mason if he could pass on the message to her that if she needed any help with the children, she can count on her to help out. Mason smiled and said thank-you, he was sure to pass that along. He said he had to get to the mercantile to grab supplies and head home. Hazel watched Mason mount his horse and wave goodbye to the children before riding away. She wondered if he knew how his eyes sparkled when he spoke of Ms. Cooliage. Hazel had a gift for seeing these things, and she smiled as she headed to her home.

-31-

Claire dressed in a simple dress of cream colors and matched a scarf of a shade darker than her dress. Placing a brown bonnet on her head she gathered some books and a writing pad with her pencil and went downstairs. Toula and Maddie were sitting at the table waiting for her to come into the room. Today Claire was going to the schoolhouse to observe a day in Stella's classroom.

Having a quick breakfast, Claire waived off the offer of a ride to the school. She said a walk will calm her nerves. Smiling at the older women, Claire tied her bonnet and gathered her books and walked out the door into the bright sunlight. Taking a steading deep breath, Claire walked down the lane towards the town.

Claire though of the way her life had changed. Not too long ago she wondered how she would approach the subject of her teaching to a man she was supposed to marry. Now here she was several months later, in a faraway world without her husband, without her family and she was headed to a school with savage children and expecting to teach. Her dream of teaching may be happening, and she had to travel to the other side of the world to do it. Laughter escaped her, nervous and unexpected.

Claire's steps slowed as she approached the church building where Stella held school classes. She could hear the children reciting the alphabet in almost perfect unison. Gathering her nerves and her skirts, Claire took one step at a time and willed her heartbeat to return to normal.

Closing the door softly behind her, she removes her bonnet and checks her scarf to make sure her face is partially covered. Hearing the children answering Stella's questions, Claire walks quietly into the one room building. She sits on an empty bench at the rear of the class as not to disturb the teachings. Here she sat for nearly half an hour totally immersed in the sounds of children wanting to learn.

Stella knew when Claire had entered the room, she just wasn't sure if Claire wanted to be introduced as soon as she entered, or if she wanted to get the feel of the classroom first. She thought her instincts were bang on, as Claire looked like she would jump out of her skin if spoke to.

Asking her class to close their McGuffey Readers, Stella announced to her class that her substitute was here and ready to be introduced to them. All heads turned to look at Claire. Face flushing, Claire rose and taking her books with her walked up the middle isle to the front of the class. She placed her books on the corner of the teacher's desk, and turned to face the children as Stella introduced her as Ms. Cooliage from Boston.

What a wide range of children in age, Claire noted. Smaller ones sat closest and the older children sat towards the back. Stella had prepared a roster of names for Claire, so that she could familiarize herself in the next few days before being handed the full duties if she chose to accept the teaching offer.

Claire noticed the two Indian boys sitting side by side on one bench behind the first set with 3 young boys on it. She glanced at the roster and saw their names. Very unusual names, she shouldn't have a problem figuring out that those were the boys names. Stella asked her class if they had any questions that they would like to ask Ms. Cooliage. Claire held her breath, expecting the usual fear of her face and barrage of unwanted questions about her accident.

She was very surprized when one of the Indian boys raised his hand to ask how far away Boston was. Another child asked her how long it took her to get here. And so went the questions. Not once did any of the children remark on her face veil, or her limp. Maybe she would be ok here in the school after all. Before Claire knew it, the school day was over. Stella dismissed her class, and when the children went out the door, she asked Claire how her first day went.

Claire was astonished at the class, their bright eyes and the eagerness to learn was refreshing to her. So used to spoiled children in uniforms thinking and knowing they are above most teachers stature in society, this was a little hard to adjust to. These children wore clean clothes, but no uniforms. They were so excited to be at school, Claire knew she would enjoy her teaching duties while Stella was away. Claire also knew it would be hard to give up the position when Stella returned. Something she jokingly told Stella. Both women were laughing like old friends as they exited the church house and walked to the pavilion in the town square. There they sat for a few moments as Stella told Claire a few stories of each child on the roster. Claire said she would arrive at the school bright and early to see the school day from start to finish.

Agreeing to accept this temporary position, the women said farewell and they would see each other in the morning before the bell for school would be rung. Claire practically skipped all the way back to the farm house, she was so happy. Full of stories of her first day she nearly burst out instantly when she saw the two women peeling potatoes on the front porch.

Toula was excited to see the sparkle in Claire's eyes as she regaled her day. Maddie smiled as she cleaned the dinner dishes from the table. In the months that Claire had been here she had prayed that something would make her young charge smile again; prayed for something to enter her soul to make her love life again. Today Maddie's prayers had been answered and she couldn't be happier.

Claire was excited for the next day to arrive, she hurried to bed and wished for sleep to come fast. Her wish was granted, and she fell into a deep sleep with a smile on her face.

-32-

The next week Claire had a routine she was happy with: morning breakfast with Toula and Maddie and then walking to school to begin teaching her class. This was Claire's dream to teach, and teaching she was doing. Her teaching degree was paying off, and the school board had sent the proper papers for her to fill out for her payment. Things were looking up. Claire was happy for the first time in nearly a year now. All it took was her family shipping her away. Even that thought could not stop her happy smile for she was a teacher.

Teaching the children was a wonderful thing, they were so interested in learning new things, and Claire was excited to find new things to share with them. Stella was leaving today, and Claire had planned a little surprise celebration for her from the classroom, and a little letter the children wrote to wish their teacher a safe travel and to have fun at the wedding.

After the early end of the school day the children gathered at the store to wave goodbye to Ms. Rhodes as she left in the stagecoach. As it was Friday, Claire announced that today was a short school day, and she will see the children on Monday. The stage rolled out of town, the children laughed and chased it for a short while and Claire walked down the road towards Aunt Maddie's house, her home now.

It was funny that she thought of this as home, these people she has lived with these past months all seemed like family to her now. She waved at Jack Stiles as she passed the mill. He was a kind man, quiet in nature, but always took the time to smile and wave hello to Claire. So different was the lifestyle here in Cougar Ridge, than her past life in Boston. She felt like she was a different person all together.

Arriving home, Claire set her school books on her dresser in her room and splashed water on her face to freshen up. She noticed how her red hair seemed softer and curlier since she moved here. Adjusting her scarf, she went to find Toula to see if she could help out with dinner preparations. She found the ladies outside under the big tree sipping cool lemonade. Dinner was simple tonight, cold chicken, potato salad and carrots, a nice cold dinner on a warm summer eve.

Claire went to bed, exhausted and happy. Tomorrow she was helping with some pie baking for Maddie's Sunday picnic, something Claire was not attending. She liked the town folk enough, everyone was friendly, but she still had a hard time sitting in the church with everyone, and attending the Sunday picnics that followed service. She enjoyed spending the Sunday wandering the property and talking to the old hound dog.

-33-

Claire had a small light breakfast with Toula and Maddie Sunday morning before the two older ladies went to church, wishing Claire would join them they said they would bring her a plate of food home from the picnic for her. Claire assured the women that she will be fine at the house alone. She was going to attempt cross stitching, something she watched Maddie do regularly. Laughing she hugged the women goodbye and watched then amble down the laneway in the single horse drawn buggy.

One good thing about being out in the Wild West was the solitude, the privacy. Claire planned on wandering down to the small little creek behind the farm house. Maddie had often mentioned how glorious it was to strip down and swim or just soak in the cool waters. Maybe today would be a good day to do just that. Everyone would be at the big church social and it was indeed too warm to be cooped up inside. Grabbing the blanket off the porch chair, Claire headed towards the path to the stream in the back of the property.

The grounds were so green and fresh, the grass felt spongy beneath her feet as she followed the faint path through the small brush. Claire spotted the small wooden bench that Aunt Maddie talked about. She sat on this bench and watched the sparkling water babble across the smooth rocks.

Hesitantly she looked around as she began to unlace her high boots. Setting them beside each other under the bench, Claire slid each stocking down her thighs and calves, pulling them off her feet. Rolling her stockings into tidy little balls, she placed them inside each boot and wiggled her toes in the soft grass.

Very nervously Claire glanced around once again, feeling very scared but at the same time very much alive for the first time in forever! Hiking up her skirts, she tentatively dipped her toes into the crystal clear water and giggled at the feeling of the rushing water playing around her feet.

Mason had arrived at the farm house to escort Claire to the social, even though Aunt Maddie and Toula both said that she wasn't feeling up to all the people yet. Mason knew the rumours about her being disfigured and basically shunned out of Boston; he knew that there was beauty under those big hats and scarves. He was planning on taking Claire out for a buggy ride if she decided that she really did not want to go to the social tonight.

It was then that Mason watched her take the plaid blanket and walk to the back of the yard. He tied the horse and buggy to the hitching post by the big elm tree, and knew where she was headed. He had built that bench for Maddie many years ago so that she could enjoy the tranquility of the stream.

Mason walked a different path, an unmarked path towards the same location. Not making a sound, he watched as Claire sat on the bench looking around her before unlacing her boots and removing her stockings. She had the creamiest, flawless skin he had ever seen. Beautiful legs.

She was giggling as the water tickled her feet. Should he announce his presence? Or should he just watch in secret a little while longer, to make sure she was ok. Surely she only intended to dip her feet and nothing more.

When she took another quick glance around, she removed her bonnet and scarf then began to unbutton her blouse and slip off her skirts. His mouth went dry, as Mason straightened and in doing so he bashed his head off the lower limb of the weeping willow tree he was crouched under. Stifling back a yelp of pain, he nearly missed seeing Claire step out of her petticoats and place them alongside her discarded bonnet and scarf on the bench.

Claire walked into the clear water and sank to her shoulders; pure delight she thought, as she allowed the water to cool her over heated skin. How horrified her mother would be if she knew what her perfect debutant daughter was doing at this moment. Well, she wasn't perfect; she would never be the perfect debutant again. She was so damaged that not only did her fiancé leave her, but her family sent her away. Only here in the far away lonely place did she feel alive again.

Lying on her back in the water she raised one leg straight up in the air and laughed loudly as the water dripped off her toes. She looked like a water sprite, splashing around without a care in the world with the sun cascading tiny rainbows around her. Mason could almost picture a halo over her head. She was a temptress floating in the water, and she had no idea how seductive she really was.

He wasn't close enough to get a real good look, but as she was climbing out of the water he could see red lines on her body and the side of her face. Scars? If so, where did they come from, who did this to her? Anger grew strong inside him, anger so severe; a need to protect her was so primal. These feelings were rising from deep inside him.

Mason needed to find out what happened to Claire, then make sure nothing or nobody would ever hurt her again. When Mason's anger haze faded, he noticed that Claire had her blouse and skirts back on. She was sitting on the blanket on the bank of the stream, dangling her feet in it still. He chose this moment to disappear into the brush and wait for her back at the house.

-34-

Claire took her time walking back to the house, she knew Aunt Maddie and Toula would be gone until dark, so she started picking the strawberries along the path back to the house. Using her bonnet as a basket she gathered a good amount. Eating as much as she picked she was laughing as she came to the side of the house. There she spotted a buggy and horse and instinctively reached to make sure her scarf was covering her face.

Mason was watching her as she emerged from the bush, eating the strawberry; its juice was still fresh on her lips. He wondered if she would taste like the strawberry she just ate. She held her bonnet in her arms filled with berries, and the plaid blanket was wrapped around her shoulders like a cape. Mason walked to her and offered to carry her berries. Claire relinquished her bonnet of berries and held the side door open for Mason to enter the kitchen.

He placed the berries in the bowl on the counter and handed Claire her bonnet. Being forever the proper lady, Claire offered Mason a glass of lemonade to drink out on the chairs under the tree in the back yard. Happily he accepted, and together they sat under the tree drinking their lemonade.

Mason told Claire that the reason he was there was to escort her to the social dance, to which she hastily declined. He then asked if she would like to go on a nice quiet buggy ride to end a Sunday evening. Claire sat for a moment, thinking about the offer. After a couple minutes, she agreed to a short ride. They take their empty glasses back into the house and Claire grabs a fresh bonnet off the coat stand in the front hall. Helping Claire into the buggy Mason sees firsthand how tiny her waist really was.

The rode down the road away from the farm house towards Mason's ranch; He pointed out his laneway as they rode past it. Claire stated how close he actually lived as she always figured he lived closer to the reserve. Mason laughed loudly at that, saying a lot of folks assumed he live on the reserve. They continued to chat about everything in Cougar Ridge.

Mason stopped the horse by just on the outskirts of town by an old tree. He pointed out the sunset over the field. The sun was golden and red with hints of orange; so vivid and clear Claire was feeling the effects in her soul. It was breathtaking, and she said as much. Mason was lost in her as she watched the sunset and spoke those words.

He asked her what had brought her to Cougar Ridge, and waited for her quiet reply. Claire steadied herself as she told Mason of her family back in Boston. Her parents, Charles and Catherine; her three older brothers Adam, Micheal and Stephan; she went into detail about each of her brothers, their lives and her house. She talked as if she were reciting from a book, it sounded so impersonal to Mason, not like it should have sounded when talking about loved ones.

Claire rushed through the part about her engagement to Brian and then the accident. She did not want to dwell on that part of her life, and then ended her story with her family sending their embarrassment of a daughter and sister to the untamed west. Mason could feel the hurt in her words even though she tried to sound strong. He wondered how a family could send an injured member away. Maybe they were ashamed? And what happened to this fiancé Brian? Why hadn't he seen this guy in town? Still a huge part of this puzzle was missing, and Mason needed to find the missing pieces.

He wanted to know about her veils and scarves. Mason decided he better just outright ask, so he did. He asked if the accident that sent her here was responsible for her covering her face all the time. Claire immediately reached for her face and Mason caught hold of her hand before it reached its target. She stiffened in his grasp but did not pull away. She felt the tenderness in his grip, she felt safe. Claire turned in the seat to face Mason, still with her hand in his. He was looking her direct in her eyes. Such a kind face she thought, so strong and sure of everything, he was like a candle in the dark, a beacon to her.

She wanted some of his strength; she needed some of his strength. Mason sensed she needed him, so he pulled her to him and cradled her slight frame in his strong arms. Holding her in a light embrace he could feel her relax and then heard her silently weeping. Protecting her was all he could think of as he tilted her face upwards to look at her. He wiped a tear from her cheek, and in doing that her scarf fell to the side exposing a red gash along her face. Mason slid a finger along the angry line. Her sudden intake of shocked breath sounded moments before he placed light kisses down the same red path his fingers just trailed.

He needed to kiss her mouth, he needed to taste her. She needed this too, he was sure. They had a connection right then and he went for the kiss. Not wanting to scare her, he placed a soft kiss on her parted lips. Fearing he would spook her he began to pull away until he felt the faint stirring of her returning a shy kiss.

When they parted, Claire looked down at her lap, ashamed of her behaviour. Mason instantly knew she was feeling guilt and he turned her face to face him. He smiled at her, and said he would like to kiss her again, but not right now; as he needed to get her home. But he was giving her fair notice that he intended to do this again! He was whistling a nice tune as he turned the horse and buggy back towards Aunt Maddie's place. Claire noticed that Mason was still holding her hand.

Claire entered the house through the front door, watching Mason drive away. Turning to go to her room she did not realise that her scarf was left behind in Mason's buggy. In a trance she sat at her bedside brushing her hair after getting into her night gown. She was climbing into bed smiling to herself, she felt butterflies... the do exist.

Mason glanced down at the seat beside him on the buggy as he pulled up to his barn, she left her scarf, and she didn't know it had come off. It was a small victory in learning about his Claire. He picked it up inhaling her scent, and tucked it into his shirt as he unhooked his horse and turned him loose in the coral. Whistling all the way into his house Mason was happily looking forward to returning the scarf to Claire come tomorrow.

For now he was going to sit outside and think about everything she had told him today. Still wondering about this missing fiancé Brian, Mason figured he would ask Maddie or Toula in the morning while Claire was teaching at the school. Plan in motion, Mason retired for the night.

-35-

Claire arrived at the school early, like always, preparing for her students arrival. Today she had planned a project for the entire class. They were going to work on welcome back cards for Ms. Rhodes return in a couple weeks. Claire figured the class could spend an hour each morning working on these, then the remainder of the school day will be spent on school studies. She was smiling as she wrote on the blackboard todays assignments.

Hazel watched Ms. Cooliage from the rear of the classroom. So happy and content, nothing like the frightened woman she saw a few months ago. She cleared her throat to give Claire notice that someone was here. Claire spun around and smiled when she saw Hazel. Calling her to come forward, the two women sat on the front row bench smiling together. Hazel was asking how the class was coming along, and if Claire needed any help. Claire assured Hazel that the class was wonderful and a dream to teach. She did have a couple concerns about the brothers from the reserve. She noticed that they were rather shy, and not really wanting to get involved in class activities.

Hazel said that she would find out what was going on, and perhaps they could meet up for lunch tomorrow to discuss what she found out. This was agreed on, and the two ladies said their farewells; Hazel returning to the post office and Claire to the rope to ring the bell as class was to start.

Mason walked over to Maddie's place his wolf at his side. Maddie and Toula were sitting on the front porch, one snapping beans, the other pealing apples. Both looked up when Mason called out. The wolf dog went loping down the pathway towards the creek. Mason sat on the top stair of the porch and removed his hat, placing it on the porch beside him. Running his hand through his thick hair he was nervous about what he was going to say.

Mason started out by saying what a wonderful day its turning out to be, the dark clouds have nearly vanished leaving a faint breeze and sunshine. Maddie sensed Mason was on a mission and smiled a knowing smile at Toula. Toula chuckled to herself and interrupted Mason's weather predictions saying he should just spit it out.

Taken aback, Mason sat there for a moment, then laughed. These women could see right through him apparently, so he better just get on with it. Taking a deep breath, Mason asked the women about Claire's accident, about the reason she is really here and about the absent fiancé. Maddie looked down at her hands as she set her bowl of beans on the table between Toula and herself. Maddie began to speak, saying that perhaps Mason should respect Claire and let her tell him if and when she is ready. Toula interrupted Maddie, saying that Maddie is wrong. Toula stood to walk the couple steps to where Mason sat, she then sat on the step beside him, and preparing to tell the story she has been wanting to tell since they arrived. Maddie sat silently, waiting and listening.

Maddie heard this all from Claire, the night she broke down. Hearing Toula's version was completely different. Toula went into detail about Claire's upbringing in a wealthy setting. How Claire's father never backed his daughter's choice in teaching and only wanted a doll for a daughter; someone to show off at parties then marry off to the right man. Enter Brian Stackhouse into the story. The way Toula talked about this fiancé, Mason could tell there were no warm feelings for him from Toula.

She continued her story with Claire going off to university and graduating with her teaching degree. On Claire's return home, the engagement and finally the accident. Toula's face showed pain as she recalled the night Claire was in surgery, the family waiting to hear if she survived. It was a very rough time in the Cooliage household; Miss Claire was never going to be the same. She continued telling Mason how Claire made it through, the weeks and months afterwards; how her friends couldn't look at her, how her fiancé disappeared. Then finally the family decision for Claire to spend time here, in Cougar Ridge, to find peace and solace in her life once again. Toula was certain that Brian was not coming back as nobody had heard from him since the accident, and Claire had returned the ugly ring before coming here.

The way Toula said it, Mason was sure Claire's family meant well when they made the very hard choice to send her so far away. Contrary to what Claire said, Mason felt her family loved her very much. He was also very sure that her companion and fiend Toula was very protective of her and loved her a great deal.

Toula must really trust Mason a lot as she told this heartbreaking story to him. Maddie was wiping away tears as Toula finished her tale. Mason had a better understanding of his Claire now. He mentioned to the women that he and Claire have made a friendship, and he just wanted to understand her better. With her face veils and scars. He told them he took her for a buggy ride, and as he fidgeted around on the porch he looked Toula in the eye when he stated matter of fact that he intended to woo her. He said he saw something special in Claire, and he was sure Claire saw something in him as well. Waiting for the women to tell him to stay clear of her, Mason looked up to see not only one of them smiling; but both. Confused, Mason waited for someone to clarify.

Maddie was first to speak. She exclaimed how marvellous this was, that she gave her blessing for him to try. Toula was a little more reserved, she said that she did like the notion of this working but she just wasn't sure, as Claire's family can be a bit judgemental and then there was the whole missing fiancé thing to worry about. Even though Claire had returned the ring, and Brian hasn't been around in a very very long time. Toula was happy at the idea, but feared something would block Claire from being happy. They decided to see what Claire thought of it all, if Claire would mention this or not. Nobody was rushing into anything.

This was agreed, and the three continued their talk on the porch. The wolf dog approached stopping short of the house, looking at Mason before a sharp bark signalling them it was time to leave. Placing his hat back on his head, Mason walked more lightly back to his ranch, his heart felt lighter knowing that there would be no resistance from Claire's guardians when it came time for him to court the lovely Miss Claire. Whistling a jaunty tune Mason started his chores before heading out to the reserve for the day. He wanted to stop by the schoolhouse on his way to the reserve, so he needed to get his chores done before school let out.

Toula and Maddie were very happy that someone saw Claire for Claire; not for her family wealth, or her beauty; but for her inner self. Mason could see past the outside scars and see into the beauty that is Claire. The women smiled and laughed together as they finished with their dinner preparations. Eagar to see this through, they planned to point Claire in the right direction.

Chores complete, Mason saddled his horse to ride into town to catch Claire before school was over. He wanted to make sure he wasn't reading into things he was feeling. Mason needed to reassure Claire that he had feelings for her, and that he wasn't going anywhere. Plan set, he rode straight into Cougar Ridge to the church which at this moment was the school. There stepping out of the white building was the reason for his smile; Claire was tying the ribbons of her bonnet as she descended the stairs. Spotting Mason she couldn't stop the smile spreading across her face.

Mason stopped his horse a mere foot away from her. He looked down at Claire and asked her how her day went. Pleasantries out of the way, Mason asked if Claire enjoyed the sunset they shared. Blushing Claire said she did. Mason then suggested they go on another buggy ride so he can show her the area, starting with the reserve. This brought Claire's head up, she was intrigued with the idea of seeing a native community up close. For all the notions she had of savages had been proven to be false stories; she has had firsthand knowledge of Indian children as two were students in her school. Not savages at all, just shy children wanting to learn. Agreeing to a Saturday ride, Mason tipped his hat and headed towards the reserve; leaving Claire to stare at the man and horse riding away.

Stopping at the post office to see if Maddie had mail, Claire spent a few moments chatting with Hazel. They were becoming fast friends and planned on having lunch at the school house the very next day. Claire was positive that the sun was shining brighter today, she was happily wandering around the town in no rush to head home for a change. Why, she may even go to church with \aunt Maddie and Toula on Sunday. Maybe it's time to stop hiding. The people of this town were not out to harm her, they were not out to run away screaming because she looked different. Claire felt she had misjudged these people, and she decided to give Cougar Ridge a chance after all. She had been here a few months now, and nothing bad had happened. Maybe she could stay here if her Aunt was willing. Would Toula be happy here? Or should she let her return to the family Estate in Boston? She will need to ask Toula someday. Gathering the letters, Claire walked down the road towards home. Yes, she was beginning to see this as home.

-36-

Micheal sat back at his desk, arms folded across his chest as he listened to his friend read from the little book the man always carried. Satisfied that everything was going well in Cougar Ridge with his sister, he thanked the big man for all his services. His friend had a knack for being discrete and at the same time getting the answers that he needed. Micheal had learned that Claire was teaching at the tiny school, and that she was fitting in well with the people there. Micheal was saddened to have also learned that during the time Claire was in the hospital, her loving fiancé had disappeared. The big man across the desk then started to say something that he thought Micheal needed to know, when Micheal's secretary knocked on the door. Excusing himself, the big man snuck out the back door as he wasn't one to be in the spotlight, preferring to be unnoticed. Micheal said goodbye, then asked his secretary to enter.

She had informed Micheal that Mr. Stackhouse had returned to his desk just this morning, with letters from family stating he had been away on urgent family matters. Micheal asked her to cancel all appointments today and that he was headed to have a talk with Brian Stackhouse. He did not think he would return to his office today.

Gathering his hat and coat, Micheal walked to the building next door, walking right past the startled charge secretary, not waiting to be introduced. He stopped directly in front of Brian's desk. Tapping his foot to gain notice, Brian looked up with a shocked look on his paling face. All the blood seemed to have drained from his face, and speech eluded him at that exact moment. Clearing his throat, Brian rose and held his hand out for Micheal to shake. Micheal looked down at the out stretched hand and ignored the gesture. Instead he politely asked Brian to gather his coat and follow him outside. Turning without waiting for Brian, Micheal walked out the front door and waved for his carriage that had been readied and waiting for his signal. Climbing in, Micheal sat and calmed his breathing while waiting for his sister's ex-fiancé to show. Brian exited the building looking a little lost at first, until he noticed Micheal was waiting inside the carriage. Swallowing a nervous lump, Brian opened the carriage door and climbed in to sit across from Micheal.

Micheal was trying very hard to rein in his anger, so he inquired about Brian's absence from the Colliage household. Wanting to rip this weasels body in half was mounting to the top of his to do list, Micheal needed to calm his boiling blood so that he can hear the poor excuse of a man sitting across from him. Actively squirming in his seat, Brian had to think of his words carefully. Now knowing that Micheal was not only his soon to be brother in law, but also his boss. How had he not known that Micheal was in charge of his career in this law firm was beyond him, still puzzling to Brian.

Brian started out by asking why Micheal had called him away from his work to join him for a carriage ride, apparently to the Cooliage Estate. Looking out the window Brian noticed where they were heading to. Gearing up for a lecture, Brian reluctantly sat waiting for Micheal to answer. He didn't have to wait long, as Micheal told Brian that he noticed that he had been absent form not only work but in Claire's life as well. He wanted to know why Brian had just disappeared at a time when he was needed most. Not meaning at work. It was Micheal's turn to sit back to wait for an answer.

A few emotions crossed over Brian's face, from shock, to fear then to calmness. Nothing was lost to Micheal's trained eye. He knew Brian was about to spin a story so great it should be recorded in print for future generations to read. True fiction at its best he thought, preparing himself for the grand tale. Brian started his story about an ailing family member away from Boston that needed him as he was the only living male relative. He needed to go to handle the family affairs. Micheal knew this was untrue, as he spoke to Brian's mother himself and she said he was away on business. Lies, nothing but lies. He would stay silent for now, let him assume he was falling for it. Micheal made all the correct comments about hoping everything went well, and that things were settled. Now it was Brian's turn to inquire on Miss Claire. He said how remiss he was in not keeping better tabs, but he was sure that the family would still think of him as close after the funeral.

Funeral? What was Brian yammering about now, Micheal thought. Brian kept talking about how he was sure Claire would have pulled through and they could have been married, he just didn't know her injuries were so severe that she could not survive. Surely this was the reason Micheal had brought Brian out to the family Estate, to discuss funeral proceedings.

Micheal asked why Brian had thought Claire was dead? Surely a fiancé would know how his soon to be wife was, after all. Shouldn't he? Putting an end to this game, Micheal came right out and said that Claire was alive and well. Not that Brian cared at all, as he couldn't even bother calling on her during these many months home. He then continued on to tell Brian that Claire had left Boston, and returned his ring. Handing the ugly monstrosity to Brian he couldn't help but smile inwardly at the utter look of confusion on Brian's face. They arrived at the Cooliage Estate and soon exited the carriage to walk silently up the stair to enter the grand home.

Forgoing formalities, there was no footman nor doorman, the pair walked right into the study to the awaiting Charles Cooliage and Stephan standing by the fire place. Micheal removed his coat and hat, and poured himself a very stiff whiskey. He needed it to calm his urge to beat the tar out of Brian. Charles motioned to Brian to sit. Doing so, Brian again asked why he was here, if not for funeral details. He still couldn't grasp the fact that Claire was both alive and gone.

Charles waited for Micheal to update them on the brief explanation as to why Brian had been away so long. No one was giving away the fact that they all knew that there was no family emergency. They knew a bold faced liar when they saw one. Ashamed that he was ready to hand over his only daughter to this louse, Charles asked what Brian intended to do with his life now that he was no longer to be wed to Claire, and now that he was no longer going to be employed at the firm. Enjoying the look of horror on Brian's face, Micheal put him out of his misery by telling him they knew there was no emergency, they knew Brian was avoiding Claire. Everyone knew Claire had been physically scarred by the accident and the decent thing that Brian should have done was to be a man and admit to not being able to deal with it, face her and tell her. But no, Brian was a coward, and he needed to explain to her family atleast. While he was stuttering and trying to word things, Micheal told him that he was finished as a trial lawyer in Boston, and his desk was being cleared out at this moment.

Brian's life was spiralling out of control; he had no idea what to say or to do. Instinct took over and he started to yell and scream at everyone at once. Threatening the Cooliage's if he can't work. Everything he had ever worked for was now gone, and it was their entire fault. He demanded to speak to Claire, so he can clear up this mess and get the wedding back on track. The three men stared at this crazed man in their midst, talking fast and wild about Claire and his wedding getting back on track? He must be insane.

Stephan motioned for Brian to leave, a carriage will take him to his home, and he was not to return here.

Outside the Cooliage house, Brian swore he would track Claire down and make things right. He had worked too long and too hard to get into this wealthy family to just let it slip by. He was hatching a plan as the carriage dropped him off at his rented home where his mother was living. How he hated this house, in this neighborhood. It was beneath his stature and he was not going to let a little thing like having to find Claire stop him from getting what he wants in life. His hand wrapped around the ring in his pocket, the ring he will make sure is placed on Claire's finger soon.

Micheal returned to his office, and his friend walked in by the back door unannounced, as usual. Greeting him with a drink, the man stated he had further information that Micheal needed to know now. Hours later, Micheal sat alone in the dark, coming to terms with everything that has been told to him. His friend had been following Brian for a long time, from when they announced the idea of Claire and Brian becoming engaged. He found out that Brian had been having secret rendezvous with another woman in the seedier part of town, an address written down on a page in front of him. It was hard to take in that this man was sneaking around with some harlot while promising a long life with his sister.

Micheal had the little book in front of him, dates, times places it was all right there. His friend had also noted in a separate area of this book all the things he noticed while spying in Cougar Ridge. Micheal was sure they had made the right choice in sending Claire away. But now he was sure they were wrong in not communicating with her, letting her know what was going on here at home. She must hate the family, thinking they shipped her off and forgot all about her. Grabbing a paper he began to pen his thoughts to his sister; telling her everything that has happened so far. He will get it out in the morning post. Promising Claire that she can return home any time she wants. Feeling better about this, Micheal began his letter to Claire.

Needing to find where Claire went, Brian calls upon the hackney driver to dig into as many places as he can to help uncover this secret. Knowing he has little money saved, he pays the man a tidy sum and promises more once he sees the outcome.

The next week went by with the delivery of his personal belonging s from the office being dropped off, and his nightly encounters with his cloaked friend at the cottage. He didn't want to give up his little love nest, but he really needed to focus on finding Claire and making her forgive him. He needed the Cooliage name to get what he deserves in life. He needed to end his visits tonight. He decided to let his lover down easily by saying he needed to go away for a bit, but will be in contact once he returns. No need to sever all ties instantly. He will need to be fulfilled once married, as he couldn't see himself having sex with that monster he plans on marrying.

A knock on his door revealed the cabbie, a piece of paper with the words Cougar Ridge was handed to him. Closing the door, Brian set forth a plan to get to Cougar Ridge and restore his life.

-37-

Claire was finally enjoying life. Ms. Rhodes had returned and resumed her teaching at the school, so Claire had her days to fill once again. She spent a lot of time wandering the town, meeting people, her friendship with Hazel was a sound true friendship. She was enjoying Sunday church services again and even attended a few of the picnics. Claire's all-time favourite thing was the buggy rides with Mason though. He made her smile, she felt butterflies when she kissed him, and they shared many kisses. Mason was proud to hold her arm as they exited church and help her into the buggy after services. They were often seen together, heading out to the reserve and just walking around town. Often dining at Christina's, everyone seemed to accept Claire as one of Cougar Ridge residents now. She was home. She was happy again.

Today Mason decided to take Claire to the bridge over the river on the reserve. Folk lore had it said that if you kissed on that bridge at sunset, and an owl hoots, you are destined to be together. He really hoped the owls were out! Arriving at Maddie's farm, Mason tied the horse and buggy to the hitch pole and knocked on the screen door. Claire came to the door wearing a very pretty yellow dress and of course, the matching veil. How he wished she would leave those hateful veils behind. She was comfortable with him touching her and kissing her, but still so insecure about her scars that she refuses to let him actually SEE her. Time heals all wounds, hopefully so does the heart. Helping Claire into the buggy, Mason waved good-bye to Toula and Maddie who stood on the porch.

Mason held Claire's hand as they rode through town. Seeing people wave to them and say hello as they drove by, Claire felt very relaxed. They stopped at the store and Claire waited in the buggy as Mason ran inside to get a few candies for the children on the reserve. Claire loved that about him, how he was always thinking about others; so different from the men in Boston. How her life had changed. And so much for the better she thought. Mason jumped back into the buggy, placing a small bag on the seat beside him he reached for Claire and handed her a broach with a wild flower encased inside a glass frame. It was so beautiful she thought as he pinned it on her dress. He gave her a quick peck on her cheek as he headed the horse in the direction of the reserve. Claire was lost in a daydream and didn't notice the stagecoach unloading a smartly dressed man who was watching her from the store porch as his bag was being set down.

Well, that was very shocking thought Brian as he picked up his bag and headed inside this run down store to inquire about proper accommodations for his stay here in this dirt village. Who was that man he saw riding away with whom he assumed was Claire? For it sure looked like Claire, dressed in common clothing nothing could hide her upbringing and though he was sure it was her, he thought she lost weight and looked rumpled. Hoping it was not Claire, Brian went to talk to the shop keeper. Such a barren place, the goods inside this store were of the worst quality he had ever seen. No decent clothing to be seen or decent tobacco; he had to wonder where in the world Claire ended up?

Tom Southwold, the shop owner had pointed Brian to the road just on the other side of the church, he was to go up that road and the first house was Agatha's Boarding House, she would surely have a room available. Brian was a little put out, having to actually walk and carry his own bag to this boarding house. Not even a cab in sight, and a boarding house. No hotel just a low class rooming house. How low did he have to sink to get Claire back? Well he will not be here long, soon he will find out where she is staying, go make his amends and book passage on the stage back to civilization. He will need to shake the dirt off his clothing once in a room. He wanted to look his best for Claire when he sees her. Tomorrow will be just a good a day to start his plan. Walking towards Agatha's complaining all the way, Brian failed to see how beautiful this tiny town really was.

Sheriff Lynwood watched the man walk out of the store and head to the boarding house. He went into the store to ask Tom who the sharp dressed man was, and if he knew why he was here in their little town. Always suspicious of newcomers, due to the recent vandalism around the area, Randal liked to know who was who. Tom said he was sure the man won't last, as he complained about everything. He chuckled when he told the sheriff of the shocked look on the rich man's face when he was told he had to actually walk and carry his own luggage to Agatha's. Promising to stop by later, Randal Lynwood left the store and decided to pay Miss Agatha a visit. Always a fan of her homemade pies, he was welcomed there anytime. Today was just as good as any day he thought as he mounted his horse to ride the short distance to the rooming house.

-38-

Hand in hand Claire and Mason walked through the reserve, saying hello to everyone and talking with each child as they handed out the small candies. So much for the savages that she read all about when growing up and hearing the horror stories of how women would be stolen and raped if they were walking alone; these people were so caring and full of life and love. Claire was humbled to know these people, and to have a friend like Hazel who explained a lot of their customs and ways; strange to Claire, but not frightening at all.

Mason was leading her to a beautiful wood bridge that crossed over a rushing stream, surrounded by trees red in colour, the leaves turning with the change of season. She often heard how beautiful the changing seasons were, but in Boston you really didn't get to see true nature. Not like her, she thought. Mason had stopped, in the centre of the bridge, pointing to the bank Claire saw a huge buck drinking from the stream. His antlers were massive and his body was larger than she would have assumed. She stood there silent for a while just watching barely breathing, afraid to break the magic of this moment. She turned to Mason to smile and stopped when she saw the look in his eyes. HE placed his big rough hands on either side of her smooth face, and slowly raised her face upwards to meet his lowering lips.

This kiss was warm, gentle and everything she could have dreamed of. The butterflies definitely do exist as they were fluttering around inside her belly and her chest. She was tingling all over, as Mason deepened the kiss. He slid his tongue gently around her lips, teasing the edges, then slowly expertly slipping inside her mouth to play a game of tag with her own tongue. How different this was from the invasive tongue thrust she experienced with Brian. Funny how she would think of that right now, but as quickly as that thought arose, it also went away. Her arms encircled Mason's neck and he deepened the kiss. Somewhere in the distance an owl hooted over and over.

The kiss was interrupted by the giggling of children as they ran past them on the bridge. Embarrassed, Claire hid her face in Mason's chest as he held her closely and laughed a deep rumble. Her scarf had fallen to the ground and Claire noticed it the same time a little girl reached for it. Hiding her scarred face in Mason's shirt Claire was ashamed to face the little girl. The little girl picked up the scarf and inhaled the pretty smell as he held it out for Claire to retrieve. Unsure why the pretty lady was hiding the girl asked Mason in her native tongue. Mason replied back in their language that Miss Claire had an accident and had a scar on her that she didn't like people seeing. Not afraid, the child tapped and tugged on Claire's sleeve until she turned to face the child.

Claire was ashamed to have to face the child, afraid she would see the horror reflected in this child's innocent face. She wasn't sure why Mason was urging her to face this little girl, but trusting him she turned. This little dark skinned girl had the biggest softest brown eyes Claire had ever seen. There was no fear in this child's eyes, only a big smile as she held the scarf out for Claire to have. That's when Claire noticed this little angel also had a large rough patch on her neck that disappeared into her dress. As the child skipped away towards the other children off the bridge, Claire turned to ask Mason what had happened to the girl. Mason explained that she had been left to die after a raid on her village.

White men had set fire to every hut and her family all died. She escaped with severe burns. She will always carry a scar, but she continues on in life, unafraid. Humbled, Claire did not put on her scarf. If a tiny child could face the world, couldn't she? One step at a time, for on the reserve she promised not to hide; she will take things slowly, as she was sure she will see rejection in some people. Mason was never so proud as he was now, walking through the reserve with the woman of his dreams on his arm and everyone here smiling at her in warm honest fashion. Her red scar full on display, she was brave for he knew how afraid she really was. His heart swelled with pride. Claire's arm tightened as they approached the buggy to return home, reading her thoughts, Mason placed her scarf around her head draping it across her scar. A single tear escaped and he captured it in a kiss as he helped her into the buggy.

Claire was certain she was in love for sure. Mason was so caring and he seemed to understand her without her even saying a word. Her mother once told her that she knew what her husband was thinking, Claire used to laugh at that, not now for she now understood. Smiling brightly she waved to the residents of the reserve as they departed. Mason was still holding her hand when they arrived at Aunt Maddie's place to find Toula waiting on the porch. Helping Claire down, mason grabbed the basket that was in the back of the buggy. Claire couldn't remember him putting it there, so she assumed one of the tribe people must have put it there. Sure enough Mason said that the women of the reserve made some breads and preserves for Maddie. Toula thanked him and asked if he was staying for dinner. Mason declined as he had chores to do on his ranch. Stating he will see them on Sunday for church. He said he will walk with them as they enjoy the walk as opposed to riding. They will be doing enough riding come winter. Winter, wow so much time has passed; Claire couldn't remember missing home at all. She wondered if they miss her.

The next day Claire and Toula walked into town, they needed to send a letter for Maddie, and get some supplies ordered at the store.

Claire was feeling so happy that she did not fasten her scarf totally; she allowed it to slip a bit and didn't bother fixing it. She was going to try to be braver each day until the day she could walk around like that happy little girl. They passed the stockyard and waved hello to Sheriff and the yard owner, Jerimiah Crawford, who were deep in conversation. At the mill Toula stopped to give Jack Stiles a pie that Maddie promised him.

They continued across the road to the post office to post the letter. Hazel noticed the subtle change in Claire's veil and smiled but kept silent in case it had slipped she didn't want to point it out. Claire chatted with Hazel for a few minutes while Toula posted the letter and checked the stack of letters that Hazel handed to her. Her sharp intake of breath brought Claire's chatter to a halt, Toula said Claire had a letter from Boston. Time stopped, as Claire reached for the letter. As if it were going to bite her, Claire held it at arm's length. Toula took the letter and placed it in her basket saying Claire can read it in the quiet of her room. They said good day to Hazel and headed toward the mercantile. Having placed their order and Tom saying that he will deliver it out today, the pair were walking past Christina's Diner when they heard someone call out Claire's name. A cloud passed over the sun and the shadow caused Claire to shiver. That voice, it sounded too familiar; but from where?

The women heard heavy footsteps as they turned to face the voice. Face to face with Brian Stackhouse. Here in Cougar Ridge. Why was he here?

-39-

Claire stood rock still, unsure of what her eyes and ears were showing here. It was Toula who was first to speak. She asked Mr. Stackhouse what had brought him all the way out to Cougar Ridge. Brian calmly said he missed Claire and wanted to concrete their wedding plans. Toula gave a quick glance at the still quiet Claire. She must be in shock as she hasn't moved a muscle. Finally as if a curtain had been raised, Claire asked Brian what wedding plans he was referring to as she had returned his ring. With that, Brian reached into his pocket to produce that hateful eyesore of a ring, and held it out to her. Mortified, Claire could only stare in repulsion at the offending gold ring. Brian lowered his hand as he advanced on Claire to engulf her in an embrace.

It was at that particular moment that Mason was riding by on his way to the reserve. He stopped his horse and looked at the pair embracing on the road in front of the diner. Toula spotted him and the pleading look in her eyes was enough for him to dismount his horse and lead it to the party of three. Brian sensing tension, released his hold on Claire and faced the brute of a man approaching them with a murderous look in his savage looking face. This Indian looked like he was out to kill. Afraid for his life, Brian stood behind Claire and Toula as the savage approached. What a gutless coward, thought Mason; hiding behind the skirts of these women... his women.

Claire stepped away from Brian and in doing so her veil slid slightly showing her red scar. Brian flinched when he saw it before she recovered the scarf. His flinching was not lost on Mason, and he seethed with a protective anger that threatened to escape. Only Claire's timid voice and hand on his arm quenched his desire to plant his fist deep into the soft flesh of this pompous ass. Toula introduced Mason to Mr. Brian Stackhouse of Boston. Brian? Oh, the missing EX fiancé; puzzle pieces are fitting nicely together. How could Claire have ever wanted to marry this blowhard? Not offering to shake hands, Mason was only concerned for Claire, he asked if she was ok, and if they needed an escort home. Brian laughed at this offer, he was astonished that such a savage would ever speak to Ms. Cooliage in such a friendly manor. Then Brian commented on Claire's dress, suggesting that she burn those rags when they return to Boston on the next stage out of this dreadful dirty hole.

Mason had had enough; he rounded on Brian and had him by the neck in an instant. It was then that Sheriff Lynwood showed up separating Brian from Mason's tight grip. The look on Mason's face was enough for the sheriff to ask the two men to go separate ways, he told Mason to continue on his way to the reserve and Brian to go back to the diner. The sheriff told Mason that he will see that the women get home. Not satisfied at all but agreeing, Mason mounted his horse and galloped full steam away from the town. Brian felt he won this battle and suggested to the lawman that the women would be safe with him as Claire was his fiancé and the black woman was her servant.

This confused Sheriff Lynwood even more, as he didn't know that Ms. Claire was engaged, and if she was he would assume it would be to Mason. Claire finally found her voice and said that she and Toula would greatly appreciate a ride home, and no she most definitely was not this man's fiancé. With that the two women walked towards the store to await the sheriff and a buggy. After a few words with Brian, the sheriff went inside the store to ask Tom for the use of his wagon to deliver the ladies home.

It was a quiet ride back to Maddie's farm. The sheriff didn't know what to say, he wasn't even sure what was going on. The women were very quiet and Claire was huddled into the back of the wagon like a lost child. Toula was afraid that Claire would revert back into her shell, and feared losing her forever. Once the wagon stopped at Maddie's place she came out to see who had stopped in. Shocked to see the sheriff in Toms wagon, and even more shocked to see the look of fear on Claire she sprung into protective mode. Demanding from Randal as to what happened to her charge. Randal removed his hat as he climbed the steps to the porch. Toula was taking Claire upstairs to her room so Maddie figured this was a good a time as any for answers. She was fuming with anger. All the hard work that poor child has done, looks now like she is back where she started.

Randal Lynwood retold the scene he witnessed, and mentioned that he was not there to know what transpired beforehand. Lynwood mentioned Brian, could it be the fiancé? Couldn't be, how would he have found her, better yet, why?

With too many questions and no answers, she thanked the sheriff and watched him lead the team away. Maddie then went to put the hot water to boil on the stove for tea then she went in search of answers. Toula poured the tea and placed a hot cup in front of Claire as she adjusted the shawl around Claire's shoulders. The child had a chill; she hadn't been able to stop the shakes since they got home. That darn dark veil was back as well. Toula was sure they had seen the last of that drat thing, as Claire was becoming more at ease with her looks around the house. She often went about without covering at all. Now she has reverted back to full coverage. All since the attack from Brian, how did he find them?

Several hours later, they managed to get Claire to bed using some of the powders left over from their first arrival. Sleep powders she didn't need any more, but Toula refused to get rid of. Thankful for them now, the two ladies went outside to sit on the porch to unwind knowing Claire will sleep until atleast noon day tomorrow. Concern showing on Toula's face, Maddie knew she too was worried about the progress being lost. As they were sipping on more tea, Maddie heard a sound. The wolf dog emerged from the tall grass followed by Mason. Dressed in his deerskin attire he truly did look like the Indian Brian thought he was. Mason asked about Claire before the women could say she was ok. He slumped in a chair, shoulders sagging in the dark. He asked for some clarification on today's events. Toula set his mind to rest when she said that Brian is unwanted, and is for sure not Claire's intended. That Claire had returned that horrid ring weeks before even arriving here.

Mixed emotions swirled in his head. The need to protect her and the desire to harm him battled for supremacy. Mason needed to go home, to clear his head and he told Toula and Maddie that he will call on Claire after lunch, to make sure all is well. He also said he would leave the wolf to stand guard; the women would be safe tonight. Toula appreciated the kindness and thanked Mason. Maddie hoped Brian was smart enough not to come poking around, she knew how to use her shotgun.

Morning came and Toula had all but forgotten the basket with the letters in it. She went to find the basket and retrieved the parcel of mail. There was a letter for Maddie, one for Claire and one for herself as well. Curious as to that letter, Toula opened it and sat down at the table to read it. It was from Jonas, he was writing to inform her that Mr. Stackhouse had returned, and went on to regale all the events that happened in Boston. He went on to inquire of Claire's wellbeing. Finishing up in saying that the family really missed her and hoped she was well. Toula decided to pen a reply before Claire awoke.

True to his word, Mason arrived shortly after noon. The weather was starting to cool off so the women were inside sitting. Mason knocked on the door and Toula went to let him in. He instantly looked up the stairs to the second floor, knowing Claire was there. He asked how she was, and before either could answer, Claire herself walked into the room, still wearing her sleep dress and house coat, complete with the offensive head covering. She approached Mason shyly, almost afraid of his reaction.

Mason noted the severe change in her, and had to quell the urge to do massive harm to Brian. He held his arms wide to hold her in a welcoming embrace. She melted into his strong warm safe arms, and wept. Mason led her to the settee and sat with her still cradled in his arms. Whispering soft words only she could hear, placing soft kisses on the top of her head, he gently removed the hideous veil placing it on the floor like a rag. Claire didn't try to stop him, this was Mason after all, and she would never hide from him again. He waited for her to calm down before asking her about Brian's arrival, and the hug he witnessed. She tensed up at the reminder, and Mason regretted his question. Claire told him about the ring and how ugly and revolting it was. How she hated it on first sight. She told him of the day she returned it, knowing that her loving fiancé couldn't stand the thought of marrying a monster. Claire then told him that's when her family shipped her away. She learned to trust strangers when she couldn't trust her family. She told him she found a family when her own threw her away.

Toula didn't have the heart to interrupt Claire to tell her how wrong she was, so she kept quiet for now. Listening to Claire and seeing how Mason calmed her better than she herself could ever do; this man was good for Claire. Maddie was busy in the kitchen preparing a light lunch of breads and cheese and cold chicken. Once she had finished, she interrupted the silence by suggesting food. Not really hungry Claire agreed as to not upset either Toula or Aunt Maddie. Mason kept a close watch on Claire noticing how little she actually ate.

Hours later when Claire was returning to semi normal, Maddie said she was going into town and wanted Toula to go with her. She suggested that Claire walk over to Mason's with him, and spend the remainder of the day away from everyone, just be with Mason. This was pleasing to both Claire and Mason, so she agreed. Going upstairs to get dressed Claire said she wouldn't be long. During that time, Toula told the other two about her letter and what was said in it. She also mentioned that Claire also had a letter from Boston. Mason took the letter and put it in his pocket, said he will make sure Claire reads it once they get to his ranch. Mason then suggested that Claire stay over at his place for the evening meal, so that the ladies can remain in town longer and not worry. All agreed, and Claire came down the stairs as Toula and Maddie were gathering their coats. Maddie handed Claire a long cloak with a hood and said the temperatures will be dropping from tonight on and she should be wearing warmer coats now. Wrapping the cloak around Claire's body, Mason led her through the tall grass towards his ranch, avoiding the main road. This was his own short cut he said.

Claire had been to Mason's ranch a few times, but had never been inside. Mason opened the huge wooden door to reveal his home. Standing inside the front door, Claire could only stare. The floors gleamed with fresh polish, the wooden beams overhead enhanced the stone of the huge fireplace centered in the middle of the great room. You could see the fire from all sides and it warmed the large room nicely. To the side of the fireplace sat a couple of overstuffed couches covered in woven blankets. A barrel cut in half with polished planks served as a low table in front of these couches.

To the rear of this great room was a large oak table carved from a large tree trunk and filed smooth. Several chairs surrounded this table. Just past the table was a kitchen. She could see a big stove and a pump on the sink. Lanterns were hung from the ceiling and Mason was lighting a couple of them. Casting a warm glow Claire felt at home here. Mason removed her cloak and draped it over the bench at the front door. Walking past the fireplace Claire noticed the bear skin lying on the floor, complete with the head and teeth. This brought a giggle from her as she told Mason how her mother would surely faint away at that sight. Claire then ran her hand over the head of the beast before touching the huge daggers that were the teeth. Sitting on the couch beside Mason, his arm protectively draped over her shoulders, she felt at home. Her stomach growled a very unladylike sound that made her laugh. Mason rose to go to his kitchen and he returned with a large pot and placed it on the fire rack. Soon wonderful aromas were filling his home. He told Claire that it was stew, and he had fresh bread for it also.

Finished their meal and now cuddling on his couch, Mason asked Claire her thoughts on her future. She was silent for a few minutes, and Mason started to think he over stepped his boundaries. Claire looked Mason in the eye when she said that she couldn't see herself living anywhere but here in Cougar Ridge. She was truly happy here, and was happier still when Mason was around. She shyly looked away when she said the last part. Mason's heart swelled, he cupped her face and turned it upwards for him to look at her. He asked softly if she could see herself living here, in this house, with him.

Mason did not realise that he was holding his breath while waiting for her answer, until she smiled and said yes. He let out his held breath and kissed her soundly. Not pulling back she kissed Mason hard. Mason turned them both so they were lying back on the soft couch, his kisses deepening. He was exploring her mouth with his own, her body with his gentle large hands, Claire was lost in deep emotions, never having felt this way before. Mason slowed his exploration, and slowed his kisses. He rose up on one elbow to look down at his Claire; her hair was in a wild array on the couch and her lips were swollen from his demanding kisses. He looked her in the eye and asked her if she had ever lain with Brian. She went still, and looked Mason directly in the face and softly said she had never lain with anyone, that no one had ever touched her the way he was doing. She told Mason that the couple times that Brian tried kissing her, she felt sullied and nauseated. She feared the day they married. She went on to say that she now knows that butterflies exist. Mason knew what she referred to, and he held her close.

Mason thought it right to ask Claire to marry him. Without needing to think she laughed and shouted yes! Mason's heart exploded, his kiss was primal and raw, and Claire met each movement with matching ones of her own. Mason picked Claire up never loosing contact with her lips. He went up the large staircase to the loft above, where he gently sat Claire on the largest bed she had ever seen. It was carved out of a red oak, a soft mattress covered in soft deerskins and sheepskins extra-large pillows filled with the softest of down feathers, Claire said it was a bed made for royalty.

-40-

Mason was proud to share the bed he carved with his future wife. He stopped and asked her if she was sure this is what she wants. Mason tossed a couple logs into the ambers of the fireplace in his room, instantly it roared to life. He approached Claire and ran his hands along her face and kissed her parted lips. Claire pushed all her debutant teachings aside and pressed her hands on his chest, testing the firmness of his muscles. She slid her hands along each arm, from his shoulders to his wrists and back to his chest. Up his neck and then ran her fingers through his hair. She touched his brow, his eyebrows and trailed her finger along his jawline before outlining his parted lips.

It had been nearly twenty years since anyone had touched him in a way that made his breath still, his heart race and the need to protect feel so strong he almost shook.

Claire stepped away from him to stand in front of his fireplace; standing so still, so unsure. He sat down on the wooden chair close to the bed. Mason almost sent her home right there. She looked so afraid, how did he stop himself from doing just that? The chair arms creaked as he physically held onto the chair to keep from rushing to her. He wasn't certain which impulse compelled him more, the one to seize her or the one to send her home.

The battle within him was strong. The love for her was stronger, he didn't want to hurt her; he wanted to cherish her forever. He wanted her first time to be special, and was sure she wanted to be married first.

So he sat and he watched her face, and the emotions showing on her lovely face. Savoring the sight of her in his bedroom, by his fire; listening to her stammer in nervousness. She babbled about everything, about nothing. She seemed scared.

Mason stood, and approached her, talking in a smooth low tone as he would to a wounded or scared animal. For right at this moment, that's how he saw her, a trapped scared creature unsure of its next move. He reached her, removing his jacket, he let it fall to the floor. Mason then removed her cardigan and let it land on his jacket on the floor. Claire's eyes followed her sweater, and Mason turned her face to look at him. He did not see her scars, he saw the uncertainty, shame and unshed tears.

Claire felt ashamed to have Mason look at her, to have him see her ruined face, old fears were creeping back in. She closed her eyes, she couldn't bear to see the look of horror then the pity. The looks of horror she had gotten used to, but it was the pity she couldn't stand. She could not bear to see pity in Mason's eyes. She kept her eyes closed tight, as tears escaped from the corners.

How could this rare creature be so afraid to show her true beauty. Yes she was scarred, but one wouldn't notice it as much as they would focus on her vivid green eyes; her face and her heavenly smile. Her unruly red curls framed all of this gorgeousness like a portrait. Her hair had grown since her arrival and it nearly covered her scars, the same ones she feared showing.

Mason saw the first tear. It was his undoing. He gently wiped it away then with the same finger he traced the jagged red line. Followed by light kisses along her face, from the trail his fingers started; from her fear at the start of the scar down to her jawline where the red line disappeared beneath her clothing to her slightly opened lips.

Claire was unprepared for the kiss. She was shocked then horrified when he touched her grotesque face, then to feel him actually kiss her deformities. It was too much to absorb. His lips met hers, warm soothing so much kindness, that Claire welcomed it by placing her arms around Mason's neck deepening the kiss.

Mason felt her final wall crumble before him. The few stolen kisses were nothing compared to this open door. Claire had removed her fear for the moment and she trusted Mason enough to allow him access to her heart. A gift he wouldn't destroy, he needed to go slow. All he wanted to do was pick Claire up and take her right there, fast and furious by the fire. Stomping down those primal thoughts and desires Mason was happy just kissing his Claire.

Yes, she was his Claire. He stepped back and her eyes opened. That's when he knew she was "his Claire". He would do anything and everything to erase the pain and shadows of her past.

Claire could see what she thought was love showing on Mason's face. It glowed from his eyes and he was breathing heavily, showing such restraint. Her heart doubled in size. No man ever had treated her with such devotion and desire. She knew she was home now. She prayed she was making the right choice. They were not married nor had they actually set a date, but Claire was sure she wanted this man. Right here right now. The need was so strong and she feared if she didn't go for it, then she never would. No man had ever made her feel as special as Mason had tonight.

Mason sensed a shift in Claire; a sparkle was in her eyes. He was confused as Claire lessened her hold on his arms and took a couple steps away to stand facing the roaring fire, her back facing Mason.

-41-

Mason's heart sank as he watched her pull away. Thoughts were running rampant through his head on what words to say or what actions to take. He stood still and silent, watching.

Claire's fingers were shaking as she began unbuttoning the pearl buttons on the front of her muslin dress. She clutched the bodice of the dress holding the fabric closed as the buttons had been released. She turned to face Mason. No words exchanged; she focused on his eyes as they seemed as if they could read her instantly. Claire had chosen this simple dress today as she was planning on staying home, not being seen by anyone; therefore not needing the underskirts, only a light chemise.

Mason's gaze was locked on her unsure eyes. He could tell that her trembling hands stole the dexterity from her movements. He was devouring every hint of skin that showed from each released button; the slim column of her throat revealed. The dress was sliding off her shoulders. The soft expanse of thin flesh stretched over her chest and collarbones, so smooth looking, nothing could contain his excitement. Even the vivid reddish uneven scar down the side didn't look out of place. Claire was lovely.

The dress dropped lower exposing the first hint of the swell of her breasts. Rising and falling with her rapid breath. Mason was trapped in her seductive trance. He couldn't move if his life depended on it. He was afraid she would spook and bolt away from him. Mason couldn't allow his desire to scare her now. He shifted his arousal slightly as to ease some of the discomfort his pants were causing him. Never taking his eyes off his fiery haired beauty standing by the fire light, Mason was lost.

The light from the lantern and the fire kissed her creamy ivory skin turning it gold, as if King Midas himself had given into temptation and touched her with his cursed fingers. The buttons of her dress were now unbuttoned to her waist, Mason could see the outline of one pink nipple perfectly against the thin white silk of her chemise, presented to him by her laced front corset. All coherent thoughts left him; evaporated like a mist under the sun's rays and everything around him receded but her.

Claire was amazed in Mason's control. She could see he was tightly reined in; a muscle jerking along his jawline was his only movement. She found it strange that the more she revealed, the bolder she became. Maybe it had something to do with the intense look on Mason's face and the bead of sweat trickling down his brow when she allowed her dress to slide down her curves and lay in a perfect puddle at her feet. Or was it the flare of his nostrils as she reached up to move her hair, unaware of how this action lifted her breasts even higher beneath her sheer chemise.

Mason was trying to calm his raging hard on; Claire was tempting his control. He removed his red plaid shirt tossing it to the floor, followed by his wide leather belt. His eyes never leaving hers.

Claire reached for the ties of her chemise only to have Mason's strong tanned hands stop her. He removed her delicate fingers from the strings and replaced them with his own. Slowly he tugged at the perfect bow to undo the silky prison holding his prize. The wait was torture to Claire, seeing his large strong dark hands slowly untying her white silk chemise strings was a huge turn on. Never one to ever think a man's hands could be sexy; she now had a new pleasure. Mason's hands were sexy, very sexy.

Claire needed to take control again. She felt strong, vulnerable and very desired. She felt pretty once again; and that gave her power. She tucked her thumbs into the band at her waist of her drawers, preparing to draw them down. Claire had her back to the fire, banked low on the hearth, closing her eyes she took a deep breath and bent to push her drawers over her hips. Claire realized as she languidly swept the lacy drawers over the slight swell of her rump and down the quivering muscles of her milky white thighs, that Mason was a man that was no stranger to women. Claire had no experience in the seduction game, and even less when it comes to the joining of a man and woman. Too late now, her chemise and her dress were in a frilly pile at her feet.

To Mason, he saw a flawless silhouette against the backdrop of the flames. His mouth went dry and pressure from his groin mounted. Claire was perfection as he looked at her. She flared out in all the right places a woman should; dipping to create curves that were a soft answer to man's hard angles. Right now his hard angle was screaming to be released from his pants.

His breath sawed in and out of his chest in tight, painful bursts; burning like it did when he would run in the winter. Frost and heat, ice in his blood and fire in his loins. Claire was melting his blood's ice, setting a fire he was barely maintaining.

Claire did her best to ignore the whisper of chilly air against the moist warm folds of her body as she stepped out of her discarded clothes. Bending her torso slightly, she plucked at the ties on her garters with unsteady fingers in order to rid herself of the cream stockings. Mason could not remain in place any longer. He approached Claire and in one swift fluid motion he picked her up in his arms and claimed her mouth in a soul searing kiss.

He managed to carry her the short distance across the large bedroom and sat her gently on the even larger bed. Watching the different emotions cross her nervous face while he removed first his boots then his pants; freeing his fully erect penis. Claire had a sharp intake of breath. She faced him wondering what came next.

She understood the culmination; she knew where this was headed and what was going to happen, in theory. But she had no idea how to get there, he needed to come to her, then he needed to be inside her. A slight tremor of fear shook through her body.

Mason saw the fear and sensed her uncertainty as he drew back the quilt on the bed and urged Claire to lie back as he took residence beside her in his massive bed. To calm her nerves, Mason began to kiss her slowly, his hands taking a joyful journey over the hills and valleys of her body; his hands and fingers playing their way down the curve of her breasts while her nipples hardened at his touch.

Claire couldn't believe what she was feeling; the thrills of sensations, the moist whisper of the pleasures to come. She no longer cared that he could see all of her… scars and all. She wanted him. Claire was not only a bashful virgin, but she was becoming a real woman. Someone desired her, found her beautiful and in some way that made all of this that much more tantalizing.

At the sound that escaped her parted lips, Mason lost his control. Hot blooded, a prowling stalking wild creature trying to a tame pet; he was poised to tear her apart. Mason knew he trembled more than she did as his hand drifted from the perfection of her breasts down the ivory expanse of her stomach; his touch light and gentle but with purpose as he continued following the candle light path to her hips and below.

Should he touch her like that, with his need for her pounding through his veins? She was perfection in his eyes. Her sex was soft, silky with red glowing hair covering pink pretty flesh nestled between that light dusting of fair curls. His mouth watered. His blood roared. His hard on pulsed in a rhythmic and uncontrolled clench and release of muscle. His curious fingers paused before dipping below her soft hair. When he encountered the moist folds, she gasped. Mason stopped breathing.

He tested that place lightly, finding a spot that quivered and pulsed at the tip of that pliable skin. Awe appeared on Claire's face as her feminine muscles clenched almost in beat with his own loin movements. Her hips rolled with instant little movements, her breath catching on sighs of appreciation. She was so wet, so ready to join him in the ecstasy he knew they could reach together.

Mason told Claire they were at a point where he was sure he could not stop, this was her one chance to stop now and deny him his prize. Claire bloomed with feelings for this strong wild man. She couldn't stop him if she wanted to, her body no longer belonged to her; it belonged to Mason. Now and forever, no matter where her future went, she would always belong to him. She couldn't speak, she nodded and Mason kissed her. Not gentle, per say, but the press of his mouth became another pleasure she was experiencing. He kissed every part of her lips; the corners, the rim, the pillowing fullness; Mason was devouring her with the efficiency of an experienced man. Claire was lost.

Mason slowed his movements; he sampled her like a man savouring a fine whiskey. His tongue thrust past her closed lips demanding entrance. Claire opened for him on a sigh of submission, her muscles pooling beneath him in a puddle of anticipation. If their consummation was anything like this wet probing kiss, then she was really looking forward to it.

In the midst of the frenzy of need building inside them, bloomed a quiet moment. One of stillness and acceptance. Her disbelieving eyes searched his face and her lips parted as though a confession hovered on her tongue, but could not escape her mouth. She felt love. For the first time ever, and it scared her.

Mason felt the shift in her and silently questioned it. He started to pull away only to be stopped by Claire's faint whispered plea for him to place his body against hers and kiss her again. Fire raged in his body, the need for control slowly evaporating. He needed to make this first time special for Claire, less painful.

Mason locked eyes with Claire as he began a slow sensuous kiss, neither breathing as his large heavy body pressed against her soft yielding one. She could feel his tempered strength. His solid muscled frame built from years outdoors, manual labour and honed to this God-like perfection that Claire sees. Lying pressed against her, Claire could feel a thick ridge of steel pressing against her soft curls between her thighs.

It pulsed in rhythm with his heart as her hand rested on his chest, the slight pulsing sent little shocks of pleasure through her already sensitized core. Eyes wide, Claire clenched the covers so tight her fingers ached. Mason's fingers traced the outer confines of her womanhood, gently parting the soft wet folds, teasing and pleasing at the same time.

With each of his caresses and every one of his kisses, the glorious sensations intensified, electrified until unable to stop herself … Claire's head jerked back and her torso arched. Her body bowed with a jerking pulsing ecstasy so acute, she felt as though she was floating. Her heart raced and her breathing was ragged. She though she heard her name, she thought she has screamed out but for the life of her she had no idea for sure.

Mason knew she had climaxed and was ready for him. He parted her legs and pressed his hardened erection at the gates of heaven. Slowly he entered her and as she tensed and clenched her muscles around his shaft she let out a primal cry, Mason's cue to dive in fast and hard, as he had breached the barrier. It will all be wonderful from here on out he whispered to her as he kissed her.

Though her flesh stretched and bled and at first there was a white hot piercing pain, now all Claire felt was pleasure. As his hot hard flesh searing all the way to her womb; she let out a soft sigh through her nose and her lashes fluttered as her hips flexed, testing the feel of him inside her.

A hot ripple of lust tore through Mason, followed by tidal waves of pleasure. Instinct won over intellect and he lifted his hips only to sink again and again. He was lost. If he had learned anything, it had been that reality always out lived a memory or even worse, a fantasy. In all his fantasies regarding Claire, NOTHING had prepared him for this.

Mason didn't pause in his slow rippling rhythm, his manhood just as hard and unyielding as his first thrust. His gasps became pants that melted into groans. He lifted his torso to look down at her, le angelic face radiantly looked back at him. She was his. This he swore as he sealed her mouth in a tender kiss. His seed further eased his way as he slid into her untried body with long deep strokes.

His mouth on hers, his tongue thrusting inside tasting the essence of her soul; thrusting to the pulse of their union, Claire could feel the waves of sensation against her spine. She feared it, like the first stirrings of an earthquake or the silent breath after a lightning strike. But there was no escape from that fear. It rushed over her helpless body like a rogue wave, rolling her in crash after crash of sensations. Mason swallowed her cries of pleasure in his kisses until abruptly he ripped his mouth away from hers and reared back, letting loose a deep animal like roar and then another. Calling his second release to the sky like a prisoner set free.

Claire's bones had turned to liquid and she wondered if she were still connected to her body; only the small errant twitches of exhaustion pulsing through her limbs reminded her that she was still connected. Mason lingered over her as they both fought to regain their breath. Peering into his clouded eyes, Claire shared an unspoken moment of awe with him.

Mason reached for the deerskin blanket that had landed on the floor, gathered Claire into his arms and covered them both in his warmth. The fire had long burnt out so they fell asleep wrapped in their own body heat. A sound deep sleep, the sleep gained from a hard day's work; but no work had ever felt so good and left Mason smiling in his sleep. Time forgotten, darkness upon them they slept.

-42-

Warmth greeted her, Claire snuggled deeper under the blanket, and a strong arm encircled her. Confusion was changed to happiness as she recalled the event that night. She was with Mason, her body ached but she felt wonderful. But what on earth was all that commotion? Mason chose that moment to wake, and glancing at the window he let out a long breath followed by a few profanities. Tossing back the cover, he got out of the bed and slid his pants on then his boots. Looking around the room he spotted his shirt and smiling at Claire he told her to stay here.

Taking the stairs two at a time he reached the front door as the banging continued. Opening the front door, there stood Maddie, arm raised in another attempt at banging on the wooden door. Anger showed in her face, and the rage in the face of Toula made Mason swallow hard. Time had gotten away from him and he failed to get Claire home. That was evident as the sun was high in the sky.

Maddie shoved her way into Mason's home, followed by Toula. As Mason was closing the door, he noticed a horse and rider approaching the porch. Curious to see who was coming now, Mason stepped out onto the porch. What the hell was Brian doing on his property, thought Mason.

Fists clenched, he waited for the man to halt the horse. Brian demanded to know where Claire was, as she was not at her residence. He was willing to come to blows with Mason if any harm had come of her. The thought of this made Mason grin, he would like nothing more than to punch that smug look off this man, but instead he warned Brian to leave the property or he would not be held responsible. As Brian was about to give a reply, the wolf emerged from the side of the house and advanced towards the horse. Sensing the danger, Brian's horse balked and shied away. Knowing when to back away, Brian sad this matter was not over and turned the horse back towards town. The great wolf climbed the porch steps and lay down.

Returning to the pair of angry women waiting inside his house, Mason steeled himself for the onslaught he knew was coming. Both women started at once, demanding to know where Claire was and why she had not returned home. Asking the ladies to sit did not go over well, they refused and it seemed to have angered them more. Mason ran his hand through his tousled hair. How was he going to get past this?

Upstairs Claire bolted upright at the sound of Aunt Maddie's angered voice. Clutching the blanket tight she glanced around looking for her dress. Knowing she didn't have the time needed to set herself in order, she decided not to hide anymore. She loved Mason, and she was pretty certain he loved her. So Claire wrapped herself in the deerskin blanket and slowly tested her wobbly legs before silently walking down the stairs.

The women were to engrossed in yelling at Mason that they missed the shocked expression on his face. When he just stood there staring, they too turned to see what he was smiling at. There at the bottom of the stairs, wrapped in the skin of an animal and looking very rumpled stood Claire. No clothing but the deerskin and no scarf covering her face. That was the first thought that crossed

Toula's mind, Claire was free. Maddie on the other hand was livid! Mason had taken advantage of her naïve niece.

Maddie turned on Mason at that moment, face redder than an apple. Mason knew he deserved everything she was yelling, for he had disgraced her in the worst way possible. It was Claire who broke the tension. It was Claire who shoved past Maddie to stand in front of Mason to shield him from the verbal abuse. Maddie stopped instantly, and looked at Claire, noticing the lack of facial covering. She broke down sobbing and hugged her niece. Confusion set into Claire and she pulled away glancing at Mason for help. All he could do was laugh and he tapped the side of his face. That's when Claire remembered she didn't cover up.

Mason spoke next. He apologized for not returning Claire, but he said he would not apologize for anything else. The night they shared was the beginning of a life time of wonderful happenings for them all, as he planned on marrying her as soon as they were able. Shock and awe showed on the faces in the room, even Claire looked shocked. He approached her and wrapped his arms around her, placing a kiss on her forehead, he suggested that she go upstairs and get dressed. In a trance Claire did as she was told.

Mason confronted the other two women and told them his feelings for Claire. He was certain she felt the same. They will wait for her to come downstairs, and then she can return to Maddie's place to freshen up. He wanted to take all three women into town for dinner at Christina's Diner to celebrate. Plus he needed to talk to the reverend about services; he also needed to speak to the elders on the reserve for a special prayer to be said at the wedding.

Claire came down the stairs shyly, not looking anyone in the face. This puzzled Mason and he went to Claire to give her the much needed reassuring hug and kiss that he knew she needed. Smiling, Claire straightened and hugged him back, saying she will see him soon. It was a question not a statement, and he smiled and told her nothing could keep him away.

Walking to Aunt Maddie's was a strained procession. None of the women seemed to know what to say. Arriving to the house, Claire noticed a horse tied to the hitching post, and reached for her shawl to cover her face. Toula glanced around looking for the owner of this horse to no avail. Maddie's back stiffened as she could not see anyone around and wondered who tied this horse here, and where did the person get to. The old hound dog was nowhere to be found, and so the three women decided to walk to the back of the house in case the person had decided to wait under the tree on a chair. Nobody was there either. They went into the house by the rear door into the kitchen.

Sitting at the table as if he belonged there, sipping a coffee he must have made was Brian Stackhouse. His coat and hat set on the sideboard table. By the looks of the coffee pot, Brian had been there a while. Anger boiled from Maddie when she demanded to know what gave him the right to barge into her home and make himself comfortable. Toula ushered Claire to go upstairs to freshen up, she also told her to remain there until called for. Claire went up like a scolded child, unsure if she was being punished or protected.

Brian smiled at the remaining ladies, not bothering to rise he said he decided to just wait here knowing the three would eventually return. Such a smug smile, like that of a weasel that ate the chicken thought Toula. Maddie took her turn to tell Brian that he needed to leave her home this instant, that he was not welcome in her home. This didn't faze him he just poured himself another cup of coffee and slowly raised it to his lips. While looking over the top of the cup at Toula, he suggested that the hired help go about her duties while he had a chat with his fiancé's guardian.

Maddie pulled a chair out and asked Toula to sit, then sat in the other chair herself, she took a steadying breath before asking once more why he was in her home. Brian set his cup down and glancing towards the stairway he said that he has come to Cougar Ridge with the blessings of Claire's family to wed her then bring her home a married woman. He snickered and evil sound when he said that it might be a bit late for a white wedding, but he was ok with her being damaged on the outside and now the inside as well.

He figured that the native had done her wrong and Brian was still willing to marry her despite her not being pure anymore. He just hoped she wasn't with child, as that would be hard to explain back in Boston. He said he will cross that particular bridge when it needs to be crossed. Shock stunned the women into silence, Brian continued as if there was nothing wrong; saying he intended to have the pastor here marry them tomorrow so that they can catch the stage out of this dirty little town.

Toula rose, knocking her chair over in the process. She rounded the table a dark look of fury showing on her usually pleasant face. Brian swore he heard her growl, but as he looked past the black woman he noted the wild beast standing in the doorway fur raised and teeth showing. Behind the beast was the native man from this morning along with, of all people, Micheal Cooliage. Brian paled, and began to feel nauseated. Not knowing what to do he sat there, waiting to be eaten by the wild animal.

Toula stopped as well when the wolf growled, turning she was extremely happy to see Mason advancing towards Brian, his fists clenched at his sides. But it was Micheal's calm voice that brought order to this crazy scene. Micheal, who appeared out of nowhere, calmly placed a hand on the shoulder of the man ahead of him. Micheal was the one who calmly asked everyone to stay put until he could get answers himself.

-43-

Claire had changed into a pretty pink day dress, and was draping a rose coloured scarf over her face when she heard the unmistakable growl of the wolf. She hurried downstairs disregarding the orders of Toula. Stopping at the sight of Brian sitting casually at their table, Claire didn't see her brother standing by Mason. Mason looked at Claire as she entered the room, instantly turning to face her, he walked around the table to be at her side. Placing his arm around her, comforting her and staking his claim at the same time. This was not lost on Claire and her pride swelled and she stood taller beside Mason.

Micheal was confused, for many reasons. Why was Brian here? His friend had mentioned that Brian had booked passage to Cougar Ridge, but didn't know why. That was when Micheal decided to arrive. His contact had said that Claire had settled in quite nicely and he was sure she would be safe. Micheal's contact had been staying at the boarding house as well for the past several months, sending weekly updates back to Micheal. When he found out that Brian was intending to show up, he needed to cut him off. Obviously Micheal was too late.

What he didn't know was who was this man standing beside his sister, branding her as his? His contact had failed to mention anything like this. Micheal demanded to know who this guy was.

Brian also was interested in the answer and he said as much. All eyes turned towards Mason as he cleared his throat.

Claire stepped out of Mason's protective shield. She walked a couple steps forward then stopped. She calmly said that Mason was the man she intended to marry as soon as it was possible. Outraged, Brian stood up yelling demanding that Micheal control his sister and make her realise she needs to return to Boston with him. Wide eyed and hysterical Brian was acting like a crazed man. Fearing for the safety of the women in the room, Mason grabbed Brian and restrained him as he dragged him out the door. Micheal stopped Claire form following them by grasping her upper arm. Claire stopped and looked at Micheal, a silent plea to let her go. He shook his head no, and sat her on the vacant chair.

Mason returned in a couple minutes saying he tied the other man to the tree like a horse. Once everyone was sure there was no threat, Mason said he would untie him. This brought a smile to Micheal's face. Micheal instantly liked this man, even though he seemed a bit too familiar with his little sister. He saw the way this man was always close enough to Claire that he was touching her.

Time for answers, Claire said. She began her tale to Micheal, from when her family exiled her to this distant place. How she hated them so. Then she began to see the beauty in this wild town, and they people in it. Claire reached up to remove her face covering, as she did so she watched for the look of horror she was sure she would see on Micheal's face. No look of horror, but a proud look and honest smile was all she saw. She told Micheal that because of the love that Mason has showed her, she was able to love herself in return. She was trying hard every day to like herself more and more.

Mason placed his hands on Claire's shoulders, and told Micheal that only just last night he had asked her to marry him, and she had agreed. Mason then told Micheal that Brian showed up the other day, and until then they had not seen hide nor hair of him. Toula said that they were going to send a telegram to the family asking them to attend the wedding, but then Brian had been waiting in the house. And from that point Micheal knew the details of the day.

Shaking his head, Micheal tried to get the idea of his sister getting married in a few days around his mind. Deciding to go untie Brian, Mason left the family to talk things out. He stepped past the group and wandered out side. His wolf had long gone and when he looked toward the tree where he had tied Brian, he noticed he too was gone. Walking around the front of the house Mason noticed that Brian's horse was also gone. Only the rented buggy was there, the store buggy that Tom likely offered to Micheal after giving him directions to the farm. Mason went in the house by the front door, to let everyone know Brian was nowhere around.

Claire was visibly relieved, as were Toula and Maddie. The only one beside Mason that looked concerned was Micheal. Micheal suggested that they all head into town to place the telegram, and have a celebration lunch at the little diner he saw on the way to Maddie's place. He had a lot to catch up on, but as far as Micheal was concerned his little sister was happy and adjusting well with life here. Perhaps she needed to leave Boston to find herself. His parents will be thrilled to hear that their daughter was happy and smiling again.

-44-

Claire sat in her room looking at her reflection in the mirror. It was hard to believe that only two weeks ago her world changed so drastically. She blushed when she thought of her night in Mason's arms, then laughed when she remembered the look on her Aunt's face when she came down Mason's stairs only wearing a deerskin. Laughing harder now, Toula entered to see what was so funny. Claire was telling Toula how she was recalling her past couple of weeks. Both women smiled and turned to the bed where they sat together. Claire was happy that her Family was due to arrive tomorrow on the stage, for Saturday she was marrying Mason. Micheal had given his blessings and sent word to the rest of the family to join them for the event. Micheal was fitting in nicely with the folks in Cougar Ridge, he was spending a lot of time with Mason seeing the area, the reserve included. It has been a busy couple of weeks.

The entire town was full of excitement placing decorations all around the tiny church and setting the pavilion in the square for the dance and party afterwards. Toula was just as proud and happier still knowing that she can stay in Cougar Ridge with Claire. Miss Maddie had said how well they got on, that she wanted Toula to remain in her home. She would be close to Claire, and yet far enough away to give the newlyweds some needed space. Claire couldn't believe how everything was falling into place.

Micheal stood at the store waiting for the stage to arrive. Agatha had cleaned the rooms just this morning and set fresh flowers to welcome the wealthy Cooliage Family into her boarding house. Micheal reflected on his time in this quaint little, getting to know Mason and the rest of the townspeople.

He was surprised how much these people cared for his sister; they didn't think of her as a snob from Boston, they didn't see her as a damaged debutant; unlike the new in Boston. He had seen the local paper from home saying that the Damaged Debutant of Boston apparently has disappeared from society for good. Well they were correct about that. Claire had left for good. Long gone was the Cooliage Debutant, for there stood a proud strong young woman, Claire Cooliage soon to be Claire Barker of Cougar Ridge. Shaking his head while smiling he turned in time to see the stage ramble to a halt in front of the store where he was waiting.

Waving out the window was his mother, as he approached the coach to open the door his mother launched herself into his arms laughing and hugging him tight. Father exited next followed by Stephan. Micheal waited to see if Adam would step out, but the driver closed the door after depositing the luggage on the porch. Before he could ask about Adam, his father told him that word was sent to Adam but no reply was received. Disappointed but understanding, Micheal placed the bags into the banker, Mr. Beacroft's wagon, so that he can take them to the boarding house. After everyone refreshed, they were to gather at Maddie's for a special dinner.

Mr. and Mrs. Beacroft were the wealthiest family around this area, the owned a beautiful property on the road by Agatha's, they heard that the Cooliage Family were coming and quickly jumped at the opportunity to offer one of their more appropriate buckboard wagons for Micheal to use while they were here. Micheal declined the offer for the family to stay at their place saying Agatha's will suit them well enough. Their thoughtfulness was not something that Micheal was expecting as most people he knew that had status were actually quite stuck up. His family included, unfortunately. The banker's family were regular people and got on well with the rest of the town, donating items when needed without having to be asked. Their wagon was of fine quality, front seat with sturdy springs and padded black leather seats; it had two more seats behind and a storage area in the rear. Two large draft horses were pulling it instead of thin legged Morgan's that most city people preferred. Still, he was thankful for their kindness.

Micheal was happy to see his family, even though they stood out like a black horse in the winter. Catherine was dressed in a navy blue travel dress with matching gloves and bonnet, a dark grey cape finished off her travel attire. Charles, ever the business man had a charcoal grey three piece suit and bowler hat, walking cane and his briefcase. Why he brought his case Micheal had no idea. Then there was Stephan, forever father's replica; wearing a dark brown three piece suit as well. Micheal chuckled as he helped his mother into the front seat of the wagon. Her hooped skirts wouldn't work well out here at all. Gathering all her material, he tucked her in and handed her the small carry bag she carried with her.

The gentlemen all climbed in and Micheal talked about the town buildings as he passed them. He decided a quick tour of the small town before heading to the Boarding house. As the stage had dropped them off at the General Store, Micheal turned the team around so that they were headed back towards the way the stage came. Having been in Cougar Ridge these past two weeks he had the pleasure of meeting everyone. He pointed out the long building saying that in fact it housed the doctor office, post office and the local newspaper. Mr. Skylar would surely want to do a story on this wedding. Past the newspaper was Christina's Diner and as Micheal said it he waved to Christina sweeping the front porch. They passed the bank where he explained that the owners of the bank loaned them this wagon and team for their stay in town. Pointing down the road leading out of town, Micheal said that road will take them to Aunt Maddie's Place and also Mason's ranch. Crossing the road Micheal had the team heading along the other side of town, passing the stockyard and the mill.

Catherine was enthralled at the pavilion in the town square; children were decorating it with pine boughs and wild flowers, she noticed that there were Indian children mixed in with the town children and asked about that. Micheal stopped the wagon just by the church and pointed to the road on the other side of the store and said that it lead to a reserve that those children lived on. He told her that this town was built close to the reserve and that the children were attending the school here. It was like nothing Catherine had ever dreamed of, they didn't look savage at all. Quite the opposite actually; these children were laughing and playing like regular children.

Smiling she knew this was a good place for her daughter. As Micheal continued, he told them that the Reverend Cooper will be presiding over the wedding, and he too stayed at Agatha's. Wondering how big this home was, Catherine was about to ask when Micheal slowed the team in front of a rather large two storey pale blue house. Agatha herself came out to welcome the Cooliage family to her home. A couple of the town children had been asked to carry the luggage to the appointed rooms and Micheal suggested they retire to their rooms to freshen up before he drove them to see Claire. He could tell his mother and father would rather head right over, but he wanted a moment alone with the other occupant of this boarding house.

Dan was an old friend of Micheal's and had been staying in Cougar Ridge since shortly after Claire's accident. Micheal had asked his friend if he could scope out the area and keep an eye on things for him. Dan had kept a low profile, and only let on he was a business man. Never interacting with the town's people he managed to keep tabs on Claire and when Brian Stackhouse arrived, he sent a telegram to Micheal right away. Brian had a room in the boarding house for just a couple weeks before he approached Claire. Dan notified Micheal the day he arrived. The rest fell into place with Micheal arriving at the right time.

Micheal saw Dan in the parlor and went to thank him for all his work, slipping him an envelope he asked if there had been any sign of the elusive Brian. Dan shook his head and said that his contact in Boston said he had returned and is trying to talk his way out of his troubles.

The two men laughed and said they would get together once they are settled back home. Shaking hands, they parted ways. Micheal went out to the buggy and climbed onto the seat. He headed to the next property to thank the Beacroft's for their kindness.

An hour later the wagon was loaded once again with the Cooliage family as they headed to Maddie's farm. Excitement radiated from the family members as they chatted the entire way. Seeing Maddie and Toula standing on the front porch; Catherine squealed a most unlady like sound causing her hand to instantly cover her mouth. The men laughed at the sound. Stopping the buggy and jumping to the ground, Micheal tied the team to the pole, and helped his mother down as the other two men exited the wagon. Maddie watched the family with wondrous pride. It had been far too long for this and she was glad the reunion was happening.

Pleasantries over with, Maddie ushered the family inside where they could sit comfortably by the warm fire. She had prepared a nice meal to celebrate and had refreshments were laid out on the side board to snack on before the main meal. She mentioned that Claire would be arriving shortly, as she wanted to make her entrance with Mason. Charles took this time to inquire about Mason. Talk turned to the man Claire was going to marry. How he lived here before the town was built, being a liaison between the natives and the army. The town sort of sprouted up around him, and he helped build it building by building. His ranch was down the road across from Maddie's place.

-45-

Mason was nervous about meeting Claire's family. He was not the typical kind of guy a young woman would introduce to her wealthy family from the big city of Boston. As they approached Maddie's farm his footstep slowed, bringing the wolf's attention full stop as well. Mason patted his loyal friend's head and motioned for him to return home, it would be better if he didn't frighten the city folk. Laughing as the wolf loped away, Mason wondered if he would be the one to frighten the family. Freshly bathed, and wearing his best pants he left his deerskin clothing at home. Removing his hat, Mason entered the home with Claire on his arm.

The front door opened and in walked Claire, holding the arm of a large man. First impression Catherine thought was handsome in a rugged outback way. Was he native? But then looking at her daughter she saw that Claire was not wearing a face scarf, she could see her daughter's pretty face and she literally glowed! Catherine rose to welcome her daughter in outstretched arms. Claire was crying as her family vied for hugging rights. Mason stood off to the side and watched this touching moment. He watched as her mother lightly touched Claire's cheek carefully avoiding the scarred side.

All eyes turned as Mason and Claire had entered. The Cooliage family all surrounded him and handshakes and hugs were given. Mason felt at ease with these people. He now knew where Claire got her kind heart. Noticing she was without facial covering made him even prouder.

They all sat in the sitting room talking about their life in the town, and soon turned to the wedding set for tomorrow. Catherine commented how the entire town had stopped to welcome them and how they were excited for the joining of Miss Claire to Mason. She was also happy to hear that Claire would be teaching alongside Miss Rhodes. Nobody mentioned Brian Stackhouse. Nothing was going to ruin this happy event. Claire seemed happy everyone was there, but Mason knew she was missing her oldest brother Adam. He was in the army and could not get away at such short notice.

Micheal couldn't help but notice the pride in Maddie's voice as she talked about Mason, and he could sense his family relaxing knowing that he was a regarded town member. He may not be wealthy in money, but he had the respect of the entire town and that meant a lot to the Cooliage family. Micheal just knew his family will accept him as he has.

Claire, finally released from her family's grasp, was sitting beside Mason during these talks, her family seemed to have accepted him, and she was happy. Maddie called saying that dinner was ready and everyone went to the dining room to eat. Talk continued around the table about Claire's time in Cougar Ridge. Claire mentioned that all her dreams have finally come true; she was happy, soon to be married to a wonderful loving man, and she has the opportunity to continue teaching. Claire's happiness showed to everyone.

Charles was finally able to relax knowing that his little girl would be fine now. He had worried all these moths, wondering if they did the right thing in sending her so far away. Now he could see it had paid off. Claire was able to heal without the Boston society treating her like a leper and shunning her. Here she grew into a woman the town people love. She was even strong enough, secure enough that she no longer felt the need to cover and hide her gorgeous face. His daughter had returned. He had this tiny town and this wild man to thank. Humbled, Charles made a mental note to say an extra prayer of thanks tonight.

Dinner was over, the night was getting late and Micheal suggested that they return to the boarding house. Tomorrow was Saturday, the day of the wedding and everyone needed to be well rested and looking their best. Catherine smiled and asked to speak to Claire in private, they went into the kitchen where Catherine clasped Claire's hands in hers. Looking at her daughter, Catherine told her that she would be honoured if she would wear her wedding dress tomorrow. Claire was stunned; she hadn't thought about something so glamourous as that dress, she had planned on wearing her yellow day dress. Her mother said she had it freshly washed and pressed and it was currently hanging in her closet at the boarding house. Claire wept openly at this wonderful offering. She hugged her mother and agreed to be at the boarding house to get fitted and ready for the wedding. Things were falling into place. This was really happening. Her family would be there to see her marry the man of her dreams.

When the wagon left with her family aboard, Claire turned to Maddie and Toula to tell them about her mother's dress. Mason wondered what the three women were talking about in such hushed tones, but figured it was better he didn't know. Smiling he walked towards the women, placing his arm around Claire he kissed her cheek and said he will see her in the church tomorrow. He whispered in her ear that after tonight, they would never be apart again. Smiling shyly, Claire watched his walk into the darkness. Climbing the stairs to her room, she wondered how she would ever fall asleep.

Fall asleep she did, and soundly too. It took both Toula and Maddie to wake her in the morning and practically needed to force the food into her. Micheal had arrived in the borrowed wagon to bring Claire to the boarding house, and Maddie told him that she and Toula will head to the church to make sure everything was ready. Claire gathered her cloak and gloves and climbed into the wagon with Micheal. Looking over her shoulder at the farmhouse she has called home for many months, Claire felt sadness for the fact that she would not be returning to her room.

Micheal reached for her hand, drawing her attention to the road ahead. Her future lay ahead; in in a few hours she would be starting her new life as Mrs. Mason Barker. A bright smile erased her sadness from the moment ago. As they passed the town square Claire took notice of all the children waving and shouting at her, she saw the pavilion glowing with fresh white paint and pretty flowers, the entire town seemed to sparkle. Maybe it was Claire's eyes that were sparkling, for today was her wedding day.

Her mother had the gown spread out on the bed; Claire remembered the framed photo that stood centre on the mantle of her parent's home. It looked like it was brand new instead of decades old. The high lace neck, the heart-shaped bodice in white silk, tiny pearl buttons secured the back and a trim waist with a flowing skirt of white silk trimmed in lace. The long tight sleeves were of sheer lace and also had tiny pearl buttons on the underside to close once her arms were inside. Her mother had a simple pearl hair clamp to secure the long veil in place. Claire had to wipe the happy tears from her eyes, this was a wonderful day for sure.

Hazel had been asked to be her maid of honour and had been asked to come by the boarding house to help get Claire ready. Catherine instantly took to Hazel and insisted to be called Catherine. Hazel stared in awe at the wondrous looking gown spread out on the bed, she now could imagine Claire living as the wealthy debutant she once said she was. She will look amazing in this dress.

Looking down at her own dress, she paled in comparison. Hazel wore a traditional Native dress complete with colourful beads sewn into the deerskin smock. It had been sun-bleached a beautiful white shade and her beaded belt had feathers on the end. Her long hair had been tied in a loose pony tail at the base of her neck and also held a feather. Feeling slightly out of place, she took a step backwards still looking down. Instantly Catherine knew what Hazel was thinking. She approached the Raven haired beauty and asked if she could possibly find a way to add a couple feathers to Claire's bouquet as Hazel looked so lovely in her dress. It would surely compliment the entire ceremony. Hazel beamed. No longer feeling out of place, she pulled a couple of her feather off her belt and twisted them into the wild flower bouquet sitting on the dressing table.

The women helped Claire into the gown, and set her red hair. Placing the veil on Claire's curls completed the picture. Claire sat there at the mirror and looked at her reflection. She spent so long wearing veils to cover her face, today this will be her final veil, and once it was lifted her new life would begin. She glanced up to see her mother holding Hazel's hand as both women nodded. A knock at the door by the Reverend Cooper announcing it was time to head to the church. He would go now so he would be at the altar with Mason. Claire, Hazel and Catherine were to arrive in the buggy with Charles and enter the church while everyone was already inside.

-46-

Beautiful fall day, perfect for a wedding. The wagon stopped outside the church, Claire noticed the railings were covered in cedar boughs and entwined with wildflowers. Someone had laid a red runner down the stairs for her to walk on, royal treatment. Stephan was at the door waiting. He held the door open to escort his mother to the front of the church to her seat. Charles placed his daughter's arm on his, kissed her cheek and followed Hazel into the small church filled with everyone in Cougar Ridge and even some from the reserve.

Walking down the aisle towards Mason, Claire's breath stopped. He looked magnificent. This was her husband and Claire straightened her back and smiled the biggest happiest smile she had ever smiled. She would keep this picture in her head forever. Mason stood at the front of the church with Reverend Cooper, to his side was Jack Stiles serving as Mason's best man. It was Mason, all Mason that Claire could not take her eyes from.

Mason stood tall and proud wearing his traditional native wedding tunic. It was buckskin tanned in two-tone beige and bleached white. Long sleeves with leather strips fringing down the seams and neckline. The chest had wooden toggles held with leather strips crossing his chest. Off each side of the neck hung two eagle feathers stark white with black tips, held onto the tunic with tanned leather and colourful beads. The tunic hung low, mid-way down Mason's thighs, his deerskin pants were tucked into calf high moccasins the laced ties adorn with smaller feathers and more colourful beads. His hair was trimmed and shiny, his face clean shaven. He was everything Claire could ever want. Embracing his native heritage and blending it with her own, this wedding was one to behold. Hazel was standing to the other side of the altar holding a fresh bouquet of wild flowers. Her dress was exquisite, Claire was proud to have her stand with her during this special day. Charles handed his daughter to Mason then kissed his daughter before sitting in the front pew beside his wife and son. The wedding was wonderful.

-47-

Mason reflected on this day as he danced with his wife in the pavilion with lantern light cascading romantic shadows on the wood floors. Music playing, friends and family dancing, wonderful smelling food lay out on tables surrounding the grounds Mason couldn't have wished for a better day. He married this wonderful woman, her family was here and she was free of her past. Claire never looked so radiant! Their wedding went off superbly, inside the small church, Reverend Cooper handled the service and stepped aside when the Shaman stepped forward to give the Indian Blessing. She looked like a princess when she walked down the aisle. When he lifted her veil he saw the love shining through her emerald green eyes, together they silently vowed this would be the last veil to ever cover her face.

Mason was dressed in his Native Celebration dress outfit, Claire in her mother's wedding dress. When the exited the church the leaves were falling from the trees and made a colourful carpet for them to walk on towards the town square. Now Mason looked out at all his friends that have come to bear witness to this happy day; binding Mason Barker and Claire Cooliage together as one. Laughter, music and happy people together... What more could they ask for?

Claire was in her glory, she was married to a wonderful man, and her family was with her. She was sad that her brother Adam couldn't make it, being in the army was a hard life, and he couldn't just get away. She was sad that none of her friends back home bothered to come. But then again, were they really her friends? They couldn't even look at her when she was at her worst, why would she want them here when she was at her best?

Smiling at her husband she vowed never to think of those dark times again, for she was no longer Boston Debutant Claire Colliage. She was now and forever going to be known as Mrs. Claire Barker of Cougar Ridge. She was dancing and enjoying the community gathering in celebration. The night continued on, and soon it was time for the married couple to ride off to their home. Everyone circled their buckboard decorated with flowers and feathers. Claire waved to everyone as they headed to Mason's ranch, their home. Promising to come to Christina's Diner tomorrow for lunch, Claire waved to her parents as Mason steered the team towards their home.

-48-

Micheal was walking towards the store when Hazel called out to him. He smiled as she approached, she was waving a piece of paper in her hand. She tried to catch her breath as she handed Micheal the telegram. Looking at his face as he read the news, she saw the colour drain from his face. He excused himself and ran as fast as he could down the road towards the boarding house. Knowing what the emergency telegram said, Hazel hoped for the best.

Claire and Mason woke to a chilly morning. Autumn had officially arrived. Smiling at his wife he said he will bank the fires and get the buggy hitched for their luncheon with her family at the diner. They had just finished a light breakfast supplied discretely by Toula this morning. Mason finding the light meal placed on the small table on the front porch in a basket. Even after such a long night, Toula had thought of them this morning. Mason knew Claire was happy that her friend and family member was planning on staying in Cougar Ridge.

Calling to Claire to hurry, Mason grabbed a wool blanket to cover his wife's lap as they drove into town. Everything seems to be new to Claire. She was seeing everything in vivid detail. She looked down at the simple gold band circling her ring finger. A simple band. Nothing more. It was perfect. Not gaudy, not heavy; it felt right. The butterflies were still present every time she kissed her husband. This is what she had dreamed of as a child. They were arrived at the diner.

Mason helped his wife from the buggy, and they walked in the door of the diner to find a quiet room. Perhaps her family were just running a little late. Mason sat his wife at a table by the window and poured her a coffee from the side board. Placing the cup on the table in front of Claire, he said he would head over to the boarding house to see what was keeping everyone. Just as Mason said that, the door jingled and Micheal stepped in. Claire could see something was wrong and her hand went to her throat as she rose from her chair.

Micheal motioned for her to sit, and he grabbed the chair beside her. He placed his hand over hers and looked at Mason. Mason sensed the news was not going to be good so he put his hands on Claire's shoulders ready to support her if needed. Micheal cleared his throat and said he received an emergency telegram early this morning. It said that Adam had been injured in battle and due to his injuries he was being sent home, as a retired Captain. He will no longer be able to serve. This news shocked Claire, and she looked to Mason for strength. Micheal said that's all he knew, and the family was heading out on the stage this afternoon, they were packing as we speak and unfortunately they needed to cancel lunch. Claire understood, and said they will see them off.

Micheal returned to the boarding house to gather the luggage and get his family in the wagon to await the stagecoach. A million thoughts running through his head, having dealt with Claire's accident and seeing first-hand what injuries can be like. He shuddered as he wondered how long Adam had been suffering, and why they weren't notified sooner.

Claire and Mason stood watching Micheal load the remaining bags into the stage coach. Hugging her family Claire wished she could be there. Mason was watching his wife say good-bye to her family and not under the happy circumstances it should have been. Stepping away he went into the store to speak to Tom.

Catherine hugged Claire, and told her that she will write as soon as she knows what is going on. They will keep Claire informed of everything. Stephan helped his mother into the coach while Charles said his good-byes to his only daughter. Mason came out of the store, and told Claire's family that they would be joining them in Boston in two weeks time, he needed to get someone to cover his ranch and they will be headed there. Tom was booking their trip as he spoke he said. Claire hugged Mason and kissed him on the mouth. She was so happy he thought of this, Catherine was thrilled they would be home. Her entire family would be together. She told Claire that she will have her rooms readied for them and they could consider this a type of homecoming, or a honey moon. Catherine asked Charles to pay for their trip as their wedding gift to them. Mason smiled knowing to deny Claire's parents this would hurt their feelings, so he thanked them and waved as they climbed into the coach.

-49-

So it was done, Charles would take care of their travel arrangements, and they were going to Boston. Mason was nervous, but ready to see where Claire grew up. Turning to go back into the store to let Tom know about the change in plans Mason reached for his wife's hand, together they would get through this. For they had the rest of their lives to be together. This was just the first chapter in the story of their life. They were going to Boston, to the Cooliage Family Estate and he would be meeting the rich and noble side of Boston. How would he measure up in their eyes he wondered. Feeling the dark change in her husband, Claire squeezed his hand. She whispered to him that he dug her out of a dark place and showed her sunshine, surely they can put up with the snobbery of the people in Boston for a short time. Laughing the newlyweds walked out of the store into the bright sunshine of the crisp autumn day, ready to embark on a lifetime together; a lifetime of new adventures, and new beginnings for both of them.

Claire Marie Cooliage Barker was now home.
Here in Cougar Ridge.

Stay Tuned

The continuing saga of the Cooliage Family Series
"Captain of Her Home"
Is due to be released spring 2019 !
Turn the page for a teaser!

Be sure to follow Debbi Haskins on her web page:
https://debbihaskins.wordpress.com

Captain of Her Home

"Cooliage Family Series"

Chapter 1

The smell of gun powder sounds of rifle fire and men yelling, horses screaming then the silence as pain ripped through his body; same visions that Adam woke to screaming in horror every night.

As she does every evening, Nurse Kit places a cool cloth over the Captain's brow and hums a soothing tune to lull him back to sleep. When he drifts back into his pain filled sleep Nurse Kit then changes the bandages and refills the water basin with fresh cold water and sets clean cloths beside it on the wash stand; ready for the next outburst of pain.

The trip back to the Captain's hometown of Boston was a very slow trek. Soon they will be settled in his childhood home, for now they were on the final train destined to the Boston terminal where his family will be waiting. Nurse Kit had been handsomely paid to be his sole caregiver on this trip and had been asked to remain on the private payroll of the Cooliage Family once they arrive in Boston. Being a widow with no children and a rented room, Kit had nothing stopping her from accepting the very generous offer. She had been caring for Captain Adam Cooliage for several months now. She can certainly do a few more, especially for such a posh family as thee Boston Cooliage Family.

Adam sat in a white wicker chair on the upper terrace of the stately Cooliage Estate. His childhood bedroom had been updated to a more sophisticated style. Adam's nurse brought his medicine and a large pitcher of ice tea. Nurse Kit set today's newspaper on his lap and poured him a tall glass of the tea. Tapping her toe, Adam grinned as he finally picked up his pills from the small silver plate and took a swallow of tea to wash them down.

Adam had grown quite accustomed to Kit's mothering ways and loved to test her kindness. In a good way though. Nurse Kit patted Adam on the head as she left him on the terrace to read his paper in the fresh morning air.

Adam's parents had told him that during his "ordeal"; it was funny that they couldn't say near death, or injury; his only sister Claire had married, and not to the fiancé that Adam had known about. So many changes since his last time home; his other two brothers, Michael a lawyer and Stephan, dad's right hand man, had been by every day filling Adam in on everything that he had missed while away in the army.

Atleast his mother had mentioned that Claire and her husband Mason were returning to Boston for their honeymoon. How he had missed his family, so many years since he had been home.

Well that all changed the day of the attack. Captain Cooliage is now retired from active service due to injuries he occurred in the line of duty. Adam must now make Boston his home once again.

Turning to his newspaper lying folded on his lap, Adam surveyed the local news. Father's company was growing according to the article about him opening another building soon. The writer had mentioned the source of the story came from Cooliage Shipping head secretary Mary Saxton.

Adam stopped reading the article and dropped the paper. Mary Saxton? Could it possibly be the same Mary? He had grown up with the Saxton children, Maxwell and his younger sister Mary. He didn't know much of Mary growing up, except that she was always following Maxwell and himself everywhere they went.

On Adam's last visit home, about six years ago, he had run into Mary at Maxwell's wedding. She sure had grown, no longer a child following them around. Adam sat back, looked out into the morning sky and thought back to Max's wedding. Six long years ago, felt like an entirely different lifetime.

Chapter 2

Maxwell Saxton sat in the salon of the Cooliage Estate talking to the mother of his best friend, as Adam came strolling in still wearing his army uniform fresh off the train. Adam set his bag on the floor, he was happy to be home even for the short two week leave he was granted to be present at his friend's wedding. Catherine Cooliage, Adam's mother, placed her hand to her heart when she saw her eldest son standing a mere four feet from her. She gathered her skirts and ran to his outreached arms.

Max walked over, smiling broadly. His coal black hair freshly cut and styled. Max's clothing top of the latest men's line. Impeccable as always, thought Adam. Pleasantries exchanged, Catherine excused herself to make sure dinner plans were set for the special return home dinner for Adam.

Adam ushered Max to his father's study and as he closed the door he noticed James, father's most trusted employee in the home, taking his bags to his room upstairs.

Door closed, Adam removed his uniform tunic and draped it over a straight back wooden chair by the door. Walking his friend over to the huge arm chairs by the fire, Adam poured each of them a drink from his father's impressive spirit selection.

Adam sat with Max for the next hour catching up on their life paths. Towards the end of their conversation, Max handed Adam his official invite to the wedding, and a hand written note detailing his duties as Best Man. This was the reason for Adam's return to Boston; his childhood best friend had requested Adam to stand beside him as he married his love of his life. He could not disappoint his friend, so he came home. Max left the Cooliage Estate and headed to his own family home to let his family know that Adam had arrived and is there for the wedding.

Dinner that night was a real feast, fit for a king. Well in his case a freshly ranked Captain returning home. Adam noticed how much his family had really changed since he left for the army years ago; but at the same time it felt like he had never left at all. The laughter and the talking during dinner was just like old times.

His father, Charles sat at the head of the grand table; Mother sat at the other end, to father's right sat Stephan the youngest son, and to father's left sat Adam. Beside Adam on his left was his younger brother Micheal and across form Micheal sat the baby of the family, and only daughter to the Cooliage Empire, Claire. She sure had grown up, she no longer had the chubby cheeks and unruly curls. Her long red hair was tied back with a pretty green velvet ribbon. His family, Adam had missed them growing into young adults.

The meal was served, talk continued around the table switching from the army to the shipping business, to Micheal's law firm and then to Max's wedding. The evening continued with stories of what had transpired during his absence. Dessert had been eaten, dishes cleared and tea and spirits served. Adam watched his mother stifle a yawn, so he then expressed his own tiredness from the travel. In fact he was exhausted from his first day back, so he retired to his rooms for the evening.

Sleep came fast, and before he knew it the birds were singing and he awoke to glorious sunshine. Today Adam was to meet Max at his family home across town to finalize his best man's duties.

Chapter 3

Washed, shaved and dressed in civilian attire Adam ventured downstairs only to find James waiting at the foot of the stairs. He informed Adam that Cook had placed a substantial breakfast in the dining hall for him with coffee as well. James also said he would have to groom ready the coach or if Adam preferred, a saddled horse. Adam said he would enjoy the saddled mount over the coach, he thanked James and followed his nose to the vast buffet set out in the dining hall. Adam sat to enjoy the wonderful foods which Cook had prepared for him. Eating alone was something foreign to him as the army ate meager meals together. His family apparently were not awake yet, so Adam enjoyed the quiet and ate his meal.

The horseback ride through the streets of Boston towards The Saxton House brought back fond memories of younger Maxwell and himself racing their mounts through these same streets. Arriving at Saxton House, Adam tied his horse to the hitching post and instructed the boy to water and feed him sparingly.

Adam raised his gloved hand to knock on the large double wooden door but did not get the chance to knock as a pretty young woman opened the door at that exact moment. An angel had opened the door, the sunlight made her golden hair glow. Her blue eyes sparkled as she smiled the most radiant smile he had ever set eyes upon. Then the angel spoke, the heavens above began to sing. Adam was lost, caught in this heavenly creatures spell.

The angel laughed; a magical sound. She asked if he remembered her. Did he? No, how could he have ever forgotten something so beautiful? She led Adam to the garden in the back of the house where Maxwell was waiting. Max stood and hugged his friend; turning to the young woman he asked Mary to leave.

Mary? No, it couldn't be. Maxwell's little sister Mary? She sure had grown! Adam was lost in thought and Max had to poke him to get his attention. They had wedding plans to discuss. Time had flown by, and next thing Adam knew Mary had re-entered the garden asking the two men to come in for dinner. Adam had no problem following Mary to the dining hall.

Throughout the entire meal Adam kept focused on everything Mary said. He noticed how her nose crinkled when she laughed. He watched her eat and drink. He could imagine doing this for a lifetime. What? Where did that thought come from? The army was his life, and that meant being alone. It was no place to have a wife and raise a family. Adam excused himself and said his good-byes. Saying he will see Max tomorrow at the church. Adam took a last sip of his water, wiped his mouth and set his napkin on his plate as he rose from the table to head to the front door.

Mary met him at the door as he was putting his coat on ready to leave. She looked out of breath, flushed and breathing heavily. She had been waiting for him. Adam approached Mary slowly, confusion showing on his face, he then stopped about a foot away from where Mary was standing. Mary closed the distance between them and placed her hands on his very wide strong shoulders. She whispered in his ear that she was so glad that he came home finally, that she missed him terribly. Then she kissed him on his shocked lips.

By the time Adam had registered what had happened, he was left standing alone at the front door. Adam rode home, he was grateful his horse knew the way back to the Estate, because he couldn't recall the ride home. Next thing Adam had realized the horse stopped at the family stable and the groom was helping Adam down. Adam whistled all the way to his room, anxious to sleep so tomorrow will arrive sooner.

Chapter 4

The wedding was perfect; Max's new wife was a real pretty woman. Shy, petite and of Italian heritage; her family were new comers to the America's having been in Boston for only two years. The wedding party and guests were instructed to return to the Saxton House for the reception. Adam couldn't wait; he was itching to ask Mary to dance.

There she was, sitting with her parents at the front side of the dance hall. Mary wore a beautiful pink satin gown, her blonde hair loosely piled on her head with soft ringlets framing her face and her lips were tinted red like strawberries. Adam had the strangest desire to see if they tasted as good as they looked!

Adam walked towards the trio of Saxton's, his eyes locked with Mary's. Her eyes were twinkling and her smile was intoxicating, she glowed. Mr. Saxton rose smiling and shook Adam's out stretched hand. After getting the happy approval of both Mary's parents, Adam escorted her to the dance floor.

Dressed in his sharply pressed Captain's uniform, his side sword perfectly polished, he felt all eyes upon them as he bowed to Mary and gently took her into his arms. The song was a slow waltz; they glided across the room as if they have danced together forever. Time stood still. Adam and Mary were in a world of their own, everyone else forgotten.

Several dances later, Adam and Mary took their glasses of punch onto the terrace. Alone, under the stars, Adam pulled Mary close for an intimate embrace and a passionate kiss. Finally coming up for air, Mary took Adam by the hand and led him down the cobblestone path towards the barn and horse paddock.

In the darkness, Adam took a horse blanket from the stable and placed it on the mound of fresh straw behind the barn. Gently lying Mary on the blanket Adam joined her. They continued their kiss, Mary was the first to break contact. Adam was breathing heavily, and the pressure from his britches was starting to hurt.

Mary must have sensed it as she placed her warm hand against the hard pulsing mound straining from inside his pants. Mary shushed Adam's refusal by kissing him hard on the lips. While at the same time she began to unbutton his pants freeing his fully grown throbbing erection.

Gasping as the cool air hit his hot flesh, he watched as Mary stepped out of her party gown; standing in front of him in all her glory. She was a picture of purity, a goddess for sure. Adam couldn't believe that Mary was offering herself to him. The moonlight was shining halos around her small round perky white breasts, adorned with light pink tiny nipples standing at attention in front of the Captain. Adams gazed left the perfect breasts to travel downward, trim tiny waistline with a cute little indent of a belly button, even lower went his gaze; to the golden hair covering her womanhood down to her strong shapely legs all the way to her tiny white toes. He looked back up the beauty in front of him, making sure this is what she was wanting, for he sure wasn't going to pass up this gift!

Adam reached for Mary and in one quick fluid motion had her on her back underneath his toned muscled body; arched above her, his eyes silently asking for her permission. Mary's hair was splayed all around like a halo's glow, her blue eyes shone with what Adam thought was love.

His kiss was gentle and tender when in reality he wanted to do nothing more than bury his hard manhood deep in her virginal passage. Adam held back, he needed to make this as painless as possible. Slow was not something Mary wanted though; she was panting and clawing at Adam like a wild animal. A woman possessed.

Their coming together was wild, wonderful and exhausting. After an hour they lay wrapped in each other's arms trying to catch their breaths. Comprehension of what had happened clearing to Adam. What had he done? He took his best friends sister's virginity in a stable, like an animal. He stood, raking his fingers through his hair. Tossing on his clothes he handed Mary her gown, while trying not to look at her, positive that if he did he would see the horror she must be realizing herself.

Adam told Mary to get dressed, that they must return before they were discovered missing. They walked in silence back along the path; neither touching the other. When they reached the house, Adam saw the tear running down her cheek and he gently wiped it away and kissed her forehead. Mary pulled away turning to leave, Adam had stopped her turning her to face him once again. Adam told Mary that come morning he was going to ask Mary's father for permission to marry her.

Shock was what he saw in her face. Then shock turned to vivid red anger, her blue eyes clouded over as she shook off his hands. Straightening her back, standing tall; she looked Adam in the eye as she told him in a flat low tone that she would not marry him. Not tomorrow or the next day, never. She would never marry him, and never wanted to see him again. Mary then turned and ran away crying into the side entrance to her home.

That memory had stayed with Adam to this day. He had never bed another woman unless he paid the whores at the saloon. No woman would ever hold his heart only to shred it.

Six years later and the thought of his Mary still aroused him, while at the same time made his blood boil with anger. Surely fate wouldn't tempt him so, would the world be so cruel? To have Mary placed back into his life, when he was only a shell of the man he used to be? He needed to find out if his father's shipping secretary was indeed Maxwell Saxton's little sister Mary... the angel in his dreams, the angel that has kept him alive during many battles through the years?

About the Author

I live in a very small town in Southwestern Ontario, Canada, and enjoy spending time with family and friends. I began writing at a very young age winning numerous short story and public speaking awards in school. As I got older I continued my writing by having a story published in Fort Lauderdale newspaper on the struggles of the homeless, and helped out at the Salvation Army. Not long after Hurricane Andrew, I returned back to Canada to raise my children. Having to work I set my writing on the back burner.

Entering this next stage in my life, being retired early I found my love for writing again. I am embarking on a new and exciting path in my writing career; solely focusing on fiction romance as I am a huge fan of romance novels. I am excited to venture into this new direction and I hope my fans and fellow readers will also enjoy my works. I look forward to sitting on my deck by the lake creating a world of romance for you to enjoy.